PAGES & CO

TILLY AND THE MAP OF STORIES

GOOD BOOKSHOPS ARE HARD TO RESIST...

Clues

Books by Anna James

PAGES & CO:

TILLY AND THE BOOKWANDERERS

TILLY AND THE LOST FAIRY TALES

TILLY AND THE MAP OF STORIES

PAGES & CO

TILLY AND THE MAP OF STORIES

ANNA JAMES

Illustrated by Paola Escobar

HarperCollins *Children's Books*

First published in Great Britain by
HarperCollins *Children's Books* in 2020
HarperCollins *Children's Books* is a division of HarperCollins*Publishers* Ltd,
HarperCollins Publishers
1 London Bridge Street
London SE1 9GF

The HarperCollins website address is
www.harpercollins.co.uk

1

ISBN 978–0–00–822994–8

Anna James and Paola Escobar assert the moral right to be identified
as the author and illustrator of the work respectively.
A CIP catalogue record for this title is available from the British Library.

Typeset in Aldus LT Std 12pt/16pt
Printed and bound in England by CPI Group (UK) Ltd, Croydon CR0 4YY
A CIP catalogue record for this title is available from the British Library.

MIX
Paper from
responsible sources
FSC™ C007454

For Adam
I love writing our story together.

Previously in Pages & Co.

In *Tilly and the Bookwanderers*, Matilda Pages discovered that she was a bookwanderer; that she could travel inside her favourite books. While looking for her missing mother with her best friend, Oskar, she discovered that her father was a fictional character and that meant she was half fictional herself.

In *Tilly and the Lost Fairy Tales*, Tilly and Oskar came up against the Underwood siblings. Melville Underwood has managed to get into power at the British Underlibrary and wants to control who has access to bookwandering. His sister, Decima, is experimenting with book magic in order to try and steal stories' innate immortality and believes that Tilly's half-fictional nature may be the key.

Tilly has found or been given several clues while bookwandering, and she and Oskar believe that there may be a map to find the Archivists, who are supposed to protect bookwandering but who haven't been heard from for many, many years.

1

A proper PLAN

'I'm looking for a book.'

Matilda Pages and her grandad looked up from writing book recommendation cards to see a man standing in front of them at the desk of Pages & Co. The shop was quiet and golden-hour sunlight dripped in through the tall windows, making everything feel sleepy and peaceful.

'Well, we can definitely help you with that,' Grandad said, glad of a customer. 'Which book was it?'

'I can't quite remember the title, I'm afraid,' the man went on. 'Or the author, now I come to think about it. But I know that it has a blue cover. Or at least I think so.'

'Can you remember *anything* about what's inside?' Grandad said encouragingly. Tilly grinned: she loved watching him work out which book someone wanted from whatever tiny bits of information they could remember.

'Not really . . .' the man said vaguely. 'How strange! I came to the shop specifically to pick this book up – it was my favourite when I was little, or was it my mum's favourite? It slips my mind. And, now I'm here, I can't remember the first thing about it. Maybe it wasn't so special after all . . .'

'Sounds like it meant a lot to you once upon a time,' Grandad said. 'I'm sure I can make some educated guesses if you can remember anything at all about it, or maybe we could help you find something different to read?'

'That's very kind of you,' the man said politely, although he was already glancing back at the door. 'But honestly – and I know this is the wrong thing to say in a bookshop – I just don't seem to care any more.'

Grandad raised an eyebrow.

'I'm sorry, I don't mean to be rude,' the man went on. 'It's just the more I think about it, the more I'm confused about what I even came in for.'

'A book,' Grandad reminded him. 'With a blue cover.'

'I'm not even sure it was blue,' the man said, shrugging. 'Oh well, thank you for your help.' And with that he was gone.

'How peculiar,' said Grandad.

'People can't remember what they're looking for all the time, though,' Tilly pointed out.

'Yes, but usually, if they've bothered to make it into the bookshop, they're a little more persistent, sometimes even quite annoyed that we can't immediately identify what they're after. *He* just seemed to forget what he even wanted as we spoke.'

'Actually, there was another customer like that,' Tilly said, remembering. 'The other day a woman was just standing, staring at a bookshelf for about ten minutes, not picking up any books or anything, and, when I asked if I could help her find something, she said she wasn't sure, and then wandered off.'

'Mmm, very strange,' said Grandad, but his attention had been distracted by a list of numbers on the screen of the till, his brow furrowed in concern. 'Well, let's hope it's not a trend,' he said. 'We've been selling fewer and fewer books over the last couple of months. Maybe it's just that it's finally getting warmer and people are getting excited about being outside. As if we didn't have enough to worry about. How are you coping without bookwandering?'

'I hate it,' Tilly said vehemently. 'I hate that I can't do it, and that I can't talk to Anne or bookwander with Oskar, and most of all I hate that the Underwoods could just take it away without asking.'

Since Melville Underwood had become Head Librarian at the British Underlibrary and made his sister, Decima, his official Advisor, they had made good on their threat to limit bookwandering by binding Source Editions. They had promised, in a series of very formal statements, that it was only a short-term measure to keep bookwandering safe while they got to grips with their new roles, but the Pages family had very little trust in statements or promises from the twins.

'Remind me how bookbinding works?' Tilly said. 'Why did somebody even invent that in the first place?!'

'It was the Bookbinders,' Grandad explained. 'That group of librarians who, years and years ago, first wanted to try to control who could bookwander. They use book magic to do it: that black sticky stuff you saw when the Underwoods were breaking up the fairy tales. It's barbaric, really, the uses they put book magic to – the very opposite of where it comes from.'

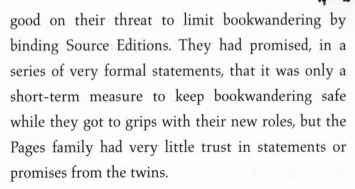

'But how does it work? Have you ever done it?'

'Books should only be bound in

the most serious of situations,' Grandad said. 'And some would say never at all. While I was in charge at the British Underlibrary, we only bound a book once and I'm still not certain it was the right thing to do. However, the process itself is fairly simple. All you have to do is trace an X of book magic over the first word of a book's Source Edition and it's like locking the door.'

'So the Underwoods have done that to all the Source Editions?'

'All the ones at the British Underlibrary, it would seem. Although, knowing them, they got some of their underlings to do it – no doubt the librarians who've gleefully revived the Bookbinder name. But don't worry, Tilly, we'll think of something soon.'

'I don't understand why you're so calm about it,' Tilly said, the anger at having her freedom to bookwander stripped from her still prickling under her skin.

'I'm not at all calm about it,' Grandad replied. 'I'm as angry as you are, but it's too big a fight to just wade into and cause more problems. We have to make sure the Sources are protected at all times, as well as the people working at the Underlibrary. We need a proper plan.'

'I *suggested* a proper plan,' Tilly said mutinously.

'I know you think that . . . I mean, I understand that you believe . . .' Grandad faltered under the apparent strain of trying to say what he meant – without actually saying what he meant.

'I know you don't believe me that the Archivists are real, or that I know how to find them,' said Tilly. 'You don't need to explain again. You're not going to convince me, though. Two separate people told me and Oskar that they use maps to tell you where they are – and I'm sure I've been sent one.'

'You weren't given a map, sweetheart,' Grandad said gently. 'You found a collection of items that you think are linked together because you want to be able to help. And we love you so much for that, but it's too great a risk to follow those clues . . . Well, we *couldn't* follow them. Where would we even start?'

Tilly rolled her eyes. 'We'd start at the Library of Congress, in America,' she explained as if speaking to a child who wasn't paying attention. 'That's where the first clue said to go. It had a . . . what did Mum call it, an American postcode?'

'A zip code,' Grandad said.

'Right, a zip code! And it had a library classmark – you said yourself that classmarks are like maps – that's how I knew!'

'We can't fly all the way to America to find a book, Tilly,' Grandad said. 'Now, give me a few moments of quiet so I can look through these sales figures again. Why don't you go and find your mum, there's a good girl?'

One of the things that Tilly loved most about her grandparents was that they almost always spoke to her as if she were a proper person who understood things, and felt things, and had good ideas. But that meant it stung even more when they spoke down to her, as though she were just too young to understand what they were dealing with.

She stood up without saying anything else, meaning to go and find Bea and talk to *her* about the map, but, before she could wander over to the stairs, the phone behind the counter started ringing.

'Good morning, Pages & Co.,' Grandad said. 'Archie speak— Oh, Seb, hello, any news? Oh . . . Right . . .' He looked up to check Tilly hadn't gone and held a hand out to tell her to stay put. 'I've got her here,' he said down the phone, and Tilly felt a wave of fear crash over her. Grandad slammed the phone down and dragged her towards the door that connected the bookshop to where the Pages family lived.

'What are you doing?' she asked, trying to wriggle out of his grasp. 'You're hurting me, Grandad!'

'I'm sorry, Tilly,' he said, 'but we need to get you hidden. Right now. That was Seb. The Underwoods are on their way here – and it's you they want.'

2

A SMALL INKLING OF DOUBT

'What do they want me for?' Tilly asked as they ran through the kitchen and up the stairs.

'I dread to think,' Grandad said, 'considering that the last time you saw them they were trying to steal your blood.'

'But it's not like they can do anything here at Pages & Co.,' Tilly said, out of breath as she jogged after Grandad right up to the top floor where her bedroom was. 'And it's not as though they've got anything to bargain with now they've already stopped us bookwandering.'

'I'm not taking that risk,' Grandad said. 'As far as

they're concerned, you are at a friend's house for tea. Your grandma and I will speak to them and find out what they want, and I'll send your mum up here to wait with you. I'll lock the door to the shop, and you must promise me that you won't come downstairs. Yes?'

'I promise,' Tilly said sincerely.

'This is the first time I've been glad that you can't bookwander, so you won't be able to disappear off somewhere,' he said grimly as he shut the door behind her firmly.

Tilly listened to his footsteps fade as he headed back downstairs, and realised she'd left her phone in the bookshop and couldn't even text her best friend, Oskar, to tell him what was happening. She had her bookcase, of course, but she wasn't sure she'd be able to sit and focus on reading when she was so anxious. Although, judging by the pile of only-just-started books by her bed, her concentration had been all over the place for a while. Tilly realised she hadn't finished a book for nearly a week – a seriously long time for a reader of her commitment.

Tilly ran her fingers along her shelves, trying to summon that faith she had always had in the serendipity of a bookshelf – that you often ended up finding exactly the right book at the right time. Maybe there was something there that would distract her. Usually, her bookcase was so full that it took quite a yank to even get a book out, but Tilly noticed there were a couple of gaps at the moment. She couldn't quite place what was missing – she must have left them downstairs or lent them to Oskar.

On one of the shelves was a curious selection of objects: the items that she was sure were clues to lead her to the Archivists. Even though Grandma and Grandad thought the Archivists were nothing more than a bookwandering fairy tale, Tilly just knew it was too much of a coincidence that these particular items had all ended up with her.

A slim book and a ball of red thread given to her by a librarian at the

French Underlibrary, a key from *The Secret Garden*, a bag of breadcrumbs from 'Hansel and Gretel'. All of them had found their way to her over the course of a few days. Surely they had to mean *something*? But, when she looked at them lined up like this, she couldn't ignore a small inkling of doubt. It was hard not to see them as Grandad did – a row of unrelated objects she'd picked up while bookwandering, smothered in wishful thinking.

Tilly sighed. Not for the first time, she wished she could bookwander – to try to find some more clues, to get Anne Shirley's take on the situation, or just to take her mind off whatever was going on downstairs in the bookshop. All of them had, of course, tried to bookwander after Seb told them what Melville had done, but it just didn't work. There was a flash of a moment where you felt the familiar pull of the story, the leap in your stomach and even the faint smell of toasting marshmallows, but then there was a feeling like an elastic band that had stretched as far as it could and you were bounced back again.

Tilly grabbed a book at random off her shelf and stared at it in frustration. It was *Alice's Adventures in Wonderland*. It was one of Tilly's favourite places to bookwander, and Alice often used to pop into the bookshop to say hello.

Tilly opened the book and, thinking about what Grandad had told her about bookbinding, stared at the first word. She could see that there was the suggestion of a shadow across it. She tried to scratch or rub it off, but nothing happened. There was still a slight mark there, echoing the book magic that had bound the Source Edition at the Underlibrary. She flicked through the pages, stopping at the familiar scene of the Mad Hatter's tea party, the first place she had ever bookwandered to.

She sat on the edge of her bed and read it aloud, trying to conjure up the feeling of awe that she'd experienced the first time she had been pulled inside the pages of a book.

'There was a table set out under a tree in front of the house, and the March Hare and the Hatter were

having tea at it: a Dormouse was sitting between
them, fast asleep, and the other two were using it as
a cushion, resting their elbows on it, and talking over
its head.'

Tilly kept reading and let herself be swept away by
the story. A few moments later, she sneezed.

'Stupid hay fever,' Tilly said to herself, brushing
away the flowers that were too close to her
face – before realising they had not been
there a moment ago.

'Where have you come from?' she said,
looking up to realise that it wasn't just flowers
that had appeared. Instead of her wooden floor,
there was a carpet of grass, fragrant and slightly
damp from the dew. More brightly coloured
flowers were sprouting up in the corners of the
room, and there was even the unmistakable sound
of birdsong in the air, even though her skylight
window was firmly closed against April showers.
The wooden legs of a table seemed to be growing
up out of the grass, creaking as they shimmered

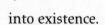

into existence.

Tilly started and the book fell shut on her bed, and in the blink of an eye it all disappeared.

'What

is

going

on?'

she whispered.

3

I'VE ALWAYS LIKED TREASURE HUNTS

Tilly sat on her bed, staring at the copy of *Alice*. She was thinking about when she'd accidentally pulled the secret garden out into her bedroom just before Christmas, and the fairytale forest that had escaped on to the train to Paris. She picked the book up again, a little gingerly, and turned over a few pages to the passage where Alice meets the tricksy caterpillar that sits on top of a mushroom.

Wanting to know more about what was happening, she tried to concentrate on pulling that scene out of the book, but all she managed was to make her bedroom smell like mushrooms. Tilly put the book down again and reached across for the large, ornate key that had stayed put even when the secret garden that had erupted into her bedroom had gone. She looked round her room, wondering if anything had been left behind this time – maybe another clue even – but there was only the faintest scent of spring grass in the air.

'I bet the Underwoods would love to know about this,' she said, smiling to herself. 'They might have been able to stop me travelling inside books, but they haven't stopped the stories coming to *me*.'

But her satisfaction in slipping round the edges of the Underwoods' rules didn't last long. After all, Melville and Decima were, at that very moment, in Pages & Co. The siblings looked like twins – both slender, blond and cold – but were less alike in character. Melville occupied the most powerful position at the Underlibrary, but it was his sister, Decima, who was the brains behind the operation.

Melville had manipulated his way to the top with sly words and charm that he turned on and off as easily as a light bulb, while it was Decima who understood book magic, and what you could do with it. She was the one who had realised that some of the everlasting nature of stories might be contained in Tilly's half-fictional blood.

Even though she was four floors up, and separated from them by several doors, at least one of which was locked, Tilly felt as though she could sense them downstairs and her knees started to fidget as she resisted the urge to go and stand up for herself. She was saved from having to decide whether to disobey Grandad by a soft knock on her door.

'It's Bea,' her mum said. 'I mean, it's Mum.'

After Bea had been away for so long, trapped in *A Little Princess* for eleven years, they still hadn't quite settled on what Tilly should call her, and sometimes neither term felt quite right.

'Come in,' Tilly called and her mum slipped round the door.

'How are you doing?' Bea asked, moving the copy of *Alice's Adventures in Wonderland* out of the way and sitting next to Tilly on the bed.

Tilly shrugged, not sure what to say. 'Kind of scared, and kind of confused, and kind of frustrated,' she said. 'I suppose?'

'All of that makes sense,' Bea said.

'Do you know what the Underwoods want?' Tilly asked.

'Not yet. Your grandad whisked me away just as they were arriving.'

'But they can't do anything bad, can they?' Tilly said. 'There are customers around.'

'I hope not,' said Bea. 'But I don't know, Tilly. Whatever they want unnerved Seb enough to call ahead. We'll find out when your grandparents come up and get us. But while we've got a moment to ourselves . . .' Bea glanced around and her eyes settled on Tilly's collection of clues. 'Tell me again what you've worked out.'

'You believe me?' Tilly said.

'I always believe you,' Bea said. 'And I want to try and understand what you're saying about the Archive, because I for one cannot bear just sitting around, waiting to see what those creepy siblings are going to do next, especially when they're so focused on *you*.'

'So, there's that string of numbers and letters that we found in that pamphlet,' Tilly said, forgetting a little of her fear as she got to explain her theory to someone who was taking it seriously. 'And Grandad said it looked like a classmark, which is how you find books in a library.'

'Right,' Bea agreed. 'And therefore you think it's telling us we need to go and find something at the Library of Congress in Washington DC, because the zip code matches the address of that building?'

'Yep, exactly,' Tilly said. 'See, it's not complicated.'

'But what about all this other stuff?' said Bea, pointing to the objects on Tilly's shelf. 'How do they all link up?'

'I don't know,' Tilly admitted. 'But surely they found their way to me on purpose? And Oskar's grandma, in Paris, she said that there's a map to the Archive.'

'How do you turn a key, a ball of thread and some breadcrumbs into a map?' Bea asked.

'Maybe map is the wrong word,' Tilly said, looking up at her mother. 'I think it might be more of a treasure hunt.'

'I've always liked treasure hunts.' Bea smiled. 'And I think it's probably fair to assume that finding the most secretive group of bookwanderers that have ever existed would involve a little more effort than following a dotted line.'

'Exactly,' Tilly said, pleased. 'But what can we do about it stuck here?'

'There are always options,' Bea said. 'And—' But she was interrupted by a knock at the door.

Tilly's bedroom door opened to show Grandma, her face pale with worry.

'They've gone,' she said quietly.

'What did they want?' asked Tilly nervously.

'Come downstairs and have a cup of tea and a slice

of cake and we'll talk properly,' Grandma said. 'We've closed the shop for the rest of the day.'

Ten minutes later, the four members of the Pages family assembled round their battered old kitchen table. Grandma had been stress-baking ever since the Source Editions had been bound and they were all picking at slices of carrot cake with cream-cheese icing, too worried to enjoy it.

'So?' Bea said, a little impatiently.

'The Underwoods are keen to understand more of your heritage, Tilly,' Grandad started. 'They were all forced smiles today, aiming to sweet-talk us on to their side.'

'They want compliance among bookwanderers,' Grandma said. 'They would like us, and you, to help them willingly.'

'But why on earth would we do that?' Tilly said, baffled.

'Well, quite,' said Grandad forcefully. 'But they're

trying to set themselves up as legitimate guardians of bookwandering, and it's not a good look to have a former Librarian and his family so publicly against them.'

'If they want to be seen as respectable, they shouldn't have tried to steal a child's blood!' Bea said angrily.

'Again, we're all on the same page,' Grandma said. And Tilly knew things were bad because usually Grandad could never resist making a joke about their surname when someone used that expression.

'They've asked that Tilly voluntarily help with their research into book magic,' he said. 'They are positioning what they're doing as an important exploration into how bookwandering works, and what book magic can do, with the suggestion being that anyone opposing them must be against progress.'

'But we already kind of knew that, didn't we?' Tilly said. 'Why did they come here? What do they want from *me*?'

'Well,' said Grandma, 'they wanted you to go

with them to the Underlibrary to see what they're working on, with one of us. That's obviously out of the question.'

'So we say no,' Tilly said. 'That's not so scary. What can they do if I don't go?'

'Stop us bookwandering,' said Grandad.

'But they already have,' Tilly pointed out.

'Temporarily,' Grandad said. 'And, if that was the whole price, then we would pay it – while we worked out what to do next. But that's not what they're threatening.'

'If we don't help,' Grandma explained, with a grim look on her face, 'then they're going to stop all children from bookwandering – *forever.*'

4

A WILD GOOSE CHASE

'All children?' said Tilly.

'Yes,' Grandad said. 'They were very specific.'

'Well, I have to go then,' Tilly said, trying to sound brave, even though her stomach had just turned inside out. She steeled herself. This was what her favourite heroines would do: sacrifice themselves for the greater good. She'd be just like . . . just like . . . Tilly found that she couldn't quite put her finger on the name, but this is what they would want. She was almost sure of it.

'No,' Bea said firmly. 'Absolutely not.'

'It's not an option, Tilly,' Grandad said, and Tilly couldn't deny the huge wave of relief that washed over her. 'Both on a personal level, because we love you and it's our job to keep you safe, and on principle, because we do not give in to people like this.'

'But how could they stop just *children* bookwandering?' Bea questioned. 'If you bind a Source Edition, you bind it. For everyone.'

'Well, they seem to be requiring people to swear loyalty to the new regime, and then they're finding a way to sneak them into bound books – or at least dangling that prospect in front of them, as they just did to us, as if it might sway our allegiance. But I'm not at all sure that they've actually worked out a way to do it. I think it's just something to string people along while they plot their next move.'

'But what exactly do they want me to do?' Tilly asked.

'We don't know,' said Grandma. 'But it can't be good, whatever it is.' She and Grandad shared a glance.

'We have to go and find the Archivists,' Tilly said firmly. 'There's nothing else to do – you have to see that now?'

'No!' Grandad snapped. 'Tilly, I need you to stop

talking about them and stay put in the real world.'

'Why won't you believe me?' Tilly said, struggling to fight back tears.

'Because there's no evidence that the Archivists are real, and I will not have us going on a wild goose chase around the world based on one scribbled note.'

'Dad . . .' Bea started.

'Not you too,' Grandad said, his head in his hands. 'You have to trust me on this.'

'I just don't understand how you can believe in bookwandering – in actual magic – and not understand that the Archivists are real,' Tilly persisted, carefully ignoring Grandma's warning glance.

'Because I have *been* bookwandering!' Grandad said. 'Because I have seen and experienced the evidence. Bookwandering is not some old wives' tale, rumour or gossip – unlike the existence of the Archivists. I love you, Tilly, but a pile of miscellaneous objects you were given or found in books does not constitute a reason to go hunting for a fairy tale.'

'Fairy tales are real!' Tilly said in frustration.

'That's not the point,' Grandad said.

'Well then, I don't know what the point is!' said Tilly.

'The point is that we're in a bit of a bind,' Grandma sighed. 'But this family is a team and together we'll come up with a plan. Archie, why don't you go and call Amelia and get her take on this new development.'

Grandad nodded. 'I'm sorry I snapped at you, Tilly,' he said, standing up. 'I just . . . I just want to keep you safe. I want to keep you all safe.'

'We'll keep each other safe,' Grandma said firmly.

'If we just sit here, trying to stay safe, they're going to keep coming back until something awful happens,' said Tilly. 'It's not enough to hide at home – we have to go and find some answers.'

After Grandad had gone back out to the empty bookshop to phone Amelia Whisper, who had been the Head Librarian before Melville had forced her out, Grandma let out a huge sigh.

'What a to-do,' she said. 'What times we're living through.'

'Why do the Head Librarians even have so much power?' Tilly asked. 'No one should be allowed to stop bookwandering.'

'You're right,' Grandma said. 'But there has to be someone in charge, and what we're learning now is that the system isn't best set up for when someone abuses that position. People are scared and so they believe the lies that the Underwoods are spewing about progress, or whatever they're dressing up their power grab as. And, of course, there are others who have always shared their opinions, but have previously – and rightfully – been too embarrassed to publicly say so until now.'

Bea had stayed quiet throughout the conversation, seemingly lost in thought, occasionally looking at Tilly without saying anything.

'Have you got plans to see Oskar soon?' she said eventually.

'He's supposed to be coming round tomorrow,' said Tilly. 'Why?'

'I was just wondering . . . It'd be nice to see him. I might just give Mary a quick ring and . . . see what her plans are,' she finished vaguely as she stood up and left the room to make the call.

Then it was just Tilly and her grandma, who stretched out her hands across the table and grasped Tilly's tightly.

'It will work itself out,' she said. 'I promise. Don't be scared.'

'I'm not,' said Tilly, although she wasn't sure if that were true. 'But I don't want bookwandering to end for children *forever* because of me. If I could stop it, surely I should try? We could at least go and see what they want.'

Grandma didn't say anything, but a look of uncertainty crossed her face.

'Did they already say what they want?' Tilly said quietly.

Grandma shrugged helplessly. 'Your grandad doesn't want you to be scared,' she said.

'I can deal with it,' Tilly said. 'And I don't think

it's fair to keep it from me.'

'I know, I know,' Grandma said, clearly conflicted. 'Anyway, I'm sure you can imagine. You know what they wanted when they lured you to the fairytale book. They think your blood, or something to do with your very nature, is the key to permanently being able to steal the true immortality of stories. It's just not worth the risk – we don't know what they're capable of.'

'And we're not going to find out,' Bea said from the doorway.

Tilly and her grandma looked up. They hadn't noticed her come back in.

'Oskar's coming round this evening for a sleepover,' Bea continued. She turned to Grandma. 'Mum, can I have a word with you and Dad in the shop?'

Tilly went to protest, but saw something in her mum's eyes that stopped her in her tracks.

'I'll go and get a bed ready,' she said instead, and Bea gave her a tight smile as she headed back into the bookshop. Tilly and Bea were still getting to know each other, but one thing Tilly knew for sure was that her mum was definitely up to something. And Tilly wanted to find out what it was.

That evening, a few hours after Oskar had arrived, and after a dinner of potato-and-spinach curry, the two friends were chatting on the sofa in front of the fireplace in Pages & Co. There were not many days left before Grandma would clear out the fire and replace it with garlands of fresh flowers, but it still felt cosy and warm for now.

Tilly had started carrying the key from *The Secret Garden* around with her as if it might suddenly reveal how she was supposed to use it, and was playing with it as they watched the flames dance.

'Do you have any more idea why you ended up with that?' Oskar asked, pointing at the key.

'No,' said Tilly with a sigh.

When she'd spoken to her mum, it had seemed so clear and so logical, but it was hard to maintain her confidence in the clues when it was questioned over and over again by her grandparents, not to mention the Underwoods' new threat adding even more pressure to what she chose to do. 'Over Christmas there was so much going on, and I was convinced it all meant something, but now I don't feel so sure.'

'There was the key, and that really thin book, and something else, right?' Oskar asked.

'The thread,' Tilly said. 'The red thread. I just can't ignore the feeling that they mean something important. I said to my mum that it seems like a treasure map, as though, if I could just work out how all the clues fit together, it would become obvious. But now we can't even bookwander, and aren't allowed at the Underlibrary, I don't know what we're supposed to do. And Grandma and Grandad are just cross about it all the time, but don't seem to be actually doing anything to stop the Underwoods.'

'Can I tell you something weird?' Oskar said.

'Of course.'

'It's just that I feel more cross about not being *allowed* to bookwander than not actually bookwandering. Does that make sense?'

'Kind of,' Tilly admitted. 'I wonder if it's like learning a language or an instrument or something, where if you don't use it you sort of forget about it. And sometimes I get this bad feeling in my stomach, but I can't work out what's causing it.'

'What a weird six months we've had,' Oskar said. 'Finding Bea, and going to Paris, and getting lost in fairy tales, and dealing with . . . what was his name?'

'Who do you mean?' Tilly asked. 'Melville?'

'No, no,' Oskar said. 'There was another man, wasn't there? I want to say he was the Underwoods' . . . butler? He had some kind of . . . hat? And was there a fire or something? Maybe I'm just getting confused with something I read in a book.'

'I have no idea who you're talking about,' Tilly said. 'What kind of hat?'

'A . . . Do you know, I can't remember,' Oskar said.

'Never mind. I'm obviously mixing him up with some other story. Strange.'

There was a fraction of a second where Tilly thought that maybe she knew what Oskar meant, but the thought vanished as quickly as it had arrived and she shrugged. There were bigger things to worry about. And so they changed the subject to what Jack had been cooking up for the bookshop café, and said no more about the man in the hat or the fire.

5

THOUGH SHE BE BUT LITTLE

Tilly woke in the middle of the night to Bea's finger on her lips. It was dark except for the gentle haze of London's streetlights soaking through the skylight.

'Is everyone okay?' Tilly whispered, glancing over at Oskar, who was snoring gently on the air bed in the other corner of the room.

Bea nodded. 'Do you trust me?' she asked very quietly, and Tilly didn't have to think twice. She nodded.

'I need you to get together some clothes and other bits very quickly and quietly, and I'll answer all your questions when we're in the taxi.'

'The *taxi*?' Tilly said, adrenalin coursing through her, ridding her of any traces of sleepiness. 'I *knew* you were up to something! Where are we going? What are we doing with Oskar?'

'He's coming too,' Bea said. 'I spoke to Mary on the phone earlier and arranged everything.'

She went over and gently shook Oskar awake. He grunted in a somewhat undignified way, which Tilly and Bea pretended they didn't hear.

'Huh?' he said, still half asleep. He took in Bea and the dark and sat upright. 'Ohhh, are we going? Mum said you'd asked if she was happy for me to go on a trip with you, but I didn't realise it was going to be in the middle of the night. Where are we going?'

He looked at Tilly, who just shrugged.

'Get dressed in something comfy,' Bea said, 'and grab anything you'd want for weather a little warmer than this. Oh, and make sure you have your passport to hand.'

'My passport?' Tilly repeated in surprise, and Bea shushed her, looking a little jumpy. 'I promise I'll explain in the taxi. But we need to get going.'

'Do . . . do Grandma and Grandad know we're

going?' Tilly asked, but she knew the answer already.

'It's time for us to take matters into our own hands,' Bea said. 'I'm going to get your toothbrushes, and I want you ready to go in ten minutes.'

Bea crept out of the bedroom, leaving Tilly and Oskar staring at each other.

'You knew we were going somewhere?' Tilly said accusingly. 'And you didn't say anything all evening!'

'I thought you knew!' he said. 'And anyway Mum just made it sound as though your family might be going to, like, the countryside for a night, not somewhere that needed a passport! Do you think I should text her?'

'Let's find out where we're going before we worry her,' Tilly said. She was nervous, but she had a feeling this was going to be their one chance and she didn't want anything getting in the way. They quickly got dressed and Tilly pulled out a few bits of clothing and shoved them into the small wheelie suitcase her mum had put out.

'Ready to go?' Bea whispered, her head round the

door, holding out a washbag for Tilly to put in her suitcase.

They nodded, fizzing with nervous excitement, and the three of them crept downstairs, through the kitchen, cold in the spring night air, and into the bookshop, which was still and dark around them. Tilly couldn't help thinking about her grandparents, and how they were going to wake up tomorrow and realise they were gone.

Hopefully, her mum had left them a note.

On the road a car was waiting in the orange puddle of a streetlight. The driver helped Bea put their bags in the boot as they slid into the taxi and it set off, heading west, out of London.

'Can you tell us what's going on now?' Tilly said, the reality of what they were doing sinking further in with every mile that they got from Pages & Co.

'I think it's time that we trust your instincts about the Archivists,' Bea said. 'There has to be a reason you can do the things you do, Tilly, and there has to be a reason why you've ended up with all those clues. Bookwanderers treat the Archivists as wishful thinking, but it makes sense to me that there are people somewhere who could stop Underlibraries doing such terrible things. I trust you, Tilly. And so does Oskar.'

'He does?' Oskar said in surprise. Tilly and Bea stared at him. 'I mean, of course I do,' he said. 'In a general sense, at least.'

'I'll take it,' Tilly grinned. 'I trust you too . . . in a general sense.'

'And anyway,' Bea went on, 'I for one am not just going to sit around, waiting for the Underwoods to do even more damage to bookwandering, and goodness knows what other problems they're causing. They clearly don't give two hoots about the impact of their actions. However –' she paused – 'I could not get your grandparents to agree. I tried one last time this afternoon, and they're convinced it's not worth the risk. But this isn't the time to be sitting around: we have to stand up to the Underwoods. Have you two ever heard the saying, "If not us, who? And if not now, when?" That's how I'm feeling. Tilly, if you think the start of the map – or the treasure hunt or whatever we want to call it – is at the Library of Congress, then that's where you need to begin.'

'Hang on,' Tilly said as Bea's words sank in. 'We're going to *America*?'

'We're going *where*?' Oskar repeated incredulously. 'Does my mum know?'

'Sort of,' Bea said, looking sheepish. 'She knows you're going abroad and that you'll be looked after. You'll meet one of my old university friends, in fact! He owns a bookshop and his husband is a librarian at the Library of Congress and I've filled them in on what's going on. They're both bookwanderers, of course. Tilly, I put your clues in your backpack – double-check you have them all?'

Tilly looked inside her backpack and made sure everything was there: the slim book, the key, the thread and the breadcrumbs.

'Got them,' she said.

'Good,' Bea said. 'Now I'll take you into the airport and get you to security, and Orlando will meet you at the other end.'

Tilly stared at her mum in horror. 'You're *not coming with us?*'

'I can't, I'm sorry. But I'll text you a photo of Orlando so you know who to look for when you get there, and I've given him a codeword too. Make sure he says "Hermia" to you.'

'Why Hermia?' asked Tilly.

'She's a character from *A Midsummer Night's Dream.*' Bea smiled. 'Another character says about her "though she be but little, she is fierce", and it's a line that makes me think of you.'

'That's very lovely and all,' Oskar said, 'but could we focus on the fact that you're sending us to America by ourselves? Why can't you come with us?'

'I have something I need to take care of here,' Bea said, determination running through her voice like **steel.**

6

AT LEAST EIGHTY PER CENT SURE

B ea refused to explain more about why she wasn't coming with them, which worried Tilly more than the trip itself.

'Does my mum know you're just putting us on a plane and leaving us?' Oskar said.

'Not in so many words,' Bea said. 'But I'm sure she'd understand.'

Oskar's face suggested he felt otherwise.

'I'll deal with your mum,' she promised. 'And you'll be totally safe in DC – you're being picked up by Orlando. He's one of the very best people I've ever known, and he knows exactly what's going on. And, crucially, his husband Jorge works at the Library of

Congress and they'll go with you.' She took a deep breath.

'We need to let you two have the space to find the Archivists,' she said. 'The clues – the map – have all ended up with you, and the Underwoods know that you're the key to all of it, and you two working together clearly terrifies them. It's not just your blood they want, Tilly: they want to stop you doing anything to get in their way, because they know that you two are the greatest threat to their plans. It's why we have to do it this way.'

'But surely you can come with us?' Tilly said, feeling incredibly overwhelmed.

'I need to stop them coming after you,' Bea said, and wouldn't go into any more detail. 'Come on, we're here.'

Tilly had never been to an airport before, let alone on an aeroplane. Bea made sure they had everything they needed, including texting them both photos of Orlando and all his details. She wasn't allowed to come through security with them, but presented a form to a security person and Tilly and Oskar were given 'Unaccompanied Minor' lanyards and told someone would help them find their gate, and that someone else would take them through customs once they landed in America.

'Stay together,' was the last thing Bea said to them. 'Trust each other and take care of each other. If anyone can find the Archivists, it's you two.'

Then she stood and watched them, until Tilly and Oskar had to turn a corner and were out of sight.

The two of them sat, a little shell-shocked, next to each other on uncomfortable plastic chairs in the huge terminal at Heathrow airport. People kept glancing at them, but no one stopped and asked if they were okay, and Tilly wasn't sure what she would say if someone did.

'Oskar,' Tilly said, very quietly. 'What if all of this *is* just wishful thinking? What if the things I've gathered aren't clues? What if Grandma and Grandad are right and it's just a pile of junk that I've convinced myself means more than it does?'

'I'm going to be blunt, Tilly,' Oskar said. 'One minute you're absolutely dead certain, and the next you're not sure at all. I get why you're worried, but now is the time to decide, one way or the other. I'd really rather not go to America unless you're, let's say, at least eighty per cent sure you're right.'

'That's fair,' Tilly nodded. 'And I reckon I am eighty per cent sure – just. And that twenty per cent means you don't get to say I told you so if I'm wrong.' She was aiming for a joke, but Oskar didn't laugh; he was still obviously finding it a little difficult to believe that his best friend's mum had just dropped him off at the airport with no warning.

'Is it weird to say I feel like I've just been kidnapped?' Oskar said.

'No,' Tilly said. 'I feel the same, and it's my mum. I'm sorry she didn't tell us what she was doing. I know this is . . . extreme. You don't have to come with me. We can call Grandma and Grandad and they'd come and pick you up straight away and you'd be home before your mum realised anything weird was going on.'

'You said *I'd* be home, not *we'd* be home,' Oskar said. 'You're going to go? Even though you're not even sure the clues mean anything? Even though we have to go and do this by ourselves?'

'I have to try,' Tilly said. She had filled him in on the visit from the Underwoods when he'd arrived at Pages & Co., and the stakes. 'I have to do something, and this is the only idea I've got so I guess this is what I'm doing. I've just realised that if the Underwoods have bound all the books at the British Underlibrary, it won't just be affecting British bookwanderers – no one will be able to bookwander into *any* copies of those books, wherever they live. Books don't know what country they're in.'

'But won't other Underlibraries try and stop them

in that case?' said Oskar. 'I can't imagine the librarians we met at the French Underlibrary would let that happen. Shouldn't we leave it up to them?'

'Maybe they haven't realised yet,' suggested Tilly. 'But no, someone must have. Maybe Mum's friend will be able to tell us what's going on in America – they must have noticed.'

'Tilly,' Oskar said, 'if you think there's something in this map, or whatever you're calling it, then I'm in too. I'd rather see what we can find than sit around at home, waiting for those two to come and find us. And I am not a fan of someone taking away my bookwandering, after I was just getting good at it.'

He paused, and Tilly thought he was about to come up with a useful idea. 'Shall we get some food?' was what he actually said. 'I hope your mum gave you some money to make up for the whole kidnapping thing.'

They found a café with an empty table and, despite everything that was going on, they couldn't entirely ignore the joy of having no adults to tell them what they could or couldn't order.

'How much have you got?' Oskar asked as Tilly took out the purse Bea had given her. 'Because I want a chocolate milkshake, and they're seven pounds fifty.'

'We've got fifty pounds in English money,' Tilly said, not sure she'd ever held so much cash before. 'And –' she looked at the other notes in the purse – 'one hundred dollars in American money.' She said this last part quietly, feeling a little bit like she was announcing a prize on a reality TV show.

'Kerching!' Oskar said. 'Waiter, I'll have one of everything!'

'I think it's for emergencies, really,' Tilly said.

'I know, I know,' Oskar said. 'But missing breakfast is an emergency. I'm going to have the full English.'

As they ordered, a couple sat down at the table next to them, grinning at each other intently, despite the early hour.

'We're on our honeymoon,' the man said to Tilly without being asked.

'Oh, congratulations!' Tilly said, feeling awkward.

'We're going to the Seychelles,' the woman said,

holding out her hand so they could see her sparkling diamond alongside a wedding ring. 'Where are you two off to?'

'And where are your parents?' the man asked. 'You're awfully young to be by yourselves at an airport.'

'Someone's meeting us at the other end,' Oskar said. 'Oh, look! Is that our food coming?' And the two of them watched the kitchen intently, hoping the couple would stop trying to make conversation. Thankfully, their food did arrive only moments later.

'I wonder what Mum's planning to say to my grandparents,' Tilly said quietly over her ham-and-cheese omelette. 'They're not going to be thrilled about this. Pretty sure dropping two twelve-year-olds off at an airport with a load of money and a photo of a man to meet in America is not traditionally seen as great parenting.'

'When you put it like that, it makes us sound like we're in a spy movie or something,' Oskar said, eyes lighting up. 'A contact on the other side of the world. An envelope full of cash. A mysterious map. I feel like

Nicolas Cage. I'm starting to get more into this whole treasure-hunt thing.'

After eating, they paid an exhausted-looking waitress and started gathering up their bags to go and wait for the person who was going to take them to their departure gate. Abruptly, as Tilly double-checked that they had their money and passports, noisy crying erupted from the table next to them and they looked over to see the newly married man in floods of tears.

'I just . . . think I've made a horrible mistake,' the woman was saying, standing up. 'I'm so sorry. It's just . . . All of a sudden, I was looking at you, and it was like . . . it was like I was looking at a stranger and I just couldn't quite remember why we got married or . . .' She tailed off, looking uncomfortable, before grabbing her bag and running out of the café. But by this point the man was drying his tears on a napkin and starting to look a bit more composed.

'Do you know,' he said to Tilly and Oskar, 'I think

she's right, really. I can't even remember why we were together when I come to think about it. Oh well!' He put some money on the table and followed her out of the café.

'That was . . . weird,' Oskar said as they headed to the information desk.

'Very,' agreed Tilly. 'How can you just forget why you're in love with someone?'

But they didn't have much time to dwell on it as they were quickly collected by an airport official and taken to their gate to board. After a lot of sitting around, waiting for their section to be called, and then a lot of standing in a queue, finally they were in their seats.

Once safely onboard, the novelty of her first plane journey wore off quickly, and so Tilly tried to lean into the strange, otherworldly experience of being on a plane. The next eight hours went by in a blur of napping, half watching films, and eating strangely textured foods that arrived at seemingly random intervals and then were whisked away.

It was only when she landed that Tilly realised she hadn't even picked up the book she'd brought with her.

7

SoUNDS LIKE A REAL MESS

The time difference meant they'd gone the wrong way in time, and it was still very early when they landed in Washington DC. They were accompanied through customs by another airport official and got through with no problems other than an extremely long queue, and a slight pause when the border security guard asked why they were visiting the US. They had Orlando's address to show him, but assumed telling him that they were on a magical treasure hunt to save bookwandering wasn't something he could type into his computer, so they just said they were visiting friends.

'Have a nice trip,' he said, stamping their passports and waving them through.

'Okay,' Tilly said, showing Oskar the photo of Orlando on her phone again as they walked out into the arrivals area. The picture showed a smiling white man with a beard and blond hair tied up in a messy bun. Tilly and Oskar looked around the bustling space anxiously, before a loud American voice boomed across the crowd.

'Beatrice Pages' daughter! I never thought I'd see the day!'

Orlando looked exactly like his photo, right down to the broad smile. He was wearing Doc Martens, worn jeans and a denim shirt open over a T-shirt. He wrapped them both up in a huge hug.

Then he paused. 'Oh sorry! Hermia! Hermia! I forgot the code word. Welcome to Washington DC!'

'Um, thanks,' said Tilly. 'I'm Tilly, obviously.'

Orlando stepped back and beamed at them. 'And . . . Oskar, right?'

'Right,' said Oskar.

'So, how are you guys doing?' Orlando said gently, clearly trying to tone down his natural exuberance –

and, to her surprise and embarrassment, Tilly burst into tears. At the sight of Tilly's tears, Oskar followed shortly afterwards. 'Hey, hey, hey!' Orlando said, looking a little nervous. 'Did something happen on the way?'

'No.' Tilly sniffed. 'We're fine. It's just . . . the whole . . . being tricked into flying to America by your own mum to save bookwandering thing.'

'It's quite a lot to deal with,' Oskar said, wiping away a tear.

'You bet,' Orlando said gently. 'Well, I think you're doing brilliantly by just getting here. And I know someone else who does too. Come meet Jorge – he'll be getting stressed about parking in the wrong place for too long, I'm sure.' He put a reassuring hand on their shoulders and guided them through the airport, to where a battered powder-blue station wagon was idling, a slender, nervous-looking man waiting in the driver's seat.

'Come on, Orlando!' the man called out of the open window. 'That security guard has been glaring at me ever since I parked up here.'

Orlando grinned, tossed their bags in the car and helped them up into the back seat. 'This is Jorge,' he said, gesturing to the driver, who was sweating slightly as he manoeuvred the car into a lane of traffic. He had light brown skin and dark curly hair and was wearing a smart button-down shirt.

'Hi,' said Jorge from the front seat, with a gentle accent that Tilly couldn't quite place. 'I promise I'll be much more welcoming once we're out of this godforsaken airport.' He gesticulated at another driver and swore out of the window, which prompted a slightly sheepish smile from Orlando. But indeed, once they'd left the maze of roads around the airport, Jorge glanced back at them, a warm smile on his face.

'Welcome,' he said. 'Sorry you had to witness that. I do not enjoy driving this beast of a car in busy areas, but Orlando insisted on us buying it. How are you both doing? Did you manage to sleep at all on the plane?'

'A little bit,' said Oskar and Tilly nodded. Although she hadn't slept much and sheer adrenalin had been keeping her alert until they landed.

'So you know my mum from university?' she said. 'We didn't get a lot of information before we left.'

'Yep,' Orlando said cheerfully, twisting round in his seat so he could look at them. 'We both worked part time at a bookstore in New York – that's how we each realised the other was a bookwanderer.'

'So, you knew Mum when . . .' Tilly tailed off, not sure how much they knew about who her father was.

'Yeah, we knew her when she was visiting *A Little Princess* and fell in love with your father,' Orlando said straightforwardly but kindly, showing that he knew Tilly was half fictional without making a fuss. 'When Bea first moved back to London, we had no idea she was even pregnant, but we kept in touch for a bit until we stopped hearing from her. We thought she'd got new friends in London; of course, it didn't even cross our minds that she was trapped in a book. But we can chat more about all of that kind of stuff later, if you want?' Orlando said. 'I have to admit we're a little bit in the dark about the plan

– Bea made it sound like everything was quite urgent.'

'Yes,' said Tilly, who was starting to struggle to keep her eyes open. 'We need to go to the Library of Congress straight away. She told you about the bookbinding, right . . .?'

'She sure did,' Orlando said. 'It sounds like a real mess. No wonder things have been off in the book world. I'm glad you guys have a plan to help.'

'Something like that,' Oskar said sleepily. Orlando eyed the two drowsy children in the back seat.

'Okay, well, why don't you two nap a little on the drive into town? We can drop your stuff off at the bookstore, which is close to the Library of Congress, and go from there.'

'Sounds good,' Tilly said, letting the rhythm of the car lull her to sleep.

'Can we . . . get some . . . food . . . too?' Oskar added, and it was not long before the two of them were fast asleep, heads resting against the car windows as they drove through Washington DC.

8

GOOD BOOKSHOPS ARE HARD TO RESIST

Orlando gently shook them awake after about forty-five minutes.

'Hey, sleepyheads,' he said. 'We've picked up some breakfast burritos for you. I thought you might like to see some of the sights as we get into the city and you can have a moment to wake up properly before we get to the store.'

He passed back two hot, foil-wrapped burritos full of spicy scrambled eggs, avocado and black beans and two glass bottles of fresh orange juice.

Tilly and Oskar ate and drank contentedly while gazing out of the windows at the cherry blossom trees that lined the road.

'Once all this bookwandering stuff is cleared up, you'll have to come back and stay – with your families – and do some proper exploring,' Orlando said as he pointed out some of the famous sights.

They saw the gigantic Lincoln Memorial – a huge stone structure that looked like something out of a Greek myth, the tall, elegant Washington Monument sticking up into the sky as though it were trying to pierce the clouds and, looking up the hill from that tower, they could just about  see the famous shape of the White House itself, where the American president lived.

Before too long, Jorge turned the car into a crisscross of streets lined with Chinese restaurants and coffee shops. They drove past a huge stadium right in the middle of the city and a tall, glass-fronted theatre before Jorge parked behind a large red-brick building, and he and Orlando helped get the luggage out of the boot.

'Enough history for now,' Orlando grinned. 'Time for the important stuff – books.'

They walked round to the front. 'For the full effect,' Orlando said proudly as they looked up at a huge building with big windows, through which they could see a busy bookshop. A large sign over the door read **'Shakespeare's Sisters'** with a large quill illustration as a logo.

'Why's it called that?' Oskar asked, staring up at the sign. 'How many sisters did Shakespeare even have?'

'Well, he had one sister who lived to be an adult,' Orlando

said. 'But that's just one of the reasons for the name. You'll see when we go inside that it's a pretty special building – it actually used to be a theatre, and we've tried to keep as much of the structure as it was – we still have the stage and everything. We've added a lot of bookshelves, of course. People come from all over to look at our Shakespeare collection.'

'So . . . why is it named after his sisters then?' Tilly asked.

'I'm getting there.' Orlando smiled. 'I'm just giving you the full spiel as it's your first time here! It's because it's not about Shakespeare's real sisters; it's about a made-up one called Judith.'

'You know the British writer Virginia Woolf?' Jorge interrupted, with a smile, seemingly used to hearing this explanation and trying to speed Orlando up a little.

The name rang a bell with Tilly, but she couldn't place it, and shook her head; she had a rule never to pretend she'd read a book that she hadn't, however tempting it sometimes was.

'She lived a while ago,' Orlando went on. 'And

part of the reason I love her is because I was named after one of her characters. But another one of her books was about women and writing, and in it she imagined what life might have been like for a made-up version of Shakespeare's sister. It's about what would have happened to a woman who wanted to be a writer in Elizabethan times and the stories she might have written if she'd had the same education and opportunities as good old Will Shakespeare. So that's what I named the shop for – all the stories that didn't make it out into the world, for one reason or another.'

'I like it.' Oskar nodded approvingly. 'But it's kind of complicated. You had to do a lot of explaining.'

'Well, we like to think it sounds good even if you're just walking past the store,' Orlando said. 'But sometimes it's worth getting the whole story, don't you think?' He gazed up at the shop. 'You know, bookstores are monuments to writers, in a way,' he said. 'Lincoln and Washington have their statues, and Shakespeare has this. It's a little less grand, but I think he'd like it anyway.'

'You sound just like Tilly's grandad,' Oskar said. 'He loves a speech about the importance of bookshops.'

Once they were inside, it was obvious the building had previously been a theatre. Although various walls had been removed, there was a huge wooden stage at the far end to where they stood, with heavy scarlet curtains framing it. But instead of actors or lights or props on the stage there were shelves and shelves of books. One wide staircase wound upwards towards a balcony, and another down to another floor. The bookshop was all artfully curated faded glamour, with a kitsch chandelier still hanging from its high ceiling and some old velvet theatre chairs arranged in pockets among the shelves for people to sit and read.

'Welcome to Shakespeare's Sisters!' Orlando said proudly. 'Let's store your stuff somewhere safe and then you can come see our Shakespeare balcony quickly before we head up to the library.'

Orlando looked so proud of his bookshop that Tilly didn't have the heart to insist that they go straight to the library to start the hunt for the Archivists.

They were already here, so what was an extra ten minutes to see the shop properly? Good bookshops are hard to resist after all.

9

I KNOW A BANK WHERE THE WILD THYME BLOWS

They left all their luggage in Orlando's locked office, but Tilly made sure that she kept the small backpack with the clues in with her.

Then they followed Orlando and Jorge up the stairs, passing an archway that revealed a small room hung with more colours and patterns of wrapping paper than Tilly could count, as well as reams and reams of ribbons and tissue paper and other accoutrements. A petite woman with warm amber-coloured skin was standing at a desk piled high with books. She had at least five different brightly coloured ribbons woven through her black hair, and was focused intently on wrapping a large hardback book in brown paper.

'Ah, that's Deepti, and our wrapping room,' Orlando said. 'If customers need a book wrapped for a special occasion, then we bring them here where they can choose how they want it.'

The woman looked up and grinned widely at them. 'Friends of yours?' she said.

'The best of friends,' Orlando said. 'This is Matilda – the daughter of one my closest friends at university. And this is Matilda's best friend, Oskar.'

'Are you guys over on vacation?' Deepti asked, and Tilly said no at the same time as Jorge said yes and Deepti raised an eyebrow. 'Well, either way, if you buy a book while you're here, be sure to come get it wrapped. I'm certain it will be on the house. By the way, Orlando, have you caught up with Candy? She was looking for you – a couple more books have gone missing over the last few days, and she thinks maybe it's a shoplifter? Although they're choosing strange books, if that's the case – anyway, you should go find her when you can so she can tell you about it.'

'Thanks, Deepti, I will,' Orlando said.

'Is Deepti a bookwanderer too?' Tilly asked as they continued up the stairs to the balcony.

'I don't think so,' he said.

'Haven't you asked?' Oskar said, surprised. 'I thought there was some kind of record of bookwanderers at the Underlibrary.'

'I'm sure there is, but I wouldn't go check up on my booksellers,' Orlando said. 'If she is, I'm sure we'll work it out at some point. I think the Pages family might have given you a false impression of how common bookwandering is! But there's probably at least one more here – booksellers are, of course, particularly likely to be bookwanderers.'

By this time, they had reached the balcony that stretched all the way round the bookshop. The shelves were full of plays by Shakespeare, in every sort of edition from cheap paperbacks to beautiful, ornate hardbacks, as well as books about Shakespeare, about the time he lived in, and lots and lots of Shakespeare merchandise.

Tilly wondered if she had time to buy a calendar

full of Shakespeare's best insults as a peace offering for Grandad before she forced herself to focus. As tired as she was, and as much as she wanted to spend hours exploring the bookshop, they had to keep going.

'It's a beautiful shop, Orlando,' she said, 'but we—'

'Thank you!' said Orlando, cutting her off. 'We're pretty proud of it. We have the best customers in the world as well. What do you think of this Shakespeare balcony, eh? Balcony, get it?'

'Huh?' Tilly said, thrown.

'Balcony!' Orlando said, delighted by his own joke. '"Romeo, Romeo, wherefore art thou Romeo . . ."?'

'Ohhhh,' Tilly said, the penny dropping. 'Yeah, I

get it. Cool, but the thing is we really need to . . .'

'Have you seen this?' asked Orlando, pulling a particularly lovely edition of *A Midsummer Night's Dream* off a shelf. 'Have you ever read it?' He opened it and put it in Tilly's hands, and she could see a beautiful illustration of the forest where the play was set.

'We read bits of it at school,' Tilly said. 'But I've not seen it on stage before. I think our teacher said it was on at the Globe, though, so I might get to see it soon. But anyway how far away did you say . . .'

'It's one of my favourite places to bookwander,' said Orlando dreamily. '"I know a bank where the wild thyme . . ."' He looked embarrassed. 'I always forget if it's "blows" or "grows" – what is it?'

'*I know a bank where the wild thyme blows . . .*' Tilly read out loud, stopping as she felt something move against her arm. She brushed it away, thinking to herself that she hoped Washington didn't have any particularly horrible types of spiders – but, instead of a spider, her hand met a thin rope of vine.

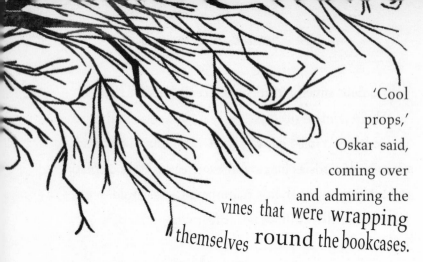

'Cool
props,'
Oskar said,
coming over
and admiring the
vines that were wrapping
themselves round the bookcases.

'How do you get them to move like that?'

'We don't,' Orlando said, staring at the foliage as it kept growing.

'Oh no,' Tilly said, realisation dawning on her as the vines snaked over the books, leaves rustling. 'It's happening again. And I barely even read anything!'

'It's happening . . . again?' repeated Orlando.

'Yeah,' Tilly said nervously. 'Sometimes . . . I seem to . . . Well, a couple of times, when I've been reading a book, the scenery has sort of, well, escaped the book a bit.'

'Ah,' Jorge said, his eyes widening. 'And this just . . . happens?'

'Well, it's only happened a few times,' Tilly said,

a little defensively. 'And never this quickly. I'm not exactly in control of it.'

'And does it just keep coming?' Orlando said, taking a step backwards as he eyed the ever-expanding forest and looking to see if any customers had noticed.

'Not usually,' Tilly said. 'But it doesn't normally happen this quickly or this much!'

'And *that* doesn't usually happen either, right?' Oskar said, pointing down at Tilly's ankle where a vine was curling itself round her leg.

'Uh, no,' Tilly said, panicking and shaking her leg, trying to free herself. 'They're not usually so . . .'

'Alive?' Jorge said, pale-faced. 'Are they hurting you?'

'No.'

'But I kind of think that's beside the point at the moment,' Oskar said, bending down and trying to pull the vine off Tilly's ankle, but another one crept out from a bookcase and wrapped itself round his wrist.

'Why is a tree trying to eat us!' Oskar said through gritted teeth, fighting a losing battle against the increasingly strong vines.

'I don't think it's the tree,' Tilly said. 'I think it's the book.'

Orlando stared at her, then down at the book in her hands. He grabbed it from her and shook it, as if that might stop the vines.

'Put it down!' said Oskar. Orlando panicked and threw it behind a bookcase instead, which did nothing to stop the twisting plants from getting a tighter and tighter hold on Tilly and Oskar.

'Sorry!' Orlando said desperately, going to retrieve the book.

'Um, a little help?' Tilly said to Jorge, who was watching all of this, mouth open in shock.

'Yeah, sorry, of course,' Jorge stammered. 'I'll go get some scissors!'

'Grab a knife too!' Orlando yelled after him while scrabbling for the book. And then, before Orlando could work out what to try next, Tilly felt a pull around her tummy button and the unmistakable smell of toasting marshmallows filled

the
air.

10

BUTTERSCOTCH AND
CAMPFIRES

The majestic ceiling of Shakespeare's Sisters dissolved away into nothingness, its bookshelves collapsing down until Tilly and Oskar found themselves, free of vines, in a forest glade that seemed too lovely to be real. They stood up and dusted themselves off, glancing around for any characters.

'That was weird,' Tilly said. 'And I feel like I'm saying that a lot at the moment.'

'Too much,' Oskar said, rubbing his wrists where the vines had got hold of him. 'But hey! At least we can bookwander!'

'That's . . . Well, that's weird too, isn't it?' Tilly said. 'Because isn't the Source Edition of *A Midsummer*

Night's Dream at the British Underlibrary, locked up with book magic?'

'Maybe they forgot this one,' Oskar said optimistically. 'Or it's because the book ate us and that doesn't count as proper bookwandering?'

'Can we think of a different way of describing it, please?' Tilly said. 'Rather than books *eating* us.'

'Sure,' Oskar said. 'I wonder why the book kidnapped us. I wonder why it . . . No, I'm out. I'm sticking with ate.'

'At least Orlando has the book,' Tilly said. 'So he can come and get us. Unless . . .'

'Unless the book *is* bound, then he won't be able to bookwander in it, will he?' Oskar finished. 'So, what do we do?'

'We need to get into the Endpapers and hope they take us to an Underlibrary,' Tilly said. 'We need to get to the end of the play. I guess we just have to let it happen and hope not too much time passes in the real world. Or that Orlando works something out.'

They looked around, trying to work out where they

were in the play at the moment. The trees surrounding them were growing closely enough that there was a mysterious feel to the place, but not so tightly packed to be intimidating. Vines wrapped round their trunks and an improbable array of delicate pastel-coloured flowers exploded in garlands from all the greenery. It looked almost as though there were strings of fairy lights threaded among the leaves, but, when Tilly got closer, she saw it was simply the late-afternoon sunlight glinting perfectly through the leaves. The grass under their feet was bright and soft and the sound of birdsong drifted on the breeze, which was refreshing but not chilly. The air somehow smelled of butterscotch and campfires.

Even though the manner of arriving there was rather disconcerting, the place itself was peaceful and lovely. Oskar elbowed Tilly and put a finger to his lips, pointing to a break in the trees, just beyond where they stood.

As they watched, two creatures emerged gracefully from either side of the clearing and met in the middle.

One was dressed in shades of brown, with a crown of twigs resting on his tightly curled hair. The other had white-blonde hair so fine that it fizzed round her head like candyfloss, just like her dress, which was floating about her in wisps of tulle.

Both figures were beautiful but sharp somehow, moving without the weight and awkwardness of a human body. They were all lightness and strangeness; Tilly felt instinctively scared of them and yet couldn't tear her eyes away.

The two circled each other, speaking too quietly for Tilly and Oskar to hear.

'What's happening?' Oskar whispered.

'I think that must be Puck,' Tilly replied, pointing at the one in brown. 'We did this in school, remember?'

'All I can remember is that there was a man who got turned into a donkey, to be honest,' Oskar said. 'And I definitely didn't picture the fairies being so . . .'

'So lovely,' Tilly finished.

'So weird,' Oskar corrected. 'There's that word again. And look, someone else is coming.'

He pointed back to the other side of the clearing, where a tall, slender man was emerging from the trees, wearing a robe made of leaves. A delicate circlet of gold sat on his head, and he was followed by other smaller sprites, who were the same size as Puck and the fairy with the candyfloss hair. He was met by a woman who approached from the other side of the glade, flanked by her own attendants. She was as tall as he was, wearing a dress of green silk that seemed to blend into the grass she stood on, so it was impossible to tell where she ended and the forest began.

'Ill met by moonlight, proud Titania,' the man said, his voice carrying easily to Tilly and Oskar, who had edged backwards so as to be hidden by the trees.

'What, jealous Oberon?' the woman replied, gesturing for the fairies gathered round her to take a step back.

'Am I not thy lord?' the man said, stepping closer to her. Tilly raised an eyebrow at Oskar.

'Then I must be thy lady,' Titania replied, the suggestion of a smile on her lips.

'*But I know when thou hast stolen away from fairy land.*'

'Are they enemies?' Oskar asked, confused. 'I thought they were married. The details, as I mentioned, are fuzzy.'

'They are,' Tilly said. 'Sort of. I don't think fairies care about marriage – but they're definitely, like, together. Romantically. Anyway, Oberon is the worst. He uses Puck to cast a spell on Titania and she falls in love with Bottom.'

'The man who gets turned into a donkey!' Oskar said. 'It's all coming back to me. I swear if I wrote a story at school with a character called Bottom who turns into a donkey, I would not be treated as a genius like Shakespeare was. Honestly, it's not fair! Can you even imagine Ms Webber's face if I called someone Bottom at school! The thing with famous writers is that—'

'Oskar, shush,' Tilly said, watching Titania and Oberon walking closer and closer to each other, speaking angry words with half-smiles and the occasional brush of a hand on an arm.

But it was too late, and Oskar's voice had carried too clearly towards the fairy king and queen so that, by the time he'd finished speaking, they were staring straight at Tilly and Oskar.

11

BEGIN AT THE BEGINNING

'*Few human mortals venture here*
For fear that they may wish to stay,' Titania said in a curious, lilting voice.

'*Why come you here without the moon*
For her light makes shadows darker?
Many choose to shelter 'neath her,
But you come with cloaks of sunlight.'

'*How long do you intend to stay?*' Oberon demanded.

'*For we have much to do today.*'

'We're really sorry,' Tilly said nervously. 'We didn't mean to disturb you.'

'But while we have your attention,' Oskar said mischievously, 'do you know a man called Bottom?'

Titania raised an elegant eyebrow at Oskar, who was struggling not to laugh. Oberon just looked annoyed.

'It seems that you have travelled far,
And must have further yet to go?' he said.
'My lady, shall you let them pass?
If your eye has not been captured.
For of late you have not rendered
Unto me what should be mine.'

Titania flicked her attention from the bookwanderers back to Oberon in annoyance and said something under her breath that made Oberon's cheeks darken with anger. Even though he was so elegant and ethereal, Tilly found him just as insufferable as she had when they read bits of the play at school. She remembered again with a flash of annoyance the way Oberon used Puck to cast a spell on Titania that made her fall in love with the man with a donkey's head.

A thought occurred to her. Given that the rules of bookwandering meant that the play had to snap back to normal after they left, so she couldn't change anything permanently, surely there was no harm in altering the story a little just this once?

'My lady,' she said, dipping into a deep, if wobbly, curtsy.

Titania said nothing, but gestured with a delicate hand to indicate that Tilly had permission to speak. Oberon was barely paying attention.

'I just thought that you'd like to know that your lord Oberon has plans to bewitch you,' Tilly said, trying to mimic the way the fairies were speaking.

Oberon let out a snort of derision. *'Imp, you know not what you say. It is not wise to question me,'* he said.

'Please speak on, child. I give you leave,' Titania said.

'Tell me more of this grievous plan.'

'He's going to ask Puck to find a flower that will make you fall in love with whoever you see next,' Tilly explained, edging backwards as Oberon stopped smirking and started to look annoyed. 'And it will be a man with a donkey's head! But, even if it was the nicest man in the world, I don't think it's very fair to make you fall in love with someone without you having any say-so!'

'You dare to spread such dreadful lies?' Oberon said, towering above them.

'I swear it's true!' Tilly said, looking at Titania, who she could see knew that Oberon had it in him.

'Uh, was this a good idea when we can't get out of the book, Tilly?' Oskar said, pulling her backwards into the trees, away from Oberon's worsening temper.

At that moment there was a crackle in the air, and all of a sudden Orlando was standing next to them, breathing heavily, and holding the copy of *A Midsummer Night's Dream* in his hand.

'You found us,' Tilly breathed in relief. 'You can bookwander!'

'Oh, thank goodness,' Orlando said. 'I didn't know how I was supposed to tell Bea that a book had eaten her daughter.'

'See,' Oskar said. 'Eaten! We got *eaten* by a book.

What took you so long?'

'I came straight away!' Orlando said. 'You know how time works in books. I was trying to follow you in the text, watching where you were going, and I wandered in as soon as I had you pinned down in a scene.'

'Okay, I'll give you the benefit of the doubt,' Oskar said. 'And anyway it was just in time – Tilly is annoying the fairy king.'

Orlando hadn't even noticed Titania and Oberon standing in the trees and nearly jumped out of his skin when he did.

'Let's go,' he said, taking Tilly and Oskar firmly by the hands.

'Make sure you don't go to sleep where he can find you!' Tilly yelled to Titania. 'And watch out for fairies with flowers!'

'*I shall not forget this kindness,*' Titania called back to Tilly.

'*And if your words prove fair not false,*
Then in your debt will I remain.
And if you find you are in need,

I now swear one gift or favour.'

She gracefully inclined her head towards Tilly, gave Oberon an icy look, and disappeared back into the forest, her green silk dress

vanishing

among

the leaves.

'It is definitely time for us to go,' Orlando said and, before Oskar or Tilly had a chance to disagree, he read the final lines of the play.

'Now to 'scape the serpent's tongue,
We will make amends ere long:
Else the Puck a liar call.
So, good night unto you all.
Give me your hands, if we be friends,
And Robin shall restore amends.'

The grand pillars and walls of Shakespeare's Sisters re-formed around them and the three of them breathed a sigh of relief.

'What on earth was that about, Tilly?' Orlando asked, pale-faced. 'I've never seen anything like it.'

'My bookwandering can be . . . unpredictable,' Tilly said, the impact of what had just happened starting to sink in. 'I guess I should be careful about reading anything until we find the Archivists – maybe they'll know how the book . . . well, how it . . .'

'Ate us,' Oskar supplied.

'How it ate us,' said Tilly, giving in.

'But how did you even get in to find us?' Oskar asked Orlando. 'Isn't the Source Edition bound at the British Underlibrary?'

'We're lucky with a lot of Shakespeare,' Orlando said, with a small smile. 'Or rather we readers are lucky – not so much the British Underlibrary. A lot of the versions of the plays that were designated as Sources were stolen from the British Library years and years ago and have never turned up. And you can't make a new Source Edition, so, as long as it's never destroyed, anyone will be able to keep bookwandering inside it. You'd better keep this,' Orlando said, giving Tilly the copy of the book. 'In case the Archivists need it to work out what happened. And I don't think I should risk having it in the store any more . . . Anyway, we clearly need to get to the Library of Congress as soon as possible before anything even stranger happens. Let's find Jorge and go.'

Seconds later, Jorge ran up the stairs.

'I have scissors!' he said, out of breath. 'And a knife!' He held up a pair of plastic scissors and a butter knife. 'Oh,' he breathed. 'You're back. Never mind.'

'Come on,' Orlando said. 'We need to go to the library. Tilly, you can tell us the plan on the way.'

'The plan?' said Tilly nervously.

'The plan to find the Archivists?' Orlando said. 'Bea said you knew how.'

'It's not so much of a plan as a . . . map,' Tilly said vaguely, trying not to worry them with how little of a plan there was.

'Okay, well, we can work with a map,' Jorge said, still trying to get his breath back. 'We know it starts at the library, yes?'

Tilly nodded.

'Knowing where you're starting from is always a

good . . . well, a good start.'

'Begin at the beginning,' Orlando said.

'And go on till you come to the end: then stop,' Tilly said, completing the quote from *Alice's Adventures in Wonderland*.

As the four of them left the bookshop, none of them heard the bookseller who picked up the phone as soon as the door had closed behind them.

'Yes,' she said into the receiver. 'They've just gone. They're going to the Library of Congress. They said something about a map.'

12

A FLAW IN THE SYSTEM

The four of them grabbed a taxi – or a cab, as Orlando called it – from outside the shop and drove through the busy streets up towards the Capitol.

Orlando was squished in the back seat with Tilly and Oskar as Jorge made sure the taxi driver parked in the most convenient spot for them to get to the library, which was just behind the beautiful white domed building where American laws were made and debated.

'So what exactly *is* the plan?' Orlando asked as they walked up the hill from the road they'd been dropped off at. 'Tilly, your mom told us a bit about what was going on, but when she called it was all very rushed, and we just kind of took a leap of faith and decided to help.'

'Whatever those people are doing at your Underlibrary, it's having an effect here too,' Jorge added. 'None of the books that have their Source Editions in London – which is a lot of them – can be bookwandered into by anyone.'

'We figured,' Oskar said. 'But, if that's the case, then why aren't you doing anything about it at your Underlibrary?' He looked at Jorge.

'I'm a regular librarian,' Jorge said. 'I don't work at the American Underlibrary. I work here at the above-ground, non-bookwanderer Library of Congress.'

'And, from what we know, our Underlibrary has *always* struggled with the control that the British Underlibrary exerts over the Sources,' Orlando said. 'Dealing with the ramifications of decisions made in London is a normal part of being a bookwanderer here.'

'Oh,' said Tilly, feeling embarrassed. 'But this is much worse than usual, isn't it?'

'Absolutely,' Orlando said. 'We may be used to dealing with the butterfly effects of the British

Underlibrary, but this is having a far wider impact than usual. Of course, we can still bookwander into any Source Editions kept here in America, but it's only through luck that we can still bookwander into Shakespeare, and a few others where Sources have been lost or forgotten. And we shouldn't have to rely on that to be able to bookwander; it's a loophole, not a solution.'

'And you're sure people can't make new Source Editions?' Tilly asked.

'No,' Jorge said. 'It's a definite flaw in the system. I don't think it was thought through very well at all, if you ask me. It's such a risk – imagine if someone found the Shakespeare ones and destroyed them, on purpose or by accident! They'd just vanish from history. I dread to think what would happen to the world if Shakespeare's plays had never existed.'

'So, that's what happens if a Source Edition is destroyed?' Oskar asked, eyes wide. 'They're just . . . gone forever? We saw a book that . . . that . . . I can't remember his name, but we saw a Source Edition get burned up and . . . What was his name, Tilly? Was that a Source Edition?'

'I don't remember,' Tilly said. 'It can't have been that important.' She shrugged; she could remember a book being burned, sort of, but the memory was hazy, as though it had happened a long time ago.

'Of course, if whatever Oskar is talking about was a Source, you wouldn't know if it was important or not,' Jorge said as they walked up to the library entrance. 'If it's gone, it's gone for good. The book no longer exists and never existed. I don't really know how it works; maybe you'd feel something if a Source that meant a lot to you was destroyed, but I hope I never find out.'

'Jorge and I met because of a book,' Orlando said. 'Jorge came to an event at the store where I was interviewing an author about their novel. I guess if that book was destroyed then we'd never have met. What a horrible idea.' He shuddered at the thought.

'All the more reason to focus,' Jorge said, squeezing Orlando's hand reassuringly. 'Now, where do we start, Tilly?'

Tilly opened her backpack and pulled out the slim book that one of the librarians had given to her at the French Underlibrary. Tucked inside was a small, crumpled bit of paper with a string of numbers and letters printed on it. This, she had been told, was a classmark – a signpost to help you find the right book in a library. Tilly felt a little bit embarrassed handing it over as though it were the key to everything, but Jorge took it reverently in his hand and studied the numbers.

'So, this should be in the stacks in the Main Reading Room,' he said. 'The last few letters are smudged, but we can get pretty close with this, at least to the right shelf, I would have thought, and hopefully the book will become obvious. We don't usually allow children under sixteen in, so I'm going to say I'm giving you a tour and let's hope the security guard is in a good mood.'

The Library of Congress was part of a collection of grand old white buildings that included the Capitol. It was much older than the current British Library and they had to go through all sorts of security scans and bag searches to even get into the building. The main hall looked like an Escher drawing with stairs and pillars stretching out as far as the eye could see, all in pale stone, with autumnal-coloured tiles on the floor.

Jorge led them from the grand entrance hall through some decidedly less grand yellow-painted corridors, then to the door to the Main Reading Room. It was one of the most beautiful rooms Tilly had ever seen: a huge, domed ceiling towered over the red-and-gilt walls, the circular space was lined with dark wooden bookcases over two floors, and statues looked down on them from brightly lit arches. In the middle of the room was a large, raised issue desk, similar to the one in the main hall at the British Underlibrary, and circles of desks radiated out from it, full of people

typing on laptops or studying piles of books and manuscripts.

Despite the size of the room and the number of people in it, it was almost silent apart from the occasional whisper from the librarians helping people, and the rustle of turning pages. Orlando and Jorge stood back to let Tilly and Oskar absorb it all.

'Is the American Underlibrary beneath here?' Tilly whispered to Jorge.

'Some of it is,' he replied quietly. 'Our small Source Library is here, but most of the actual work in terms of bookwanderers and keeping track of libraries and bookstores happens at our New York branch – underneath the New York Public Library.'

'Have you ever been?' Oskar asked.

Jorge shook his head. 'I may be a bookwanderer, but I'm only moonlighting as a literary mystery solver. I'm useful to this mission because of my knowledge of classmarks, not magic. Although I'd say they're much the same thing, right? Sorry, sorry, just a little librarian joke,' he said. 'The point is that I don't usually get involved in all the politics – but these are exceptional circumstances.'

The four of them approached a desk where a librarian and a security guard were stationed, and Jorge spoke quietly to them, showing his ID badge and pointing back at the group. The guard shrugged his agreement, the librarian smiled, and Jorge turned back and gave them a thumbs up.

'Sorry to be a cliché,' he said as they went in, 'but please, do try and be quiet. It is a library.'

Orlando, Tilly and Oskar followed Jorge through the rings of workstations and chairs and past the large raised desk where a librarian looked imperiously down at them as they went by. They headed to the opposite side of the room and passed under one of the smaller archways that broke up the walls of bookshelves. Out of the grandeur of the main room were smaller rows of shelves linked with arched passageways, and metal staircases up to the second level. Tilly felt the same sense of awe and wonder that came over her when she had first visited the British Underlibrary. She reminded herself that all libraries held more magic than just bookwandering.

As they walked, Jorge kept checking numbers on the ends of shelves, and on the spines of books.

'Okay,' he whispered, 'this classmark takes us to ancient literary history, but there's a fair few books it *could* be, considering we don't know the last couple of letters, which might give us the author's surname, so it's difficult to know where to even . . .'

'What about this one?' Oskar said, pointing at a thin navy-blue book with a small gold labyrinth embossed on its spine.

13

THE LIBRARY OF ALEXANDRIA

Oskar slid the book off the shelf. It was clothbound, with no writing on the spine or covers, just another labyrinth in gold marked on the front. The pages were crinkled, as though the book had been dropped in the bath and dried out on a radiator. The first page just said 'The Library at Alexandria', with no author listed.

'Oh,' Jorge said in surprise. 'I must admit, I thought it would be harder than that. Are you sure it's right? Tilly?'

'Well, a picture of a maze has to be a good sign, yes? I mean, it sort of fits with the whole map thing.'

'Do you mind if I take a look?' Jorge asked, and

Oskar passed him the book. He flicked it open with a careful librarian's touch and looked through the first pages with a sharp librarian's eye. He frowned. 'There's no bibliographic data here – no date of printing, no publisher, nothing you'd usually expect to find. Although we have all sorts here from before that was common practice. More concerning is that it's not supposed to be here.'

'What do you mean?' Tilly asked. 'Someone's put it back in the wrong place?'

'No, I mean it shouldn't be here at all,' Jorge said, flicking through the whole book.

'But I thought this was a library,' Oskar said, confused.

'It is,' Jorge said. 'But libraries aren't just random piles of books. There's a reason the items in a library are called a collection. Even though we're the second biggest library in the world – after your British Library – there's still care and thought put into every book or manuscript or letter that's kept here. And there's a record of everything. This book doesn't have any classmark; it doesn't have a stamp showing it's part of our collection, or a borrowing record; it doesn't have *anything* to show that it's officially here. It's either ended up here by accident, or it's been hidden here on purpose.'

'Considering we were pointed exactly to this spot, I'm assuming it's the latter,' Orlando said too loudly, his voice echoing through the stacks. They got a glare from someone working on a desk a few metres from them. 'Sorry,' he whispered, holding up a palm in apology.

'Anyway,' Oskar whispered, 'it's great that we've found it and all, but what do we do next?'

The three of them looked at Tilly and she swallowed nervously. She held her hand out for the book, hoping the answer would present itself. She hadn't been expecting a big flashing sign inside the library to tell her what to do, but she had assumed if *this* hunch was right, then the next steps would follow on easily.

'Do we have to read it?' she said. 'Can we take it home with us?'

'Probably,' Jorge said. 'If it's not an official item in the library's collection, then we shouldn't be stopped.'

'But do we have time?' Orlando asked.

'Do you know where the Library of Alexandria is?' Tilly asked.

'It's not where, it's when that's the question,' Jorge said. 'It was a library in Ancient Egypt that was accidentally burned down when Julius Caesar set fire to some ships in the nearby harbour and it spread to the library.'

'So, are we supposed to bookwander there?' Tilly asked nervously. 'If that's what this book is about?'

'Do they want us to stop the fire?' suggested Oskar.

'That wouldn't be possible,' Orlando said. 'Not in any real sense. If you bookwander inside a non-fiction book, you're not really travelling to that time or place – you're still just going into that particular book, that writer's version of events, their ideas. We can't actually travel in time, or change history, which is probably for the best, all things considered. What do you want to do, Tilly?'

Tilly had seen Orlando and Jorge exchange an anxious glance when they realised that she didn't have a fully formed plan, and had no more idea what to do with the book than they did. Tilly wondered, not for the first time, what her mum had told them about how much she knew, and whether there might have been some slight exaggeration along the way.

'Shall we . . . just bookwander inside it then?' Tilly said, trying to sound confident, and not sure what else they were supposed to try.

'Sure,' Orlando said hesitantly. 'Do you want to start at the beginning?'

'We start here,' Oskar said, pointing at a page as Tilly flicked through.

'How do you know?'

'Because there's another shiny maze thing,' Oskar said. 'What does it say underneath it?'

'*Many wanderers*

found what they were looking for at the Great Library of Alexandria,' Jorge read over Tilly's shoulder. *'It was a place where questions were asked and answered, stories started and ended.'*

'That seems pretty clear to me,' Oskar said enthusiastically.

'Shall we?' said Orlando, offering an arm to Tilly with a grin.

The four of them formed a small circle, linking arms.

'Tilly, I reckon you should do the honours,' Oskar said. 'It seems like it doesn't hurt to have the person with the special magical powers do it.'

Tilly felt her cheeks flush in embarrassment, but couldn't argue with his logic, considering her half-fictional nature had got them out of a few scrapes before. Albeit mainly ones that it had got them into in the first place.

'So, I'll just start reading from here?' she said quietly. 'Just after that line about stories starting and ending?'

'Seems sensible,' Orlando said. 'Or as sensible as any other option. Nothing ventured, nothing gained.'

Oskar gave her a quick thumbs up and a nod.

'And everyone stays together once we're in there,' added Jorge, clearly nervous about what they might find. 'So we can get out quickly if we need to.'

Tilly nodded, thought of her family back home and started to read.

'The Library at Alexandria was designed as a home for the great thinkers and scholars of the day. They were able to live and work with an unprecedented amount of freedom for the time . . .'

14

SIGNPOSTS

The beautiful wooden shelves of the Main Reading Room folded themselves down, just as usual, and there was the familiar smell of toasted marshmallows and the slight lurch in her stomach that Tilly barely noticed any more.

'It's just normal bookwandering,' Oskar said, his voice caught between relief and disappointment.

'So far,' Jorge said carefully.

The four of them were standing in a beautiful building of pale stone. The air was hot and dry and smelled of the sea. Towering columns held up the ceiling, and through large windows was a great swathe of pink-tinged sky as the sun set over a wide harbour full of majestic white-sailed ships. There

was no one in view, but the sounds of people talking and working and moving about echoed through the space.

Tilly felt a layer of contentment settle over the top of her worry as the warmth of the air and the background bustle of industry soothed her. The hall was full of high wooden shelves all packed with piles and piles of scrolls, and it was hard to argue that it felt like the sort of place where a secretive group of bookwanderers might choose to hide.

The scrolls were all different sizes and heaped up in messy stacks that were clearly making Jorge's librarian's fingers itch. The papers were wrapped round long wooden sticks and most of them had small tags tied to them to help identify them.

'What are they made of?' Oskar asked, touching the edge of the closest scroll. 'It's not regular paper.'

'Paper has only just been invented,' Jorge explained. 'This is papyrus – it's made out of a kind of reed from Egypt and, although it's pretty delicate, it was the best thing for writing on until paper was used more widely. People used clay tablets sometimes too – and, of course, everything was written by hand.'

'So the Archivists are here somewhere?' Oskar asked. 'Do they have, like, an office or something?'

'I have a feeling that would be way too easy,' Orlando said. 'Considering how long it's been since anyone even claims to have seen or spoken to them, and that most people think they're not much more than a legend. Honestly, Tilly, until your mom called me, I couldn't have told you the last time someone even mentioned the Archivists to me. But clearly something or someone pointed us towards the book that brought us here. Your instincts have proved true so far, so what's your gut telling you?'

'I . . . don't know,' said Tilly hopelessly.

'What about the rest of the clues?' Oskar encouraged her. 'Eighty per cent, remember!'

Tilly nodded, trying to summon the confidence she'd felt when she'd first worked out that they needed to come to the Library of Congress to start the treasure hunt.

'These things are less . . . conclusive,' she warned Orlando and Jorge. 'They're all things that have just turned up in unusual circumstances, more than *clues* per se.'

'Well, let's have a look,' Orlando said, and Tilly opened up her backpack. She pulled everything out of the main pocket except for the copy of *A Midsummer Night's Dream* that Orlando had given to her. Assembled on the stone floor, they did not look especially inspiring.

'Right,' Tilly said, trying to stay calm. 'Well, the note got us here, so let's assume that's its only purpose for now. It came tucked into this pamphlet-y sort of thing about the history of libraries and, considering we're in a really old library, I think maybe that was all part of the same clue.'

'So what's left?' Orlando asked.

'A key from *The Secret Garden*, a bag of breadcrumbs from Hansel and Gretel, and a ball of string from a librarian in Paris,' Oskar said, pointing to each one in turn.

Tilly tried to ignore the concerned looks on Orlando and Jorge's faces.

'Is there a connection between how you got them?' Jorge asked. 'In any way at all?'

'Not really,' Tilly said. 'The thread and the pamphlet were both given to me by a Librarian at the French Underlibrary, which is why I was so sure they were linked. And then the key was left behind after I accidentally pulled the secret garden into my bedroom . . .'

'Like you did in the store?' Orlando asked.

'Except it wasn't trying to suck us in,' Tilly said. 'But yes, essentially the same thing. Except the key was left behind when the rest of the garden disappeared. And the breadcrumbs were in a book of fairy tales. That was in Paris too, but aside from the French thing . . .' She tailed off.

'Basically, no,' Oskar supplied. 'There's no real connection.'

'Maybe we should think about the French link a bit more?' Orlando said uncertainly.

'Except . . . Hang on . . .' Tilly said slowly. 'If classmarks are like maps to help you find the right book . . . Well, what if these are the signposts?' she said. 'Just slightly . . . unusual ones. The breadcrumbs are how Hansel and Gretel get out of the woods they're lost in, and the key helps Mary Lennox find her way into the secret garden. They both help characters find their way! So that just leaves the thread.'

'It's Theseus and the Minotaur!' Oskar yelped in excitement. 'Don't you remember when we did Greek myths at school? Ari . . . Ari . . . That princess lady gave him the red thread to help him find his way out of the Minotaur's . . .'

'. . . labyrinth!' Tilly finished triumphantly.

'You two are a force to be reckoned with when you put your heads together,' Orlando said, impressed.

Tilly and Oskar gave each other a high-five.

'So we're looking for . . . a labyrinth or a forest or a door?' Tilly said. 'A door seems most likely in a library?'

'Shall we split up and go look?' Orlando said.

Oskar rolled his eyes. 'Come on,' he said. 'Even if you haven't seen any horror films, you should know that's the cardinal rule. Bad things happen when the heroes don't stay together.'

On Oskar's instruction, the four of them stuck close together as they walked through the huge library. The sun continued to set, casting great slices of pink-and-purple light on to the white stone walls. While the sound of voices never ebbed or died away, they didn't encounter a single person. A door seemed the most likely option, but they looked for anything that might link to one of the clues – a door or a maze, or another labyrinth symbol – but most of the library was open and unlocked. Great halls connected with archways and walkways, there was nothing hidden away or out of bounds, and the initial excitement about decoding the clues quickly started to fade.

'Oskar,' Tilly said quietly as they walked. 'You don't think the key is a mistake, do you?'

'What do you mean?'

'Like a red herring in a murder mystery. The other things were all given to me, but the key just got left behind.'

'Tell me again exactly what happened when you found it?' Oskar said.

Tilly thought back. 'I was reading *The Secret Garden* with my mum in my bedroom and the garden started spilling out of the book, and just growing around us. It was amazing – not like the vines in Shakespeare's Sisters. I didn't notice the key straight away. I only saw it in the morning, just sitting on my bedside table.'

'And no character came out of the book with it?'

'No, it's not like when Anne or Alice visit the bookshop – that happens to all bookwanderers. It's like the story *itself* is breaking out of the pages. And it's not supposed to happen outside the bookshop anyway.'

'As far as I see it, our only option is to just run with what we've got,' Oskar said. 'And, if it doesn't work, we'll try something different. What else can we do?' He tried to give her an encouraging smile before walking ahead to keep looking for a door.

'I suppose so,' Tilly said to herself, although she didn't feel very reassured.

But Oskar was right about one thing – they didn't have an alternative plan. This library was certainly the path to somewhere, and they just had to hope it led to the Archivists.

So, without anything else to try, they kept walking. Jorge suggested checking the tags on the scrolls for more of the labyrinth symbols, but there were thousands upon thousands of scrolls and even Jorge couldn't work out the pattern to how they were stored. Not to mention that the majority of the writing was in languages and alphabets they couldn't even begin to understand.

'Do you know,' said Tilly, 'reading books has given me a very inaccurate view of how much admin there is in adventuring. When did you last read a chapter in a book where people just had to carefully look for something?'

'Well, that's because it sounds incredibly boring,' Oskar said. 'Just like this is. If we were in a film right now, this would all be turned into an inspirational montage.'

'Sadly, we're not characters in a book or a blockbuster,' Jorge said. 'So we have to put the work in.'

'If we *were* in a book, there'd be some sort of wise old librarian – probably with a cane and a beard – who would turn up and silently and mysteriously point us towards it,' Orlando said, trying to lighten the mood.

'Or one of us would fall over in a charming sort of way and tread on a foot sensor or something,' Jorge suggested, smiling at Orlando.

'Or something would start glowing mysteriously right about now,' Oskar said hopefully, looking around as if he could wish it into existence. 'Hang on . . . I actually *can* see something glowing.'

They all looked over to where he was pointing and he was right: there was a definite glow visible on the far wall.

'That way!' Oskar yelled triumphantly and started to run towards it.

But Tilly paused, sniffing the air around her. She turned to Orlando and Jorge.

'Is it just me, or can you smell something burning?'

15

WE SHOULD'VE SEEN THIS ONE COMING

Oskar quickly realised the same thing and skidded to a stop.

'The library's on fire!' he yelled back at them.

'Didn't you say that it's basically famous for burning down?' Tilly said to Jorge, who nodded.

'We maybe should've seen this one coming,' he said.

Smoke was starting to billow through the hall and a visible line of fire was edging across the shelves, the dry scrolls all erupting into flames, passing it on to the other scrolls they were piled up and on and under so quickly that it was hard to keep track of where the edge of the fire was, or where it was heading next.

'We need to leave, Tilly. Get the book ready – I'll go grab Oskar,' Orlando said.

'Guys! Guys!' Oskar shouted from across the hall.

'Oskar, come away from the fire!!" Orlando yelled, running towards him.

'No, look!' Oskar said, pulling his arm out of Orlando's grip and gesturing in front of him. 'There, beyond the fire.'

Orlando squinted, trying to make out what Oskar was pointing at.

'I can't see anything,' he said, the smoke stinging his eyes.

'There's a door,' Oskar said, coughing as the smoke continued to encroach on them.

'It could be any door,' Orlando said. 'It's not worth the risk – we need to get into the book Tilly has.'

'But look!' Oskar said, increasingly frustrated,

pointing again as Tilly and Jorge ran up to join them, their tops pulled up round their mouths to try to stop them from breathing in the smoke.

And there, glinting in the firelight, was the unmistakable golden labyrinth that had been printed on the book that had led them here.

'But how do we get to it!' Tilly said in despair. 'We can't walk through the fire. It's real!'

'We have to go back,' Orlando said firmly, tugging Tilly and Oskar away from the growing flames. 'We can't get to it this way and I will not be calling up Bea to tell her you died in a fire in a library in Ancient Egypt! We need to get away from the flames and go back, and then we can try again.'

'What happens if it doesn't work again?' Tilly said.

'We're leaving,' Orlando said. 'Now read us out, Tilly!'

She turned to the last page of the slim book and started to read, but, when she got to the very last word, nothing happened.

'It's not working!' she said, panicking.

'Try again!' Jorge coughed, keeping a tight hold on everyone.

She read again, starting a bit further back as if a longer run-up might help, but again – nothing. The burning library stayed solidly around them, viciously hot. She double-checked it was definitely the last page, and that there wasn't anything that had been ripped out, and held the book up helplessly to the others to show there was nothing else.

'We need to get out of the building then!' Orlando shouted. 'And we can work out how to get out of the book once we're safe.'

They ran back towards the hall they'd first entered, which had plenty of archways that led outside, but an almighty rumbling started to echo around them and suddenly the shelves began to collapse, burning scrolls and fiery embers flung into the air, raining down on the four bookwanderers.

Orlando and Jorge instinctively leaned over Tilly and Oskar, trying to shield them from the worst of the burning papyrus. But, just as the four of them, holding tightly on to each other, braced for the impact, a familiar smell caught in the back of Tilly's throat. It wasn't charred paper and ash, but toasting marshmallows. She opened her eyes to see the burning shelves click-clacking down underneath them to reveal the Library of Congress with its neatly bound books and air conditioning. The four of them were in a huddle on the floor, breathing heavily and covered with smudges of soot and ash.

Orlando couldn't help but burst out laughing in sheer relief, and everyone in the room immediately turned to glare at them.

'There!' a voice shouted and, before they knew what was happening, a group of five people in uniforms and riot gear charged towards them across the Main Reading Room.

16

COVERT OPERATIONS

'Who are *they*?' Orlando said to Jorge, quickly pushing Tilly and Oskar behind him.

'I've no idea,' Jorge said. 'I've never seen people dressed like that at the library before. It's just out of the frying pan into the fire.'

'Actually, it would be the other way round,' Oskar piped up from behind the two men. 'Because we've just come from a literal fire, making this the frying pan.'

'Thanks for that,' Tilly said sarcastically.

'You're welcome,' Oskar said, with a thumbs up.

The guards ran over and quickly surrounded them. The librarians, meanwhile, were ushering the other users of the Main Reading Room out, and soon it was just them left.

One guard stepped forward and lifted the visor on her helmet. 'You're wanted downstairs,' she said.

'Downstairs?' Jorge repeated, confused. 'Who are you?'

'We report to the Head Librarian of the American Underlibrary, and he has some questions for you,' the woman said. 'Follow me.'

She gestured for some of the guards to fall in behind them to make sure no one made a run for it, and the group walked through the now-empty Reading Room and into the corridor, where people were standing silently, craning their necks to see who had caused such a reaction. They were clearly surprised to watch two children being escorted out of the room.

'Do you still have the book?' Orlando said under his breath to Tilly as they walked. She nodded and gestured to her pocket.

'Good,' whispered Orlando. 'Keep it ready.'

They were marched along until they reached a door marked '**Supply Closet**'. Tilly thought of the entrance to the British Underlibrary, which was hidden in a locked area and down a seemingly out-of-order lift, and so wasn't at all surprised that they initially walked into an actual cleaning-supply cupboard, piled with cleaning products. The leader of the guards slid away a metal trolley full of hand towels to reveal a door. Behind that was a lift, much like the one at the British Underlibrary, all shiny wood and copper detailing.

'The blond guy goes with the girl,' the leader barked. 'And the boy with the other one.' She pushed Tilly and Orlando into the lift with two guards and waited behind with Oskar and Jorge. It was silent in the lift down, and Tilly felt terrified, until Orlando's warm hand found hers and gave it a squeeze.

'Try to stay calm,' Orlando said quietly. 'Just pay attention to me, okay?' Orlando seemed to have something in mind, which made Tilly feel a little calmer, but she had no idea how he could possibly get them all of out of this safely.

The lift juddered to a stop and the doors pinged open, letting them out into a broad, carpeted corridor with statues of grumpy-looking men dotted along the sides. Orlando and Tilly followed the two guards into a circular room hung with velvet drapes. The logo of the American Underlibrary – an oak tree in the centre of an open book – was woven into the carpet, and a huge wooden desk stood opposite them. Behind it sat a stony-faced black man with salt-and-pepper hair, wearing an immaculate suit. Two other men in suits stood behind him.

The man behind the desk didn't stand up, or speak – just watched them walk towards him. A few moments later, Jorge and Oskar joined them. The guards clicked their heels, saluted and left the room.

'Welcome to the American Underlibrary,' the man said. 'My name is Jacob Johnson, and I am the Librarian here. I apologise for the rather abrupt manner of your arrival, but I have been given intelligence that informs me you were engaging in covert operations here in the Library of Congress.'

'No!' Tilly said. 'I promise we weren't. Or rather we were – but we're not hiding it from you! We just can't have our Librarian find out – he's the one that's stopping everyone from bookwandering – we're trying to stop him!'

'That makes everything much clearer, I thank you,' Jacob said, nodding his head briskly.

'Oh,' said Tilly. 'Um, good.'

'Yes,' continued Jacob. 'I'm glad to hear from your own mouths that you are working in opposition to Melville. He did warn me that you might try to lie about your purpose.'

'He . . . he warned you?' Oskar repeated, confused.

'Why, yes,' Jacob said. 'I spoke to him on the telephone only a few hours ago – after we learned you were on your way here. Sadly, we weren't fast enough to intercept you before you left the bookstore, but luckily you came straight here. And now I have the great pleasure of informing my friend and colleague in London that I have you in my custody.'

'Your friend?' Tilly said, a horrible, icy feeling

taking over her whole body.

'Of course,' Jacob said. 'We've been working together for a while now. I think you'll find we're both most satisfied with the results so far.'

17

NEW FRONTIERS OF BOOK MAGIC

There was a moment of awful silence as the four of them digested what Jacob had just told them.

'You're . . . working together?' Tilly managed to stammer.

'We have always been great allies of the British Underlibrary,' Jacob said calmly.

'But . . . what they're doing there stops bookwanderers here from being able to bookwander into all kinds of books!' Oskar said, outraged.

'I assure you, I understand that,' replied Jacob. 'They asked for my blessing on the decision before they bound the books. For now, American bookwanderers are able to travel into the books that are held here, and I watch the results of Mr and Ms Underwood's grand experiment with interest.'

'But what's in it for you?' Oskar asked coldly.

'I realise it's difficult for children to understand complex issues such as these,' Jacob said, and Orlando and Jorge had to put their hands on Tilly and Oskar's shoulders to stop them from exploding in anger. 'But,' Jacob went on, 'what the Underwoods are attempting to do is noble indeed, and in the service of all bookwanderers.'

'What lies have they told you?' Orlando said, his voice full of barely suppressed rage.

'Do not presume to think I'm naive, or have been hoodwinked,' Jacob said. 'I have made it very clear to them that my support is not a blank cheque, but for now I'm a willing partner in their endeavour. And what I have been promised, in return for my support and guidance as they explore the new frontiers of book magic, is not your business – and it is arrogance indeed to suggest otherwise.'

'But how did you know we were going to be here?' Jorge asked.

'We have such sweet and helpful friends in all quarters,' Jacob smiled. 'Including at your lovely bookstore, Shakespeare's Sisters.'

Orlando turned very pale. 'Someone at the store told you we were coming?' he whispered. 'Who?'

'I shall let you talk to your co-workers yourself,' Jacob said. 'For now, I imagine you'll want their aid running the store while you are indisposed.'

'Indisposed?' repeated Jorge.

'Oh, none of you are going anywhere. You must understand: my friends are keen to know what young Ms Pages is up to, and what has called her over to this side of the world,' Jacob said. 'Something I'm interested to know myself.' He paused as if waiting for them to voluntarily explain their whole plan.

Tilly felt Orlando take a step closer to her and find her hand. He squeezed it gently, and she looked up at him questioningly.

'Jorge, why don't you tell Mr Johnson more about

what we were doing,' he said.

Jorge looked utterly baffled, but evidently trusted Orlando enough to run with whatever he was planning, and so started to bluster about research and libraries and bookwandering. It wasn't very convincing, but it provided just enough time for Orlando to speak to Tilly.

'You and Oskar need to go,' he said, so quietly that Tilly was worried she'd misunderstand what he was trying to tell her. 'Do you think you can find your way back to that door before the fire spreads?' he whispered.

Tilly nodded, understanding what he was suggesting. She reached out her other hand to grab Oskar as subtly as she could.

Jacob either didn't notice or didn't care, but Oskar immediately realised that she was trying to communicate with him.

'Trust your instincts,' Orlando whispered. 'We'll take care of things here. NOW!'

And with that final yell he pushed Tilly and Oskar

behind him and spread his arms wide. Tilly was ready and, before Jacob's guards were out from behind the desk, she had the right page open and was reading aloud the sentence to take them back to the Library of Alexandria. She just caught sight of Orlando restraining the two guards who were trying to grab them before the walls slid down around them and they were back in the great pale hall, the sun only just beginning to set again, and this time they knew exactly where they needed to go.

For a beat, the two of them just stood, staring at each other, breathing heavily.

'I . . .' Tilly started, feeling like she was in shock.

'I know,' said Oskar. 'We can talk about it later. Right now, we need to find that door before the fire starts, because we do *not* want to pop back up in the Underlibrary.'

'Are Orlando and Jorge going to be okay?' Tilly said.

'Yeah,' Oskar said, although he didn't sound very convinced. 'I'm sure they can look after themselves, and they wanted us to keep going, right? And they don't know how to find the Archivists – because *we* don't know – so they can't give that away. As soon as we're out of here, we can call your mum and tell her what's happened. Hopefully, she'll have some other friends who can check in on them or something. But, Tilly, we really need to go now. There's no point in Orlando and Jorge sacrificing themselves for us to go and waste what they've done.'

Tilly nodded and steeled herself. 'It was this way,' she said, and the two of them ran through great halls of scrolls, bathed in deepening twilight shadows.

As they got to the door, they could start to smell the faint tang of acrid smoke, but they couldn't yet see it, or any flames. The door was plain and small, covered in peeling paint in a similar dark blue to the book, and with the same golden labyrinth painted on it. There were no other markings, no signs or instructions, just a keyhole.

'What were you saying about the key being a red herring?' Oskar grinned at her as Tilly fished in her backpack to pull out the large brass key from *The Secret Garden*.

She slotted it neatly into the keyhole, which turned with a satisfying click as the door mechanism was released.

She pushed gently, and they stepped through the door into darkness, leaving the Great Library of Alexandria

burning

behind

them.

18

A STORY WITHIN A STORY

Wherever they were, it was thankfully not back at the Library of Congress with Jacob Johnson. It took a few seconds for Tilly's and Oskar's eyes to adjust to the strange light and make out their surroundings. It seemed to be a forest, except everything was completely drained of colour, as though they'd stepped into a black-and-white film.

'Are we outside?' Tilly asked uncertainly.

'I . . . I'm not sure,' said Oskar quietly. Even though there was no sight or sound of anyone else, there was an uneasy feeling in the air, as though they were somewhere they weren't supposed to be. It was dark above their heads, but there was no moon or stars, only emptiness.

'Are we back in *A Midsummer Night's Dream*?' Tilly asked, and indeed the clearing they were standing in did look remarkably like the glade that they had only recently visited, only a completely unsaturated one, all blacks and white and greys and silence. A silence that was even deeper than just the mere absence of sound: it was a heavy, insistent silence, pushing down on them.

'Is that sky?' Tilly said, craning her neck to stare up into the vast blackness over their heads.

Oskar waved his hands over his head as though seeing if he might come into contact with some invisible ceiling. The strange half-light seemed to be emanating from the forest itself, and they could see for at least six metres or so all around.

'The trees are . . . glowing?' Oskar said, walking warily towards one and reaching out a tentative finger to feel it. 'Oh!' he gasped in amazement. 'It's made out of paper!'

Tilly carefully touched the trunk to find that he was right. It was like the most incredibly realistic paper

model of a
tree, from
its gnarled
and knotted
bark to its delicate,
twisted branches and
the translucent leaves
above their heads.
Everything they could
see was made from white
paper with black writing on it,
the thickness and amount of which
gave shade and shape to the forest.

Tilly bent down to touch the grass
and it too was made of paper – the softest
tissue paper she had ever felt – and the
flowers clustered round the base of the
trees were made of dainty paper petals.

'Are we in a book?' Oskar asked in
awe. 'Or did someone make this?'

'I don't know,' Tilly said

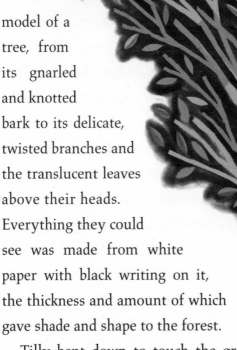

in wonderment. 'It would take a lifetime to create something like this, surely?'

'It must be a book,' Oskar said. 'Even though we didn't bookwander in the proper way. It's like we used the back door.'

'A story within a story,' Tilly said. 'This *must* be where the Archivists are. Hidden in layers of stories. I just don't understand why they're hiding.'

'Maybe they're not,' Oskar suggested. 'Maybe they're lost.'

'So how do we find them?'

'We keep wandering?'

There didn't seem to be anything else for it so they set off in a random direction, the paper grass crunching softly underneath their feet as they walked, the strange gleam remaining constant until they saw a golden light through the trees.

This, it turned out, was coming from a lamppost glowing in the middle of a clearing. It was made of paper, but somehow it wasn't burning up, the paper candle just charring the paper at the top without spreading.

'How strange,' Tilly said. 'But something about it is so familiar. I feel like when you can't quite remember the right word for something, but it's on the tip of your tongue. As if I've read this book, but years and years ago.'

They kept walking, and every few moments they happened across something else perched among the paper trees. They passed a long trestle table, two of its legs buckled so that the origami cups and saucers on top had slid down into a messy heap in the grass. They saw an armchair sitting in the pool of light cast by a tall paper lamp by its side, and more than one empty bookcase, some carved into tree trunks, some leaning up against them, and some lying toppled on the ground. They stopped and wondered at a huge plant made of coarse card that stretched up into the sky, reaching so high that its top disappeared into the inky blackness. The strangest thing that they saw was a whole pirate ship on the grass, listing to one side, paper vines growing up its sides rooting it to the ground like an ancient temple reclaimed by the forest. A huge anchor lay abandoned beside it, grown over with delicate tissue wildflowers.

'Have you noticed?' Tilly said, the pirate ship being the final element that allowed her to work out the pattern.

'Noticed what?'

'That we keep passing things from books we've bookwandered into?'

'Ohhhh!' Oskar said. 'That's what I haven't been able to put my finger on. But . . . how could it be so personal to us? That doesn't make any sense.'

'Unless someone knows we're coming,' Tilly said. 'NOT THAT IT'S MUCH USE IF YOU DON'T SHOW US HOW TO GET TO YOU!' she yelled up into the sky.

'Tilly!' said Oskar, stopping suddenly and grabbing her arm, yanking her backwards.

'Hey!' she said. 'That hurt!'

'Sorry, but I think I've had an . . . What do you call it? An epiphany! I've had an epiphany!'

'And . . .?' Tilly prompted.

'Well, what helped us get to the Library of Alexandria?'

'The classmark,' Tilly said.

'And what got us here?'

'The key.'

'So what else do we have?'

'The thread and . . . the breadcrumbs!'

'Exactly!' Oskar said triumphantly. 'And what did Hansel and Gretel use the breadcrumbs for? To get out of a forest!' He gestured around them. 'And where are we?'

'No, no, I'm up to speed!' Tilly said. 'I'm there.'

'I'm just enjoying explaining,' said Oskar.

'The only problem is that Hansel and Gretel used the breadcrumbs to get *out*,' Tilly said. 'And we're not trying to get out of somewhere – we're trying to get in.'

'Fair point, but considering we have absolutely zero idea where in this forest we need to go, and that the clues have helped us so far, what's the harm in trying? The worst-case scenario is that we keep a trail of where we've been, so we don't retrace our steps while we're searching.'

Tilly couldn't argue with that logic and put her bag

down, opening it up to fish out the breadcrumbs. She passed them to Oskar.

'Would you like to do the honours?' she said, smiling.

'At least there aren't any paper birds to eat them,' he said. 'Or any . . .' He stopped and stared at the ground where he'd just thrown the first handful of breadcrumbs.

'Not again,' he said, backing away.

Tilly looked down to see a thick paper vine creeping over her foot. She shook it off, but it kept coming towards her. It was somehow even more sinister when it was made from paper and ink, even though it moved much more slowly than the vines in the bookshop. And this time no one knew where they were.

'Maybe it's just friendly?' Oskar suggested from a safe distance.

'I am not taking that risk,' Tilly said. 'Let's go.'

She grabbed her bag from the grass and the two of them started running, Oskar tossing breadcrumbs over his shoulder as they went.

In their rush to escape the creeping paper vines, neither of them noticed the ball of red thread that had rolled out of Tilly's open backpack and been left behind,

scarlet

like a pool

of blood

against

the

white

paper

grass.

19

READERS HAVE TO SET THEIR OWN COMPASS

After a few moments, the forest seemed to have stopped trying to grab hold of them, and Tilly and Oskar were able to slow down.

'Do you think I should be worried about this?' asked Tilly.

'Uhhh,' Oskar said, clearly torn between telling the truth and not wanting to exacerbate Tilly's concern. 'Well, let's just say that we've dealt with worse.'

'But where would the vines even be trying to take me?'

'I think we're going deeper and deeper into stories here,' Oskar said. 'So maybe they want to take you inside another layer of books? We can ask the Archivists if they know . . . Hang on, you don't think it's the Archivists who are trying to grab you, do you?'

'I'm not a big fan of their methods if they are,' Tilly said. 'But I suppose better them than the Underwoods.'

'Honestly, I'm getting to the point where I'm not sure I even want to find the Archive if this is how you have to get there, sneaky vines or no sneaky vines,' Oskar said. 'We have no real idea about how to reach them, we're just getting more and more lost, and now we're being chased by either evil or grumpy plants. We were promised a map, but this is like being given a map in another language, drawn by someone who's never been there before, that's then been ripped up and glued back together in the wrong order.'

Tilly paused. What Oskar said had rung a bell in her head.

'It's all about maps,' she said. 'Do you remember what Grandad always says about bookshops? He says that they're like a map – but that readers have to set their own compass. Maybe that's what we need to do – work out how to set the compass. We need to plot our own course.'

'That's all well and good in theory,' Oskar said, 'but how do we even *do* that? You can't just say something inspirational and expect it to fix everything. Unless you've been hiding an actual compass in your bag?'

'I meant it more straightforwardly,' Tilly said, ignoring the dig about inspirational comments. 'I think we should use the pirate ship as our compass. It's huge and easy to find, and somewhere to shelter too, if we need it. Let's follow the breadcrumbs back there.'

'Shouldn't we have passed it by now?' Oskar said a little nervously as they followed the breadcrumb trail. They'd been walking for what felt like ages, much longer than when they'd first come this way, and there was still no sign of the pirate ship. They had passed an old-fashioned school desk tipped on its side, ink dripping out of a hole in the top, and a broken swing dangling from a thick tree branch, neither of which they'd seen before. 'And is it just me or are there considerably more breadcrumbs on the ground than I put there?'

Oskar was right. Instead of the rushed scattering of breadcrumbs he had left as they'd run from the vines, there was now what was undeniably a path made of their breadcrumbs mixed in with tiny screwed-up bits of paper. And it was definitely not taking them back the way they'd come.

But the one thing both Tilly and Oskar knew from reading a lot of books was that if, while on a magical treasure hunt, a path appears in front of you, you should definitely follow it. It became more and more distinct, the breadcrumbs fading away completely into a paper trail that wound through the trees. They were paper silver birches with translucent layers of tissue wrapped in peeling layers. As they walked, the trees started to form an archway over their heads, not stretching out for them like the vines, but twisting gracefully over their heads as if to shelter them.

'Do you know what this reminds me of?' Oskar said.

'Anne's birch path?' Tilly said, thinking the same thing. 'Do you remember when bookwandering was all fun and uncomplicated and we could just go and explore with Anne?'

'I'm not sure it's ever really been uncomplicated,' said Oskar. 'But it's also never stopped being fun, don't you think? I know everything feels really intense at the moment, but would you rather have lived a life where you didn't get to walk through a paper forest? If I had the option, I'd still choose this.'

'Me too,' Tilly said, realising it was true. 'Every time.'

The path through the paper birches curved round ahead of them, the trees growing closer and closer together so that, before long, they could no longer see through them and they were entirely encased in the silvery walkway. The path wound into tighter and tighter curves as though they were moving into the middle of a circle, before they stumbled out into a small clearing, entirely lined with paper trees, knit together to form a wall of bright whiteness.

The only thing in the middle was an archway. It looked like it was made of white stone, but on closer inspection it, too, was paper.

Tilly and Oskar wordlessly approached it. From where they'd entered the clearing, you could see through the arch to the trees behind it. They walked all the way round it and nothing changed except an almost imperceptible shimmer in the air between the pillars, not unlike the secret passage that linked the British Underlibrary to Pages & Co.

Oskar shrugged at Tilly and she returned the gesture, and, without needing to say anything, they took each other's hands and

^stepped

through.

20

The Last Clue

There was a split second when they were in two worlds at once, the silver birches behind them still visible, and the high walls of the arch on either side of them, but then Tilly and Oskar felt a shiver run through their bodies and they were through.

In many ways, the place they found themselves in had the same feel as the paper forest: the empty dark non-sky; the complete lack of people or noise; and the fact that everything was still in shades of black and white. The difference was that everything was made of stone, not paper; stern and ancient rather than wild and whimsical. They were surrounded by walls of pale stone towering above them and their feet were on a road made of the same material. The archway itself had melted back into the wall behind them as soon as they'd passed through, leaving solid walls on both sides of them and a dead-end behind.

'On the plus side,' Oskar said, with a small wobble in his voice, 'no one seems to be following us any more.'

'And at least there's only one way to go this time,' Tilly said, and they set off up the road, for lack of any other option.

'Do we just assume something will happen?' Oskar said. 'Should we be using the red thread, do you think?'

'But we're not in a maze,' Tilly said. 'There's no turns or breaks or bends. I don't want to risk using it wrong.'

'Fine,' Oskar said. 'But I don't want to just keep walking forever, trying to stay calm and optimistic. Because you'll get more and more anxious, and then you'll go all quiet and, let's be honest, probably get a little bit passive-aggressive. And *I'll* start talking more and more, and making worse and worse jokes to try and help, and I'll be annoying both of us equally, and then, after hours and hours and hours . . . Oh. Never mind.'

They paused as they'd both seen at the same time that a little further ahead there was another archway.

'Is this it?' Oskar asked as they walked towards it. 'Surely there can't be another layer to this.'

'But we haven't used the thread yet,' Tilly pointed out. 'I think this is the last layer. The last clue. Look.'

As they peered through the archway, they could see that several walled pathways split off from it, all turning sharply so you could only see a few metres down any of the options. They could see the solemn branches of a few paper trees poking above the walls, and a couple of plants made of twisted paper were stationed at the entrance.

'I think we can safely say this is the labyrinth,' Tilly said. 'It must be – and they're going to be in the middle, I can feel it.'

'At least it's obvious what clue we have to use,' Oskar said. 'And even how we use it. We've cracked it, Tilly!' He gave Tilly a high-five and unzipped the bag on her back to fish out the last clue.

Tilly finally felt some sort of sense of achievement and clarity. Each clue had matched a layer of stories, and now they had a ball of thread and a labyrinth – it couldn't be more obvious.

The great pale stones of the entrance stretched high above their heads, but Tilly couldn't help but feel excitement rather than fear now it was so clear where they were supposed to go. The symbol of the

labyrinth had guided them to this central point, this dusty, stone place that felt as though no other people had passed this way for decades, if not longer.

The Library of Alexandria had still felt alive, somehow, but these stone passages were devoid of noise or natural light or anything that felt familiar. They were deep inside stories now, and there was only one way to . . .

'I can't find it,' Oskar said, interrupting Tilly's train of thought.

'What?' Tilly said, her optimism popping like a balloon.

'The thread. It's not here.'

She looked at him, and the bag in his hand. 'But it *must* be there. We haven't even got it out before. It was definitely there when we were in Alexandria.'

'But we've been pulling things in and out of your bag all day,' Oskar pointed out. 'And running around and running away; it must have fallen out when you were getting something else.'

'Oh, so it's my fault?' Tilly snapped.

'Well, it's not mine!' Oskar retorted.

'Why is it always my responsibility to keep track of everything!'

'Because people keep giving you magical presents!' Oskar said. 'And, wherever you go, special things happen, and you're always the key to everything! None of that happens to me!'

'I didn't ask for any of it!' Tilly said, close to tears. 'Everyone expects me to just work everything out! "Oh, Tilly's not normal – her bookwandering doesn't work right; she's the best person to solve all these stupid magical puzzles." I don't want to be half fictional!' And she couldn't stop the tears running down her cheeks in frustration and disappointment.

'I know,' Oskar said quietly. 'Sorry, I didn't mean that I think it's all up to you. It's just that . . . you know, I want to be useful, not just someone who ends up being dragged along.'

'But you're useful all the time!' Tilly said, surprised that he felt like that. 'I wouldn't have worked out the clues without you. I wouldn't have found the door in the Library of Alexandria without you. There's no way I'd be stuck in a deserted stone labyrinth if it wasn't for you. I couldn't do *any* of this without you. Not to mention, like you said, that I'd probably get very anxious and passive-aggressive and no one would give me any magical presents any more.' She tried a small smile, and Oskar leaned over and gave her a hug.

'The thing is,' he said, 'that if someone has gone to all this effort to give you these clues *surely* they're not going to leave us stranded. So, let's just have a go at the maze without the thread. We can ad-lib. I've done the maze at Hampton Court Palace so I'm pretty confident, actually. Now, my tactic is always to . . .'

But Oskar's description of his tactics was drowned out by a high-pitched whistle. A whistle that sounded very much like it was coming from a steam train, and one that was awfully close. Once the whistle had subsided, there was the unmistakable noise of clickety-clacking and the huffing-and-chuffing of a train pulling into a station.

'COULD YOU PLEASE STOP GETTING WEIRDER EVERY SINGLE SECOND!' Tilly yelled at the sky, pounding her foot on the stones underneath them.

'Did you . . . Did you just stamp your foot?' Oskar asked in delight. 'Seriously, I haven't seen anyone do that in ages! Actually, I don't think I've ever seen *anyone* do it in real life.'

'I'm very cross,' Tilly said, trying not to laugh. 'But come on – why is there a train here! What do you use red thread for on a train?!'

'I haven't the foggiest idea,' Oskar said. 'But shall we go and see if we can cadge a lift?' And at that they both burst out into near-hysterical laughter. 'Come on, Tilly,' said Oskar, crying with laughter. '*Obviously*, there's a train station here in this mysterious stone city by the paper forest. I can't believe you didn't work it out already!'

'Maybe the Three Bears were supposed to give me a train timetable,' Tilly said, her stomach starting to hurt from laughing so hard.

'Only grown-ups would come up with something like this,' Oskar said. 'If I was an Archivist, do you know what the system would be? A nice email saying what you needed, or a text message checking if they could help. Maybe an online FAQ.'

'I feel very light-headed,' Tilly said, leaning against the wall. 'Do you feel light-headed? Why am I laughing so much?'

'I don't think it's good for us to be diving so deep within stories,' said Oskar.  'You're not even supposed to bookwander into one book inside another book, remember? And goodness knows how we're going to get back out again.'

'No offence, Oskar,' Tilly said, 'but I am *not* going into that labyrinth without the thread, however many mazes you've done. So, as a train must be going *somewhere*, I suggest we go and find it.'

'I second that motion,' Oskar said. 'Now, if you were a train station in an imaginary maze, where would you be?'

'I would put myself right where I needed to be,' said Tilly wistfully. 'Somewhere just behind here, across the road from the imaginary labyrinth. Can you imagine if we could . . .'

'Tilly, turn round,' Oskar said quietly.

Behind them was another archway that led to a neat, stone-gravelled path curving away from them. One that had definitely not been there before. 'No big deal, but did you just wish that into existence?' Oskar asked.

'That's impossible,' said Tilly. 'It must have been there . . . But it wasn't, was it?'

'Does it work with other things?' Oskar said hopefully. 'I'm imagining a veggie burger with sweet potato fries and a Fanta orange.' And suddenly, at his feet, there was a tray of food. 'This is the BEST!' he shouted. 'How did we only work this out now?' He grabbed the burger and shoved it in his mouth jubilantly before his joy turned to a grimace and he spat it out again. 'It's made of paper,' he said, looking as though someone had just cancelled Christmas.

'How about . . . I imagine a ball of red thread that will lead us through the labyrinth?' Tilly said, and Oskar gave her a thumbs up, still picking bits of wet paper out of his teeth.

A ball of thread rolled past their feet – however it wasn't red, and it was also made of paper.

'I don't fancy our chances with that,' Oskar said. 'And honestly, at this point, I really don't trust whoever or whatever is sending these things. Who sends a paper burger? It's just cruel. I vote we go through there and find the train.'

Tilly nodded and, with only a brief look over their shoulders, they left the labyrinth behind them and crossed through the freshly imagined arch and into what was definitely a train station, complete with a train that was gloriously and blissfully not made of paper. It was resolutely made out of what trains were supposed to be made out of: steel and wood and smoke and paint. They stood agog until a boy, who looked about their own age, swung out of one of the doors.

'Are you coming then?' he called.

'ALL ABoARD!'

21

THE SESQUIPEDALIAN

For a moment, Tilly and Oskar couldn't do anything but stand and stare at the train. It was unusually long, with many more carriages than they were used to seeing at stations in London. And it wasn't just the number of carriages that stood out, but their appearance; each one looked as though it had come from a different train. There were old-fashioned black carriages, a sleek section of shiny, matching ones towards the front, shaky wooden carriages, ones covered in brightly coloured peeling paint, some with windows, some without, and none of them looked like they should fit together at all, let alone stay on a train track and keep moving forward.

The boy who had called to them – and who was waiting impatiently for a response – was tall and wiry, with copper-coloured skin and messy dark brown curls falling over thick-rimmed glasses.

'We can't wait for you!' he called. 'We've just paused to drop something off! You're looking at a one-time-only opportunity to hitch a ride on the Sesquipedalian!'

'The what?!' Oskar called as another squeal from the train's whistle echoed in the air and a plume of glittering smoke billowed overhead as the train prepared to depart.

'The Sesquipedalian! And it's about to leave.'

'Are we getting on?' Tilly asked Oskar.

'It's a real train, complete with a real person, going somewhere that isn't *here*,' Oskar said. 'What are we waiting for?'

'But the Archivists . . .' said Tilly as they walked towards it.

'Maybe that boy knows how to find them?' Oskar suggested. 'If he's here, then he must know something useful.'

Tilly couldn't shake the thought of her mum, not to mention Orlando and Jorge, and how disappointed they'd be if she failed in the search for the Archivists. But she couldn't disagree with Oskar's logic, and she didn't fancy getting lost in the labyrinth with no food or water or any way of contacting other people. The lure of a moving vehicle, not to mention another real person who might know more, was too tempting.

The train had started to shudder back to life and was moving slowly along the platform, meaning Tilly and Oskar had to break into a jog to catch up.

'Come on!' the boy called, his arm outstretched to help them onboard.

'You go first,' Tilly said, giving Oskar a shove so he was able to grab the boy's hand and yank himself up on to the wooden platform on the back of the last carriage. Tilly gritted her teeth and picked up speed, holding out her hand for Oskar and the boy. Her fingers were just brushing theirs as the train jolted forward and she lost contact again.

'I am not getting stuck here by myself!' she

shouted, and summoned a last burst of energy. Just as the train rolled out of the station, the boys managed to get a secure grasp on her wrists and hoisted her up off the ground and on to the train, the three of them crashing to the floor in an undignified heap.

After they had disentangled their limbs, Tilly and Oskar stood up and faced the boy who had helped them. He was wearing a slightly-too-small assortment of clothing: bottle-green trousers held up with braces over a not-very-clean white T-shirt. A mustard-yellow scarf was wrapped round his neck several times, matching the fingerless gloves on his hands. On his feet were brown boots, one with normal brown laces, and the other tied up with a purple ribbon instead. He looked like . . . Well, he looked like a character from a book, Tilly couldn't help but think.

'I'm Milo,' he said, sticking a slightly greasy hand out for them to shake. 'Welcome aboard the Sesquipedalian.'

Tilly introduced herself and Oskar.

'And I'm sorry,' she said. 'Welcome aboard the what?'

'The Sess-quip-a-day-li-an,' Milo said, sounding it out for them slowly. 'It means long words, or the sort of person who loves using long words. But we call her Quip for short.'

'I'm gonna stick with Quip,' Oskar said, shaking Milo's hand. 'Thanks for having us.'

'You're welcome,' said Milo. 'So, what were you two doing in the labyrinth? You're lucky we were passing – this is a very new route for us.'

Tilly and Oskar exchanged a look, unsure of how much it was safe to tell Milo. He was certainly friendly, but, after everything they'd been through so far, they were hesitant to share what they were up to with a stranger.

'We're . . . looking for someone,' Tilly said vaguely. 'Or rather some people. We think. And we were given a map that brought us here. But we got a bit lost and none of the usual bookwandering rules seem to apply.'

'What's bookwandering?' Milo asked, frowning at them.

'*Oh no,*' breathed Oskar.

'You're . . . not a bookwanderer?' Tilly said in horror.

'Ah no, I'm sorry,' Milo said, breaking into a grin. 'I'm just teasing! Of course I'm a bookwanderer. How do you think someone ends up on a train that travels through stories without being a bookwanderer?'

'So that's what this train does?' Tilly asked in wonder, not even bothering to be annoyed by the joke.

'Yup,' said Milo proudly.

'But we've never heard of you before,' Tilly said. 'And my grandad used to be the Librarian at the British Underlibrary.' Tilly could have sworn she saw Milo wrinkle his nose at the mention of the Underlibrary.

'Well, if you've come from the highfalutin' official end of things, it's no surprise you've never heard of us. In fact, I'd be worried if you had. We operate on a strict need-to-know basis.'

'There are official and unofficial bits of bookwandering?' Oskar asked.

'Obviously,' said Milo. 'Pretty much everything has its official and unofficial bits, its open streets and its hidden alleyways, its rules – and its rule breakers. And the Quip and those who know of her are definitely from, if you'll excuse the pun, the wrong side of the tracks.'

'So, what do you actually do?' Tilly asked.

'We're in the business of the lost and forgotten,' Milo said. 'Stories and books in particular. And sometimes lost-and-forgotten people too; those who need helping from one place to another, or have something to hide. People come to us because we know how to find things. And how to lose things. And we have an *excellent* success rate; we can get almost anywhere with this train.'

Tilly and Oskar looked at each other. Perhaps all hope of getting to the Archivists wasn't quite lost.

22

UP TO NO GOOD

'So . . . the Underlibraries don't know that you exist?' Tilly asked as the train started speeding up through a narrow tunnel of stone.

'Nope,' Milo said. 'We do have the occasional client who's taking care of some personal business and would prefer to remain anonymous. But no, Horatio goes to great pains to make sure we go as undetected as possible.'

'Who's Horatio?' Oskar asked.

'He owns Quip,' Milo explained. 'And runs the business. He's also my uncle, but he likes to pretend that's not the case, so, if you do meet him, I wouldn't bring it up. But you should hope you *don't* meet him, as he won't be too thrilled to find two stowaways. No one's allowed onboard for free – ever. But don't worry, you can hang out in my quarters until the next stop or . . . Well, where are you going?'

'Depends what the options are,' Tilly pointed out.

'The Quip can go anywhere you can imagine,' Milo said. 'But I don't get told the routes. And this is only the second time we've been to that labyrinth place. The first time we stopped there, we then went on to a big old building where Horatio had a meeting. He called it the Archive, but he didn't let me off the train. And then I suppose we'll go on to . . .'

Tilly glanced at Oskar, whose eyebrows were raised.

'So we're going to that Archive place next?' she asked, trying to sound casual.

'I don't really know,' said Milo. 'I don't get told very much. The routes don't always stay the same, but it's where we ended up last time we came via the labyrinth. But it took, what, maybe half an hour to get there? So, why don't you come in off the back of the train and we can have a cup of tea?'

Tilly and Oskar swapped another meaningful look as they followed Milo through the wooden door and into the final carriage of the train, which was almost pitch-black as it only had small slits for windows running along its top edges.

'This is just a storage carriage!' called Milo. 'Try not to bang into any—'

'Ow!' yelped Oskar, catching his knee painfully on the corner of some anonymous object.

'Too late!' Milo said cheerily. 'Just follow the sound of my voice!'

'Hey, Milo!' Oskar shouted. 'Do you have any biscuits?'

'So many biscuits!' replied Milo. 'Well, some biscuits! A biscuit! Probably! Do you mind if they're a bit soft?'

As he spoke, he yanked open a door at the other end of the carriage and they could make out his silhouette a few metres ahead as they picked their way through the carriage. It was piled high with boxes, broken shelves, piles and piles of papers and things Tilly couldn't even start to put a name to. Once they were out the other side, there was a narrow gap to jump over, which Milo helped Tilly and Oskar cross safely.

'Welcome to my home!' he said proudly as he swung open the door.

They were standing in a tiny, cosy snug of a room.

'It used to be a sleeper carriage for two people,' Milo explained, with a slightly embarrassed shrug. 'But I took out the bottom bunk and made it just right for me. I've been fixing it and making it home ever since I started living here.'

'When was that?' Oskar asked.

'When I was six,' Milo said. 'That was when Horatio unofficially adopted me, and I came to live with him on the Quip.' Tilly noticed that he didn't mention his parents and knew enough about complicated parental situations to understand that she shouldn't ask any more questions just yet – and Oskar had been friends with Tilly long enough to know the same. Milo would tell them more if and when he wanted to.

They focused instead on his room. Now he'd pointed it out, it was obvious that his bed, which was tucked up towards the ceiling, had previously been the top half of a set of bunks. But now there was a small desk underneath it, complete with an inkpot, quill and a pile of parchment. Next to it was a full-to-bursting bookcase, with another pushed up against the far wall of the small carriage. A tiny kitchen area took up one corner, with a kettle, a hotplate and a glass bottle of milk in a bucket of icy water. A cracked mirror hung on one wall, and the rest of the wood panels were decorated with what looked like Christmas-tree lights (with quite a few bulbs missing), postcards of places from around the world and a vintage London Underground poster tacked up above the door.

Not much of the floor was visible underneath the squishy cushions and blankets heaped in a cacophony of clashing colours. The room seemed set up so that you could sit down whenever the mood struck you and curl up with a book – which was evidently what Milo often did, judging by the fact that several paperbacks were strewn across the floor, some with pages splayed open to show notes and underlinings in them. A marmalade tabby was curled up asleep on the largest of the cushions.

'That's Hester,' Milo said. 'She's technically the train cat, not mine, but I'm pretty sure I'm the only one who feeds her, so she spends most of her time in here.'

Tilly picked up one of the books to see what Milo was reading. It was a copy of *The Railway Children* by E. Nesbit.

'It's one of my favourites,' said Milo.

'Mine too,' Tilly agreed happily. 'Although I see you're a corner-folder. Just as I was starting to like you.'

'Oh, I'm sorry,' Milo said, taking the book and straightening it out. 'I just forget where I've put my bookmark sometimes and . . .'

'Only teasing,' Tilly grinned. 'Needed to get you back for pretending you didn't know what bookwandering was. You can do as you like with your own books! They're not museum objects!'

'To be fair, some of the books on Quip are,' Milo said.

'What do you mean?' asked Oskar.

'Well, some of the books we carry are rather precious and some are . . . borrowed . . . from other establishments,' Milo said carefully. 'Or liberated, as Horatio says.'

'You steal books?' Tilly said in horror.

'No!' said Milo, sounding affronted. 'But sometimes, if people find themselves in possession of a stolen book that they might like to be taken elsewhere, or sometimes, if we stumble across a book and it's not entirely clear where it's come from, we might help it on its journey.'

'So you're book smugglers?' Oskar asked, impressed.

'At your service,' said Milo. 'Although Horatio doesn't like that word.'

'So, saying you trade in lost-and-forgotten books is actually a very fancy way of dressing up the fact that you steal books?' Tilly said, unsure how she felt about the whole set-up. She couldn't help but think about how her grandparents would react.

'But we do deal in lost-and-forgotten books,' Milo said defensively. 'I wasn't lying, and it's not like we're petty thieves. Most of what we do is tracking down stories that people thought might have been lost forever and taking care of them! We've saved so many books and stories from being forgotten. Really you should think of us as book . . . rescuers.'

'But how do books get lost or forgotten?' Oskar asked.

'For all sorts of reasons,' Milo said. 'Authors hide away books they never published, or stories are censored, or burned, or sometimes manuscripts end up in suitcases or stolen or just misplaced. We help find them. Every book that is read and loved and shared strengthens the magic of bookwandering. Surely you know that? And every book that gets lost or forgotten means the magic of stories loses a tiny bit of its power. We help keep imagination in balance. Or we try to anyway . . . Imagination can be a bit unpredictable, as I'm sure you know. But yes, we do get unusual requests from some of our more . . . private clients, only it's not just stealing books, I swear. Anyway, I don't know what you're up on your high horse for – you're clearly up to no good!'

'What do you mean?' Tilly said, offended.

'We picked you up in that labyrinth, all by yourselves, and you're being very cagey about why you were there or who you're looking for.'

'Actually, for your information, we're up to very good,' Tilly said awkwardly but incredibly self-righteously.

'We're trying to save bookwandering.'

'What, all of it?' said Milo. 'Does it need saving?'

'It would seem that way,' Oskar said. 'And, if you're so clued into all that stuff you were saying about keeping imagination in balance, then you must be aware that something's up. How about you tell us what *you* know, and we'll return the favour – see if we can't help each other out?'

'I'm game if you are,' Milo said, gauging Tilly's response.

'Deal,' she said, and she and Oskar each took one of Milo's hands and the three of them shook on it as the Sesquipedalian

rumbled

its way

down

the tracks.

23

A SHORT CUT

They looked at each other, not wanting to be the first one to reveal their secrets.

'Just so you know,' Tilly said, 'my mum knows where we are.'

'She knows you're onboard the Quip?' Milo said, confused.

'Well, no, not that bit,' Tilly admitted. 'But she knows what we're looking for, and where we started, and we have friends there who know every step we took until we got on this train,' she said, slightly fudging the details about how much Orlando and Jorge knew.

'I'm not trying to kidnap you,' Milo said, looking a little offended. 'You do remember that I just helped you get out of the labyrinth? And you should go first anyway as you're on my train. What are you up to?'

Tilly glanced at Oskar and he gave her a nod. She took a deep breath. 'We're trying to find the Archivists,' she said.

'Would they be the Archivists who reside at the aforementioned Archive?' Milo said.

'We don't really know,' Tilly admitted. 'We hope so. You said you'd been there before; do you know much about it?'

'Like I said, I didn't get off the train,' said Milo. 'All I saw was a big old building we'd never been to before, and I know that Horatio was in there for a couple of hours. He doesn't tell me anything about his meetings, before you ask.'

'Well, we know that they help bookwanderers,' Oskar said. 'We're following a sort of map to try and find them – that's how we ended up in the labyrinth – although it looks like we've found a short cut.'

'What do you need help with?' Milo said. 'That whole saving bookwandering thing you mentioned?'

Tilly nodded. 'There's been a coup at the British Underlibrary,' she began. 'These awful people have taken over and have stopped everyone bookwandering – and they're threatening to stop children bookwandering *ever again* unless . . . Well, unless everyone agrees to help them,' she finished, not wanting to tell Milo the truth about her parents and what the Underwoods wanted from her.

'But if they've stopped people bookwandering,' Milo said slowly, 'that means they've been binding books?'

'Yes,' Oskar said. 'And they've convinced the American Librarian to help them too.'

'But binding books . . . that's basically evil,' Milo said, looking pale. 'You may think you're above what we do onboard the Quip, but we would *never* bind a book. We keep stories circulating, as they're supposed to. But –' he paused – 'it figures that something like that has happened. As I said, Horatio doesn't tell me much, but the Quip has definitely been quieter over the last few months, not to mention Horatio is always in a bad mood – or a worse mood than usual anyway. He would never tell me, but after spending so much time with him I'm pretty sure there's something more serious than usual bothering him.'

'See, I knew you knew something!' Oskar said.

'I never said I didn't!' Milo grinned.

'Grandad said that Pages & Co. – that's our bookshop – was selling fewer books too,' Tilly said thoughtfully. She cast her mind back to the strange encounter with the man in the shop, who had forgotten the book he came in for. 'I wonder if it's all linked.'

'I thought you said your grandad worked at the Underlibrary?' Milo asked.

'He used to,' Tilly explained. 'But he retired and now he runs our bookshop with my grandma. There was an amazing Librarian who was in charge called Amelia, but the Underwoods – that's who's in control now – forced her out. And now everything's a horrible mess.'

'Well, that's what you get for trusting the Underlibraries,' said Milo, a little sanctimoniously.

'That's rich coming from you,' Oskar said. 'They're great when they have the right people in charge!'

'That's the problem,' Milo pointed out. 'How do you keep the right people in charge, and who decides who they are? What happens when people like the Underwoods end up in power? This mess you're trying to fix is what happens.'

'We knew someone else who thought that,' Tilly said. 'We met a bookseller in Paris who wouldn't register with an Underlibrary and got permanently withdrawn.'

'And then she got pushed into the Endpapers!' Oskar said. 'By the Underwoods.'

'How exactly does one get *pushed* into the Endpapers?' Milo asked.

'The Underwoods were causing problems even before they bound all the books,' Tilly said. 'They were messing up fairy tales on purpose so they could harvest the book magic that was leaking out where they broke them apart. And the Endpapers started overflowing into the actual book because of the mess

they made and, when Gretchen tried to stop them, they . . . well, they pushed her in. Just like it sounds.'

'Hang on,' Milo said. 'Gretchen . . . Gretchen . . . Short hair, big glasses?'

'Yes!' Oskar said. 'Do you know her? Has she been on the train?'

'Sort of,' said Milo. 'We picked her up from the Endpapers a few months ago. She hadn't booked a journey, but Horatio will let people cadge a ride if they're happy to pay.'

'So, she's okay?' Tilly asked, a wave of relief washing over her.

'We dropped her off back in Paris, I think,' Milo nodded. 'At her bookshop.'

'Hang on, did you just say there's a *train station* in the Endpapers?' Oskar asked, incredulous.

'Obviously not a permanent one for regular trains,' Milo said. 'But, like I said before, the Quip can stop almost anywhere, so long as you can imagine it. We run on magic, not coal.'

'Book magic?' Oskar asked.

'Yup,' Milo said. 'One-hundred-per-cent environmentally friendly magic.'

'But how come you're allowed to use book magic?' asked Tilly. 'Especially for something illegal. I thought it was incredibly hard to get permission to use it?'

'Oh, that's the easy part,' said Milo, with a grin. 'We don't *ask* permission.'

24

SOMEONE WHO KNOWS SOMEONE WHO KNOWS SOMEONE

'But . . .' said Oskar. 'Even if the Underwoods are doing bad stuff, the rules are there for a reason.'

Milo waved this away. 'Oh, most of the rules aren't really *real* anyway.'

'What does that even mean?' Oskar said. 'You don't get to just say whether rules are real or not.'

'So who does?' Milo asked. 'The Underlibraries?'

'Well, yes!' Tilly said. 'Someone has to be in charge!'

'If you ask my uncle, he'd tell you that wasn't necessarily true,' said Milo. 'It's not my fault if you can't see outside the box.'

'I don't think you get to be all high and mighty,' Oskar said. 'You do steal books as a job.'

'It's not my job,' Milo said. 'Or at least I don't earn any money from it.'

'Nothing?' Tilly asked.

'What would I spend it on?' said Milo. 'Horatio gives me somewhere to live and food to eat and I get to travel to amazing places with him, and that's a significantly better situation than where I was before.' He paused as if waiting for them to ask about it. 'Aren't you going to ask me where I was before?'

'If you want to tell us,' Tilly said carefully. 'You don't have to, though.'

'I was in an orphanage for the children of bookwanderers who have died inside books,' Milo said abruptly. 'Kids who couldn't be put back into the real world because what had happened to their parents would cause too many questions to be asked, and focus too much attention on corners people didn't want others looking into. I can't even *remember* my parents. All I know is that, until I was six, I was in an awful, cold place full of other kids who didn't know who they were or where they'd come from, and only thought of books as something that had taken their families away. And then Horatio came and found me and brought me here, and so I won't ever complain about it.'

'I get it,' said Tilly.

'Do you?' Milo said, a little sharply.

'Well, no, not exactly,' she said. 'But I didn't know my parents until last year. I grew up with my grandparents, but my mum was trapped in a book and we only found her last year, and my dad . . .' She tailed off. 'Well, he died. So, I don't know what it's like to be you, but I know what it's like to not really know who you are. Thanks for telling us.'

Milo shrugged as if it were no big deal, but Tilly could see his shoulders relax, a weight taken off him by sharing who he was, and people accepting him as such.

'Anyway, that's enough of that for now,' he said. 'I promised you a cup of tea and a biscuit.'

He filled up the kettle from a hose that came

through the window and set it on the hotplate to boil.

'There's a bucket on the roof,' he explained, gesturing to the hose.

'Is it . . . clean?' Oskar asked nervously.

'Oh yes,' Milo said. 'We're in pure Story here, nothing to pollute it. And we're boiling it anyway, so don't worry. Now, biscuits. Biscuits . . .' He started rooting through various drawers and under piles of books and eventually pulled out an already-opened packet of custard creams.

He offered them to Oskar, who emptied a pile of crumbs into his hand.

'Ah,' Milo said. 'Sorry. We do have a dining car, but I'm not really allowed to use it when we have guests onboard.'

'There are other people on the train?' Tilly asked, surprised.

'Of course,' said Milo. 'What did you think all these carriages were, just books?'

Tilly shrugged, that being exactly what she'd imagined.

'We have guest quarters for people of varying means; we have the aforementioned dining car; we have many, many book carriages. And there are rooms for people to meet in, to do business in; there's the conservation carriage, even a printing press carriage and the engine, of course. Good thing about running through Story, and running off its magic, is that we have a fair amount of room for expanding and evolving, depending on what people need. Or want. Once you've saved bookwandering, and all of that, you should book a trip and you can see Quip properly.'

'How do we do that?' Oskar asked. 'Is there, like, a website, or something?'

'Yes, just type in magicalbooktrain.com,' Milo said sarcastically. 'No, there isn't a website! But, if you ask around, you'll find that you know someone who knows someone who knows someone, I'm sure.'

25

FUELLED BY IDEAS

The kettle started to whistle and, as Milo poured the hot water into a teapot, Tilly and Oskar looked at everything tacked to his walls.

'Is this map . . . moving?' Tilly asked, noticing a half-unfolded map on Milo's desk. It had coloured lines crisscrossing each other in a rainbow tangle.

'Probably,' Milo said, wiping out three mugs with the end of his scarf. 'There wouldn't be space to keep track of everywhere we go or can go, so it updates as we travel. Can you see the steam?'

They peered closer and, on a lavender line, there it was – a small plume of black, glittery steam chugging along. Oskar held his finger to it and jerked back.

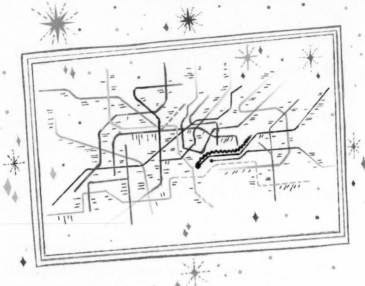

'It's hot!' he said.

'The train *is* burning book magic,' said Milo. 'So, yeah, it's hot.'

'I'm really not sure you're supposed to be burning books,' Tilly said.

'We're not burning *books*,' Milo said, outraged. 'We're not barbarians.'

'Well, how are you burning book magic?'

'I don't know how *you* access book magic, but here we do it the civilised way, straight from the source.'

Tilly and Oskar looked blankly at him.

'We're fuelled by ideas. By imagination,' he explained.

'What?' Oskar said, confused. 'How does that work?'

'It's how you pay to travel on the Sesquipedalian, or to use our services,' Milo explained. 'Depending on what you want, or where you want to travel, you pay in ideas. That's why Horatio can't see you – he's very strict about payment. No exceptions – ever.'

'But . . . I thought that book magic came from books,' said Tilly.

'It can do,' Milo said. 'We could just shove books into the engine if we wanted to – or in an emergency, I suppose, but I think our system works a bit better.'

'The Underlibrary told us that it was a precious resource, though,' Tilly pushed on.

'It's precious because of what it can do,' Milo said. 'But the world would be in a lot of problems if it ran out of imagination, and that's what book magic is really, at its very core. It's not a finite resource, printed in books and ink. Really, we should call it something else – books are often the way the magic is contained, but it's stories really, not the books, and it's in every bookwanderer – it's in every reader, if they knew how to access it. The Underlibraries have either forgotten that or they're choosing not to share it with most people. So, if—'

He was interrupted by a bellow from outside.

'MILO!' the rough voice shouted. 'Where are you, boy? We're about to get to the Archive and I need you ready to unload!'

'We're at the Archive *now*?' Tilly said in a whisper. 'Why didn't you tell us!'

'I didn't know!' Milo said. 'Quick! If Horatio's coming in here, you need to hide. Now!'

26

THERE'S ENOUGH MAGIC TO GO ROUND

All Milo's former confidence and good humour melted away like an ice lolly on a hot day. Previously, with his height and way of talking like a grown-up, Tilly had found it hard to believe he was the same age as them, but the sound of his uncle's voice seemed to turn him into a little boy, terrified of getting into trouble.

'Come on, please,' Milo urged. '*Please*. Quickly.'

It would have been cruel to do anything other than what Milo was asking. There was the sound of a door smashing shut very close by, and Milo gestured urgently at them, with panicked eyes. Tilly slid herself into a narrow crack behind the bed, taking cover behind the frayed velvet curtains that hung down from the window, while Oskar burrowed his way under a pile of blankets.

Milo was heaping more on top of him just as the door to the carriage was flung open. Tilly could barely breathe, the musty scent of the curtains filling her nostrils, and she hoped she wouldn't sneeze or cough while Horatio was in the room.

'There you are, boy,' a gruff voice said. 'Didn't you hear the bell ring? We're just about to get into the Archive.'

'Sorry, I must have been lost in a book,' Milo said, a small wobble in his voice. 'What's at the Archive anyway?'

'Opportunities,' Horatio said. 'Not that it's any of your business.'

Tilly smiled to herself behind the curtain at Milo trying to find out more information for them.

'Are we going to keep coming back here?' Milo asked.

'Not sure yet,' said Horatio. 'It's a new port of

call and a lucrative one, I think. I came across a map of sorts while I was sourcing something for Mr Gentlemoon and it brought us here, where I met a most interesting woman. I need you to get the books she requested and then get us ready to go. I can't imagine I'll be here too long. Pay attention, boy! Why are you sweating so much? It's not like you've been working hard enough. What have you even been doing since we left the labyrinth? Why aren't you ready to go?'

'Sorry, Uncle,' Milo said. 'I must've lost track of time.'

'What've I told you about calling me that?' said Horatio. 'Use my name. I'm not interested in any of this sentimentality. I didn't take you out of that place for your own entertainment or mine, boy. I needed an extra body to help on board and that arrangement works for both of us, not to mention I'm repaying my debt to your parents as I said I would. Now, come on,' he said. 'Don't irritate me, boy.' There was the sound of a door slamming and then a few beats before Milo came and uncovered them from their hiding places.

'I'm sorry you had to hear that,' he said, looking embarrassed. 'He's . . . well, anyway, it doesn't matter to you what he's like. He's my only family and I'd rather be on the Quip than back in the orphanage any day, so it is what it is.' He plastered an unconvincing smile on to his face. 'I've got to start getting the boxes ready. You two can wait here until we stop and then hop off the back – just like how you got on. I'd really appreciate it if you could try to stay out of sight.'

'Of course,' said Tilly as they followed Milo back out of his carriage, across the gap and into the dark storage carriage.

'Just stay in here until we stop,' Milo said in the gloom. 'It was really nice to meet you guys – I hope that you find the answers you're looking for, and that you get home safe afterwards. And remember, there's always enough magic to go around!'

Then he gave them a wistful smile and a wave and

headed back to whatever task Horatio had waiting for him.

'Should we take him with us?' Tilly asked Oskar quietly. Even though they'd barely spent any time with him, her heart felt unbearably sad for him. She knew the pain of not knowing where you come from and struggling to find a place in the world. While at first glance living on a book-smuggling train seemed like the greatest adventure you could possibly hope for, she couldn't imagine it helped him feel as if he knew what home was.

'We can't,' Oskar said. 'He's not an abandoned kitten, Tilly. We'd just be ripping him out of his life and what would he do? Come and live with you? With me?'

'I'm sure Grandma and Grandad would let him stay at Pages & Co.,' Tilly said, but she knew that that wasn't the point.

'He'll find his own home one day,' Oskar said.

'Since when did you get so wise?' laughed Tilly, poking him in the ribs.

'Since I started reading all these books and going on these big life-and-death adventures, I reckon.' Oskar grinned. 'I talk in inspirational quotes nowadays, so you'd better get used to it. But, more importantly – this is it, Tilly.'

'We're finally going to find the Archivists,' she said.

'Do . . . do we have a plan?'

'I'm sort of hoping it just becomes obvious, and whoever sent me the clues is there and is expecting us.'

'I hope so,' Oskar said. 'And I hope they have biscuits. Because, much as I liked Milo, those custard creams were very disappointing.'

They heard the train brakes squeal as they slowed, and Tilly peeped through the window to see a station that felt like the direct opposite of the one they'd boarded in the labyrinth. Instead of stark white stone and emptiness, it had a beautifully paved platform surrounded by red brick, with ivy creeping up its walls. An ornate golden gate hung open and a woman in black stood there, waiting. As the train came to a complete stop, Tilly and Oskar crept out of the back door and slid off the platform on to the tracks.

'How on earth are we going to get through those gates without him noticing?' Oskar said, pointing to the man, who was evidently Horatio, climbing down from the engine and striding across the platform to shake hands with the woman in black.

They'd only heard his voice when hiding in Milo's carriage. Now they could see that he was tall and thin like his nephew, with the same warm copper skin tone and dark hair, although his curls were going grey and he'd clearly made more of an attempt to get them under control – though without a huge amount of success. He was wearing a plain but expensive-looking black wool coat and smiled broadly at the woman as they shook hands.

'Do we just wait for the train to leave?' Oskar said.

'That could take ages,' said Tilly. 'Presumably, those two aren't just going to stand there – they'll go inside, wherever inside is, and we can make a dash for it.'

As Tilly predicted, after a few moments of pleasantries, the woman and Horatio turned and walked through the golden gates.

'Now!' hissed Tilly and the two of the scrambled up on to the platform and ran towards the gates. Tilly took a quick glance over her shoulder and saw Milo starting to lug large boxes from a carriage further down the train. He noticed them running and gave them a thumbs up before turning back to the boxes.

Tilly and Oskar reached the gates, and ran through them, nearly with the back of Horatio and the woman in black.

'Ah, you must be Matilda and Oskar,' the woman said, not seeming at all surprised to see them, and smiling warmly. 'Welcome to the Archive. I'm so glad you finally got here.'

27

THE BIBLIOGNOST

'You two were on my train?' Horatio said, raising his eyebrows.

'Um. Yes,' said Tilly. 'Sorry.'

He ignored her, turning instead to the woman. 'And you know them?'

'Yes,' she confirmed. 'I've actually been waiting for them. I had thought they were coming via the labyrinth, although I saw there was a last-minute detour.'

'We . . . um . . . did come via the labyrinth?' Oskar tried hopefully, wanting to protect Milo.

'The end of the labyrinth is on the other side of the Archive, I'm afraid.' She smiled. 'But what good fortune that the Sesquipedalian was passing through.'

'They owe me payment,' Horatio said brusquely.

'Surely you can waive it this one time?' the woman said.

'That's not how it works,' Horatio replied sternly.

'How about this then,' she said. 'I'll pay for them. And I'll warrant you'd rather have my payment than theirs.'

Horatio grunted his assent and turned his attention back to Tilly and Oskar. 'Did that boy of mine help you?' he asked. 'He can't seem to resist when it comes to waifs and strays.'

'No,' Oskar lied. 'Milo didn't know anything.' There was a pause as Oskar realised the mistake he'd made by using Milo's name. 'Or . . . rather . . . he didn't *help* us or anything. He told us we had to get off as soon as we stopped when he realised we were onboard.'

'A likely story,' Horatio huffed. 'But I'll deal with him later.'

'Honestly, it's not his fault,' said Tilly.

'It's no concern of yours, regardless,' Horatio said.

'Now, Horatio,' the woman said, 'let's all go inside and I'll get Tilly and Oskar comfortable, and we can have our conversation privately and then I believe you have some other meetings while you're here?'

Again, Horatio only grunted his agreement, while glaring at Tilly and Oskar.

The woman turned and led the way. Beyond the golden gates a grand red-brick building was visible. It looked like an old university with large windows, more ivy climbing up the walls, and carefully tended gardens leading down to the train station. Although it was a little imposing, after burning ancient libraries, forests made of paper and labyrinths of white stone, it seemed refreshingly normal at first glance.

But, as they got nearer, it became obvious that something wasn't quite right. Some of the flowers were shrivelled and dead, fading to black and white, almost as though they were back in the paper forest itself. Down one wall of the building there was a great crack that ran straight from the roof to the ground, and the ivy that looked so beautiful from a distance wasn't quite as orderly as it first appeared. There were places where it was invading the windows and other smaller cracks in the wall, and some windows where it seemed to be growing from the inside out. When they turned a corner, they could see a great heap of rubble on the far side of the building where a huge chunk of it had tumbled down.

'I'm afraid we're not looking our best at the moment,' the woman said. 'Some, well, some structural difficulties.'

Tilly and Oskar followed her and Horatio through the gardens, the two adults talking quietly in front of them, their conversation disguised by the swishing of the woman's skirt on the gravel path. She was wearing a bizarre combination of clothes – all black – that seemed pulled from completely different times and places. From the back, her full skirt was ruffled and extravagant, but it was short at the front and she was wearing it over a pair of black trousers with heeled boots. She wore a corset over a T-shirt that fell loosely over her back and shoulders so that a golden tattoo of a labyrinth was showing at the base of her neck. Her hair was jet-black and her skin was porcelain-white, and if it wasn't for the tattoo she would almost look like she was in black and white too.

They walked up a sweeping set of stairs and the woman in black pushed open a pair of creaking double doors to let them into a large entrance hall.

'Welcome to the Archive,' the woman said. 'I'm so sorry – I haven't even introduced myself properly. I am the Bibliognost.'

'That's your name?' Tilly said, confused.

'No, that's my job,' she said. 'My name is Artemis. Now, if you two follow me, I'm just going to speak with Mr Bolt very quickly and make sure he's happy, and then I'll be back with you as soon possible.'

Artemis led them through to another smaller room lined with bookshelves, with two comfortable-

looking sofas facing each other next
to a roaring fire. On the coffee table
between the sofas were a large plate of
biscuits and two mugs of hot chocolate.

'Please do stay in here for now,' Artemis
said. 'I'll be back very shortly.' She let herself out and
closed the door behind her.

'Well!' Oskar. 'What do you think?'

'About what?'

'About all of it!'

'I'm not sure it's what I was expecting. She
obviously knew we were coming, so that's reassuring,
right?'

'I think so,' Oskar said, studying the biscuit choice.
'She certainly sounds like she knows what's going on.
Is she an Archivist, do you think? Are there more of
them?'

'She did say that Horatio had more meetings, so
I guess there must be other people somewhere. And
this place is huge. Although have you noticed that it
seems all fancy, but it's not quite right? It's falling

apart. Look.' Tilly gestured to another crack that whispered its way down the wood panelling. She stood and inspected it closely and saw that there was a faint, sparkly substance at its edges.

'It looks a bit like the cracks we saw in the fairy tales,' she said to Oskar. 'But it's sort of glittery dust, not sticky book magic. Maybe it's because we're so far inside stories?'

Oskar nodded as he munched on a Viennese sandwich. 'Whatever happens next, Tilly,' he said, 'we should remember that we actually managed to get here, despite everything, and I think that's pretty impressive, to be honest. We said we would, and we did.'

Twenty minutes later, though, they were starting to feel rather bored, not to mention very sleepy. After the epic journey to get here, it felt a little anticlimactic to be sitting on their own, eating biscuits.

To stop herself from dozing off, Tilly stayed on her feet and explored the room. There was a large desk beneath a gable window that was very neat and held only a small pile of papers. There were fine cracks in the windowpane that spilled a spiderweb of shadows on to the sheets of paper. Tilly picked up the top one to see a list of what appeared to be book titles written in very neat handwriting, although none of the names were familiar to her.

- *Roseberry Topping* by Patrick Bray (1987)
- *Danger on the River* by Lyra Lake (1866)
- *Kin* by A. M. C. Collier (1895)
- *The Penguin* by Eve Tsang (1928)

'Have you ever heard of any of these books, Oskar?' Tilly asked, reading out more names to him.

'Nope,' Oskar replied drowsily. 'But there are a lot of books out there; we must only have heard of a tiny fraction of them.'

'I suppose,' Tilly said. 'I wonder what they are, though.'

'They're books that I am trying to find,' Artemis said, having come back into the room without either of them hearing her. 'Books that have gone missing.'

'Are they special in some way?' Tilly asked.

'I don't think so, individually,' Artemis said. 'But their disappearance is very strange because I don't mean that just one copy of these books is missing; I mean *all* of them are. They have vanished and it's very hard to work out what has happened because the books are so obscure that there's barely any reference to them. Here at the Archive we are able to keep track of a lot of things, so at least we know they *did* once exist, but there are certain things hidden from us, and these books – and goodness knows what else – are being concealed in those shadows.'

'And that's why Horatio is here,' Oskar said, joining the dots. 'Because he finds lost-and-forgotten books.'

'Exactly,' said Artemis.

'So why are *we* here?' Tilly said. 'You did send us the clues, right?'

'I sent you a map, yes,' Artemis confirmed.

'I mean, I think calling it a map is a bit strong,' Oskar said. 'It wasn't exactly obvious how to get here.'

'It is a map for those who know how to read it,' Artemis replied. 'And here you are.'

'Were the vines from you too?' asked Tilly.

'The vines?' Artemis repeated, confused.

'When we were in DC, part of *A Midsummer Night's Dream* came out of the book and dragged us in,' Oskar explained.

'And, when we were in the paper forest, one tried to get hold of us,' Tilly added. 'The vine was trying to twist round my ankle, like they did in the bookshop.'

'That most certainly wasn't me,' Artemis said. 'That's not my style of getting someone's attention at all.'

'But, if it wasn't you, who was it?' asked Oskar.

'I wonder . . .' Artemis started. 'I have a theory,' she said, 'but I might need to explain a bit more about the Archive before it makes sense.'

'Okay,' Tilly said, not sure what other option they had. 'I'm sorry, I don't mean to be rude, but you didn't actually answer the question about why we're here. I understand that if those books are all going missing you need Horatio to help find them, but how do we fit in? Is it something to do with what's going on at the Underlibrary? That's why we've come after all!'

'What is going on at your Underlibrary?' Artemis asked, and Tilly felt wrong-footed all over again. Why on earth were they here if not to fix what was happening at the British Underlibrary?

'You . . . don't know?' Oskar said slowly.

'I'm afraid not. Are books going missing there too? That would be an interesting piece to the puzzle.'

'Who knows!' Tilly said, frustration building. 'But there are awful people in charge, who tricked their way into the job, and are using book magic so they can stay in power forever! They've stopped people from bookwandering!'

'Ah, that does make sense,' Artemis said. 'I wondered why you weren't bookwandering any more.'

'But . . . that's the whole problem!' Tilly said.

'That's why we're here! So you can help us! I thought that's why you sent me all those clues!'

Artemis looked thoughtful. 'No. There are obviously even more layers to this problem than I had anticipated. When did the Underwoods take over?'

'Just before Christmas,' said Tilly.

'Hmm,' said Artemis. 'Just before books began to go missing at a greater rate, as far as I can tell. I'll need you to tell me a little more about what they're doing.'

'But I still don't understand how you don't already know, but you *did* know that we weren't bookwandering,' Tilly said in frustration.

'I think the best way for me to answer that is to show you,' Artemis said, seemingly unmoved by Tilly's exasperation.

'Follow

me.'

28

MADE of IMAGINATION

Tilly and Oskar stood up and walked through the door after Artemis. She took them down a long corridor to a large set of wooden double doors painted white. Artemis pushed them open, and in front of them was just bright whiteness, so dazzling that they were forced to squint until their eyes got used to the glare. As their eyesight adjusted, they could see a room come into focus in front of them. A room with no windows and high ceilings – and rows and rows of shelves full of large books bound in white. The floor was whitewashed wood and there was no other decoration or furniture apart from the shelves. Despite the lack of colour, the room still somehow had a sense of warmth and friendliness, as though it were inviting you in.

'Welcome to the Archive,' Artemis smiled.

'So, what exactly is archived here?' Tilly asked.

'In this hall are the histories of every bookwanderer since this Archive began,' Artemis explained.

'What do you mean, *histories*?' asked Oskar.

'Records of every time a bookwanderer travels inside a book,' Artemis said as if that made it any easier to understand. 'That's how I knew you two weren't bookwandering any more.'

'But how?' Tilly asked. 'How did you know?'

'I didn't,' Artemis said, 'but the Archive does. This place is built out of story magic; the same magic you use every time you bookwander. It's all pulled from the same magic source, and so the Archive can see how you're using that magic, and records it here.'

'So, there's one of these books for me and Tilly?' Oskar asked, unnerved. 'Can we see them?'

'I'm not technically permitted to show any bookwanderer their record,' said Artemis. 'But, considering the circumstances, perhaps I can make an exception, so you can understand what I know. And I can tell you a bit more about how the Archive came to be as we walk.'

She led the way down the long row of shelves.

'Legend says that the original Archivist was a bookwanderer who was trying to escape death,' Artemis explained in her low, soothing voice. 'Not because of any of what one might call the usual reasons, but because he was haunted by all the books he would never have time to read. And so he burrowed his way down into layer upon layer of stories, as far as he could reach – stories inside stories, and books within books. He didn't care if it proved impossible to find his way back – he never wanted to leave. He carved out a space inside Story, and sent messages back to his trusted friends so that they, too, could find their way if they wished, and for a while it was a place to write and read and talk and share ideas, and it became suffused with the magic of books and stories and imagination.'

'Suffused?' Tilly asked, not quite understanding the word.

'I mean that magic attracts magic, and so it gradually spread through this whole place until it was part of its very foundations.'

'So the Archive is made of magic?' Oskar clarified.

'Yes – it's made of imagination,' Artemis said. 'And imagination is pure magic. Now, the people who were living and working here were able to experiment with that magic, outside the boundaries of the usual rules of time and life. And one of the things that they created was this – a way to channel the magic into these records so that all the adventures of bookwanderers past and future were saved. And so the man's refuge became known as the Archive. A constantly updated record of all bookwandering.'

'But doesn't that mean you know where every bookwanderer is?' asked Tilly.

'No. We only know where they bookwander *to* – the Archive can only see you when you're in stories. It isn't watching you go about your daily life – it couldn't even if it wanted to. And, of course, that means it can see you while you're here, and I could monitor your journey here as soon as you reached the Library of Alexandria.'

'So are the people who invented these records still here somewhere?' Tilly asked.

'No,' Artemis said. 'The founder was not fundamentally of the world of story and imagination, and the real world eventually found him and claimed him back, and he died. But the Archive stayed – it had enough story magic in its foundations to keep it going until now. Being a reader or a writer is to be part of an everlasting chain of stories passed down from friend to friend, or grandparent to grandchild, or librarian to reader – but something is sapping that magic, something is breaking that chain, and the Archive is crumbling – as though there's not enough imagination to sustain it. Ah –' she paused – 'here we are.'

Artemis stopped in front of a shelf that looked identical to all the others. The volumes all had the same golden labyrinth symbol embossed on their sides as well as a long number. Artemis pulled down a volume and flicked it open and it settled naturally about two thirds of the way through its pages. Tilly and Oskar watched in amazement as words appeared on the page in front of their eyes, as if written by an invisible quill.

'*Matilda is shown her volume in the Archive by the Bibliognost,*' it said.

'It knows I'm here?' Tilly said, feeling deeply unsettled.

'*Matilda queries the mechanism of the Archive,*' the book wrote, '*and questions its knowledge of her presence.*' Then a word started to be written before vanishing again, like it had been rubbed out.

'What was it going to say?' Tilly asked.

'You must have changed your mind about something,' Artemis said cheerfully, closing the book.

'I don't like that at all,' said Oskar. 'It's like it's one step ahead of us.'

'Can I see what it's said about me in the past?' Tilly asked.

'And can I see mine?' Oskar added.

'I'm afraid not,' Artemis said. 'As I said, I shouldn't really be showing you your volume at all, but I need you to see this so you understand what I am able to see.'

'But it knew what I was going to do before I did,' Tilly said.

'Not quite.'

'So, how come you don't know about the Underwoods?' Tilly asked. 'Don't they have records?'

'They do,' Artemis said, 'but the Archive has a blind spot. No record of how book magic is channelled at the Underlibraries – for bookwandering or any other purpose – can be monitored here.'

'Why not?' Oskar asked. 'That would seem kind of useful.'

'It would indeed be very useful,' Artemis said. 'But, decades ago, the Underlibraries decided to use great quantities of book magic to cloak themselves, and the Archive is unable to record anything that takes place under that protective shield.'

'But why not?' Tilly repeated.

'Because they didn't want our interference,' Artemis said. 'The resources of the Archive used to draw bookwanderers here – for advice, for guidance, for reference. We existed above the politics of different countries and policies, and the Underlibraries increasingly resented our position. They wanted to be able to get on with their own plans, even if it meant damaging stories or bookwanderers, and they didn't want any evidence of what they'd done. Look.'

She opened Tilly's archive again and found a different page. On it there was a description of when Tilly and Oskar had bookwandered right to the edge of *Alice's Adventures in Wonderland* and into the Endpapers. But the record simply stopped when they reached the Endpapers, saying only, '*As a half-fictional person, Matilda was propelled from the Endpapers to the British Underlibrary, alongside Oskar Roux.*'

And then it stopped, and only picked up again once they'd bookwandered into *A Little Princess* to rescue Bea.

'So . . . you know I'm half fictional,' Tilly said. 'Of course you do.'

'Yes,' Artemis said gently. 'I have been following how your bookwandering abilities have manifested as best I can, and I sent you the map in the hope that your skills might be of use in helping me work out why the magic is leaking out of the Archive, and if it has anything to do with all the missing books. Speaking of which, Tilly, in answer to your earlier query about the vines: you remember I just told you that the original Archivist was not of Story and so he was ultimately claimed back by the outside world? Well, I think perhaps that the reverse is happening to you: Story is trying to reclaim you.'

'What?' said Tilly.

'You are half fictional – half from the world of Story. And I think Story is trying to take you back – to claim you as one of its own.'

Tilly stared at her. 'But why now?' she asked in horror.

'You've been making your presence known since

you learned you were a bookwanderer. And now, travelling through layers of stories in order to visit us here, has made you even more visible,' Artemis answered. 'I can only apologise if my desire for you to visit has exacerbated matters. It may also be linked to the disruption going on in Story. After all, its very foundations are being shaken. It may settle down once we've sorted this out, and so now we have one more reason to solve this mystery.'

'You said that the original Archivist isn't here any more,' Oskar said. 'So, are there still people here apart from you? Other Archivists?'

'Oh yes,' Artemis said. 'And I think it's perhaps time that you met some of them.'

Artemis carefully replaced Tilly's record on the shelf and the three of them walked back through the glistening white room to the main entrance hall, which seemed dark and old-fashioned in comparison. As they walked up the grand central staircase, Artemis's foot went right through the wood, but she simply shook it out again and carried on.

'Mind your step,' she said over her shoulder to Tilly and Oskar.

'This place is weird,' Oskar whispered to Tilly.

'I know,' Tilly said. 'I don't know what I was expecting, but it wasn't this.'

'Now, I'm not sure where any of the Archivists will be at any given moment,' Artemis went on. 'And it's a long time since most of them have had any visitors, so they mainly keep to their rooms. But we might find some of them in the library. Shall we see?'

She gestured at a door with a neat wooden plaque next to it that did indeed read '**Library**'. There was a bloom of mould on the paint where the sign was fixed to the wall. Artemis opened the door for them, and they entered a beautiful library that on the surface looked like the perfect place to relax and read – apart from the fact that there were two men shouting at each other in the middle of the room.

One of them was wearing a loose-fitting shirt tucked into velvet trousers that stopped at his knee,

and stockings. He had quite long hair and an earring in one ear. The other, his dark hair slicked down from a severe centre parting, was wearing a sharply cut suit and holding a champagne glass.

'The thing is, Will, old sport,' the one holding the champagne glass said with a strong American accent, leaning insouciantly on the mantelpiece, 'is that you're just NOT LISTENING.' A bit of champagne sloshed out of his glass as he raised his voice.

'No, it is you who listens not,' the man called Will

retorted. 'And, if you persist in ignorance, I shall have no choice but to believe you do it to cause me harm.'

'Boy, if I get under your skin, it's merely a bonus,' the American man replied. 'You sure do overestimate how much time I spend thinking about your feelings.'

'Nay, only a fool would believe that,' Will said. 'And you cast about in pursuit of distraction. If you were the gentleman you profess to be, it would be the time to confess 'twas you, and you alone, who cast my good ruff into yonder fishing pond.'

'I will do nothing of the sort, old sport,' the American said. 'For it ain't my fault!'

Artemis coughed and the two men noticed the new arrivals.

'Come now, gentlemen,' Artemis said. 'We have guests. Now, Tilly, Oskar, this is Scott Fitzgerald, over by the fireplace, and Will Shakespeare, two of our Archivists.'

29

UNREAD STORIES

'Is this all a very, very complicated practical joke?'
Oskar said to Tilly in disbelief. 'Because I thought
she just said that was William Shakespeare.'

'Young sir,' Will said, coming over and bowing
deeply before them. 'Truly, I feel that I am suffering
at the service of some other man's twisted humour
many days, but I assure you we are who we claim to
be. To imprison writers in a purgatory such as this goes
against all I hold dear as a good English gentleman.
Imagine! I was lying on my deathbed, waiting to
shuffle off this mortal coil, and behold! I awaken here.
With only men such as this for company,' he said,
gesturing at Scott, who rolled his eyes behind Will's
back. 'He has been here an infinitesimal fraction of

time compared to what I have been forced to endure, and as such has no excuse for the abominable way he behaves.'

'How long have you been here?' Tilly asked.

'This marks somewhere just beyond my four hundredth year,' Will said wearily. 'One rather loses a sense of time for want of anything to busy the mind with.'

'Aren't you supposed to be helping bookwandering?' Tilly said quietly. 'That's sort of what we'd been led to believe.'

'It is true that we helped those who sought aid of us for a time,' Will said. 'But the true purpose of our existence here has been lost to myth, I fear. I know the good lady Artemis tends to the Archive, but what use it is to us I do not know, for no one comes to consult it any more. A hall of unread stories, unwillingly given by their subjects. Once we were glad to aid those who worked in the service of the written or spoken word, and invited those who wished to write and read and explore ideas to do so alongside us, the greatest minds of our times. But the limits of our aid were exhausted, our motives were questioned and, if those who live continue in their folly – as they are fated to do – then who are we to realign the stars?'

'If I had known what was waiting here for me,' Scott chimed in, 'then I think I would've made more of an effort to stay alive, to be sure. When I was among the living, I wanted everyone to know my name, but if I'd understood what was in store for me, I'm not sure I would have chosen the same profession.'

'On that we can be agreed,' said Will. 'But people love what you've written!' Tilly said, horrified at the idea of a world without *The Great Gatsby* or *Romeo and Juliet*. 'Oh, you flatter me, child,' Will said, clearly pleased at the praise. 'But what worth have stories when all is reduced to dust?

You write and the people applaud, but it is a dangerous thing to believe that they care. When I lived, I thought, as you still do, that stories could alter the very movement of the heavens. But the world will not be changed, however much we wish it so. What are books or plays or sonnets but a few hours of trifling pleasure in exchange for a brief moment of forgetfulness?'

'Hear, hear, old sport,' Scott said, toasting the air with his nearly empty champagne flute.

'My lady,' Will said to Artemis, 'if you perchance see Jane or Charles, will you tell them that I seek their company. I tire of Americans.'

The two men started arguing again, but Artemis shushed them.

'I was hoping, Will, that you might give Tilly and Oskar here a quick tour round the Archive. I thought you'd be more excited to see some new people; it's been so long since we've had visitors. And, as you just said yourself, you need a change of company. Why don't you go and see if you can find Jane or Charles yourself, and take Tilly and Oskar with you?'

'Am I to be a nursemaid to children now?' he protested.

'Tilly and Oskar are fine young people who have travelled very far to speak to us,' Artemis replied. 'And, if you don't wish to talk to them, you will have very little grounds for complaints about boredom or your purpose here in the future.'

'Very well,' Will said. 'If only to give myself some respite from this *old sport*,' he finished sarcastically.

'Wonderful, I'll leave you three to it,' Artemis said. 'Will, if you bring them back downstairs to the reception room when you're done, I'll come and find you there.'

'I imagine it will only be a brief turn about the place,' Will said wearily. 'For there is very little of interest to show you.'

Tilly had thought visiting the Library of Alexandria was unusual, but that had been topped by a forest made of paper, which in turn had seemed normal when they travelled on a train through stories, and now she was getting a tour of a building with William Shakespeare.

'I must apologise,' Will said as they walked along a corridor leading from the library. 'You will think ill of me. It has been a long while since we had guests here, and I have allowed that gentleman to worry his way 'neath my skin. We were the closest of friends when first he arrived, but our friendship has soured so, and everything he says makes me wish to plunge myself into the fishing pond after my poor, unfortunate ruff.'

Will was tracing his hand listlessly along the wall as he walked and dragging his feet, more like a petulant teenager than the world's most famous playwright.

'So, who chooses which writers get to be Archivists?' Tilly asked, trying to find out more about how it all worked, and what the Archivists could possibly do to help with their situation.

'Oh, it is a magic unknown to me,' Will said disconsolately. 'I suppose those of us who were so fortunate in life as to think we held the minds and hearts of our public are now taunted by that very fact. The lady Artemis tells us it is not the doing of any man or woman, but that this abode is a resting place of imagination that draws us to it – the same energy that creates that confounded Archive downstairs. She says it as though it should be considered a great compliment to be here, and I grant you, in years gone by, there were times of such merriment and inspiration, with guests and gatherings and masques and balls.'

'Why did it change?' Tilly asked.

'It is hard to know now; it happened by such small moments,' Will said. 'But there were those who wished us to solve all the world's ills and would not take to heart that perfection is an impossible goal. We had not the power to solve what was brought before us, and those who wander in books became disillusioned, and angry, and sought power and opportunity, not wisdom and solace.' He paused to look down at Tilly and Oskar. 'Was a map sent to you?'

'Yes,' Tilly said. 'Sort of – more a collection of clues.'

'We had such larks designing those maps,' Will said wistfully. 'We would come together and create charts of such beauty and intricacy, which we would send out through stories in order to aid the wanderers who were looking to find their way here. But, as their resentment grew, we created fewer maps, and allowed fewer ways to find us. We buried ourselves deeper and deeper within tales, and so we no longer resided in books within books, but in the very fabric of Story. And now look: it frays around us, and we cannot leave but I fear we cannot stay.'

'Why can't you leave?' asked Oskar.

'Several dear friends have attempted departures over the years,' Will explained. 'And, despite the pleas of those who have seen it occur, we were forced over and over again to watch our allies dissolve into the air around us in front of our very eyes. I do not wish such a fate upon myself, even if this is the only alternative. Ay, my friends and allies and this very

Archive collapse around us, and we have nothing to save ourselves with!' he wailed.

He pointed dramatically to a crack running down the wall. 'For even our words have no might against the destruction of imagination!' he finished. The crack was actually not that large, and Will gave it a bit of a bang with his fist. It looked as though he were trying to work the bash into his expression of woe, but Tilly couldn't help notice that he looked more satisfied when a bit of plaster tumbled poetically from the ceiling, as if to emphasise his point.

30

ERRANT INK
SPLOTCHES

'Where dost thou hail from?' Will said as he led them up a spiral staircase.

'We live in London,' Oskar answered.

'Ah, such times I have spent in our fair capital,' Will said dreamily. 'Do you know that they used to stage my plays there for thousands?'

'Yes, because they still—' Tilly began.

'And even Good Queen Bess used to come and favour us with her presence,' Will continued, lost in his memories and entirely ignoring Tilly's reply. 'They were the days of heady joy and those I long to return to. And now I rot here, constrained within these crumbling walls.'

'You can't even bookwander?' Oskar asked.

'Alas, no,' Will said. 'There is no way at all to leave this cursèd place save in our own imaginations.'

'So, you just sit here and complain and have arguments?' Tilly said.

'Do you think I should do otherwise?' He stared down at her.

'Actually, yes I do,' she said, trying to sound braver than she felt about disagreeing with Shakespeare. 'I think you should help us, for one. What was the point of sending us a map?'

'It was the good lady who sent that forth, I am sure,' Will said. 'Not I. If I were to have my say . . . Ah, here comes Jane. You would do well to be polite and charming to her, for her tongue is sharp and I do not like to be on the wrong side of it.'

A woman in a neat, floral, empire-line dress with a lace trim was approaching down the corridor. When she saw them, she stopped and bobbed a curtsy.

'Jane,' said Will, folding himself into an elaborate bow. 'Art thou well? The day is fine, is it not?'

'It is not so fine to my eyes,' the woman said, with a sigh.

'Oh, Jane, you and your wit!' Will said, laughing awkwardly, and blushing a little.

'If you see that as wit, I should think I will avoid your plays,' she said. 'Now, who are our guests?'

'I'm Tilly,' Tilly said.

'And I'm Oskar.'

'My name is Jane,' the woman said. 'Jane Austen.'

'My mum loves you,' Tilly said nervously, feeling as though she were meeting a celebrity, which she supposed she was.

'How lovely,' Jane said, clearly pleased. 'Always cheering to know one's words are still read. I struggled to find success while I was truly alive, but I am glad that people have found comfort and enjoyment in my books since.'

'Yes, very much so,' Tilly reassured her.

'Miss Artemis knows much of the world outside the Archive. However, she says too much knowledge of how our work fares suits us ill,' continued Jane.

'But I doubt her motivations, would you not agree, sir?'

'I would,' Will said. 'Most vehemently.'

'Now, if you will excuse me,' Jane said. 'I have been practising my French, and Alexandre and I have a bet running as to how much whisky Ernest has drunk today.'

'Isn't she glorious?' Will said, watching her walk away. 'Now, I believe I cannot put the task at hand off any further. It is, I assume, the reason as to why the lady Artemis bade me accompany you. Her motivations are more transparent than she believes. I think I shall regret asking the question, but will press on regardless. Tell me why you have come. But I shall not be able to assist you – know that before you speak.'

'It's the British Underlibrary,' Tilly started.

'It's been taken over by this creepy brother and sister who are binding all the books so no one can bookwander without their permission,' Oskar went on.

'And they don't want children to be able to bookwander at all,' Tilly finished.

'People have tried worse,' Will said. 'And people have tried much the same, over and over – where is the imagination? 'Tis ever power or immortality.'

'They want both,' said Oskar.

'They so often do.' Will nodded.

'So, what do we do about it?' Tilly persisted.

'Oh, if you wait long enough, they will wear themselves out, or die in some sort of contrivance of their own making,' said Will. 'There are tomes and tomes in the Archive that tell this same story over and over, as many times as you would care to read it.'

'But what about *now*?' Tilly said, starting to feel more angry than disappointed.

'We are all but errant ink splotches on the pages of history,' Will said. 'Except for myself and the others here naturally. And look where that has got us. This too shall pass, I promise you.'

'I'm sorry,' Tilly said, 'but I'm going to have to respectfully disagree with you.'

'Me too,' Oskar said, folding his arms.

'I mean, it's just not good enough,' Tilly went on. 'Where would the world be if everyone just sat back and said, "Oh, this too shall pass? No one would have invented anything, or travelled anywhere, or written anything. Did you write your plays because you didn't care?'

'I used to care, my child,' Will said. 'I assure you. But it will take you only to trouble and heartache. I now seek an easier path.'

'I refuse to believe that the man who wrote *A Midsummer Night's Dream* thinks a nice, quiet life caring about nothing and nobody is the best option,' said Tilly.

'Does bookwandering mean *anything* to you any more?' Oskar said. 'Or even people reading? The Underwoods want to steal everything good from stories and use it for themselves. They don't care about anyone else – to be honest, they sound a lot like you except less posh.'

Will shrugged, but he looked a little flustered.

'You cannot possibly begin to fathom the torment of existing here,' he said. 'I was as you were, propelled by belief in lofty ideals. But I have had them punctured by those who visited this place. To abide here in our loneliness is preferable to becoming embroiled once more in the squabbles and battles of people whose lives are a mere blink of an eye. I would refuse to believe a single man who does not act solely in his own interest exists, even were he to parade before me. I admire your faith, I do, but 'tis misplaced.'

'Listen,' Tilly said sternly, 'I did not fly all the way to America, escape a burning library – twice! – nearly get stuck in a forest made of paper – and a labyrinth! – or stow away on an illegal magical train only to get here and have you tell me you don't care and won't help!'

'I can tell you nothing else,' Will said. 'There is nothing to see that will cheer you, only further people that will thwart you as I have, and I do not care to witness that. Let us return you to the lady Artemis, who can herself explain why she has made you undertake this arduous journey with no hope of success. Perhaps she is as bored as the rest of us, and merely toys with you.' He sighed. 'I pity you, I do, but there is nothing more to be said, and I have no desire to entertain you any longer.'

31

FRAYING THE VERY FABRIC OF STORIES

Shakespeare deposited Tilly and Oskar back in the room with the fireplace – and the biscuits – where Artemis was waiting, and left.

'How did you get on with Will?' she asked.

'He's not interested in helping us at all,' Tilly said, feeling utterly dispirited.

'Ah,' Artemis said. 'And you told him why you had come?'

'As much as we know why we've come!' Tilly said. 'Which isn't much!'

'We thought the Archive was to help bookwanderers,' Oskar said. 'But it's just some dusty old creepy spy library sending out unnecessarily complicated maps.'

'We used to send much simpler maps into the world

that allowed bookwanderers to find us,' Artemis said. 'They were simply paths through books within books. But people began to trade them and sell them and organise visits here to demand access to the Archive. To study the stories of their enemies, to try to read their own stories before they were finished and affect the outcomes, and so on. As a result, we sent fewer and fewer maps out, and most of the ones that already exist have been lost or destroyed.'

'So what do we do now?' Tilly said. 'You sent us a map because something is going horribly wrong and there are books going missing. You asked Horatio to help find the books, I get that, but what are we doing here?'

'I think it is your particular set of skills that we need, Tilly,' Artemis said. 'You are able to bring items *outside* the books you wander into – something I tested for myself by sending you clues you had to extract from stories. If books are being hidden somewhere outside the usual places, I think it is the combination of your abilities, and Mr Bolt's ability to track books down, that may provide the solution.'

'So, you think the missing books are being hidden inside *other* books?' Oskar said.

'I do,' Artemis confirmed. 'Although I can't see inside the Underlibraries, if the books were there, they wouldn't be causing all of this chaos; they wouldn't be fraying the very fabric of Story. They're being hidden somewhere deeper than that, somewhere so deep that it's as if they've vanished; otherwise the world of imagination would not be suffering so much.'

Some of the pieces of the puzzle started to click together in Tilly's mind.

'If something's causing the world of imagination to fall apart, that could be why people are buying fewer books at Pages & Co., right?' she asked.

'Yes, absolutely,' Artemis agreed. 'If imagination is being sapped from the world somehow, then people will start to care less about stories, without even realising why.'

'And, if a book has disappeared, it could make someone forget all about it?' she went on, thinking about the man who had forgotten which book he was looking for.

'Yes, to some degree,' Artemis explained. 'It's not an exact science, and it does depend where these books have been hidden, but if they're being taken out of the chain of readers and writers then it's almost like they were never written, and any effects they might have had on a person – or the world – would vanish as well. That's why it's so imperative that we retrieve them. And, Tilly, I think you might be the only person who can.'

'So, you brought us here to help *you*, not the other way round?' Tilly asked. 'It's just a bonus if this sorts out the Underwoods too?'

'From what you have told me, I think all of this is connected, one way or another,' Artemis said. 'So, it's a case of us all helping each other. I would much rather not have people such as the Underwoods in charge of any Underlibrary, however fractured our relationship with that institution is. We're all on the same side here, I promise.'

'Does Horatio know about this plan?' Tilly asked, feeling rather uncomfortable about the prospect of having to trust Milo's uncle.

'Most of it, yes,' Artemis replied. 'Of course, there will be similar gaps in his knowledge to mine, in terms of what's happening with the Underwood siblings and what has gone on at the Underlibrary. And I think it's time to fill those in if—'

But she was interrupted by Horatio bursting into the room without knocking, trailed by a flustered-looking Will.

'My good lady,' Will said, 'this gentleman from the train claims that he must speak with you now. I asked him to remember his manners, and that you are entertaining our young guests, but he would have none of it.

'Don't worry,' Artemis said. 'We were just about to come and look for Mr Bolt anyway, as the time has come to formulate our plan. Will, Tilly and Oskar tell me you don't wish to offer your assistance, so you are welcome to leave us to it.'

'I think it is probably wise if I stay and ensure this gentleman does not cause more mischief,' said Will.

'As you wish,' Artemis replied, with a small smile. 'Tilly, Oskar, would you permit me to fill in the gaps for Mr Bolt?'

Tilly didn't trust Horatio Bolt at all: he seemed rude and unkind, and she didn't like how he spoke to Milo. She looked at Oskar and could see from his face that he agreed. But it was impossible to say any of that in front of Horatio, and if, after they'd come all this way, Artemis felt that he could help to find the missing books and stop the Underwoods, then Tilly wasn't sure they had much choice. She shrugged her agreement.

Artemis proceeded to share what she had learned about what was happening at the British Underlibrary, occasionally pausing to ask Tilly and Oskar for more details. Horatio listened and nodded, but said nothing.

'Now, Mr Bolt,' Artemis finished, 'you know that I have commissioned you to try and find some of these books. As you all know, my theory is that these volumes are being hidden somewhere that breaks all the rules of Story, and that is why *all* copies of some books are disappearing, why the Archive is crumbling around us, and why the very foundations of Story seem to be under threat. These missing books are the crucial element and, when we find them, all will become clear, I am sure of it.'

'While I'm genuinely interested in these theories,' Horatio said, 'I'm not sure how they alter what we've already discussed; I have already taken on your commission to find these books. You've paid me my deposit, and therefore I don't need to understand your reasoning.'

'I'm coming to that, Mr Bolt,' Artemis went on. 'As I've established, if rare books are being removed or hidden from the chain of readers and writers, the repercussions are grave. What you don't know, Mr Bolt, is what Tilly can do to help. She has some wonderful and unusual skills: she has found that she's able to bring items she finds inside books out with her. Between the two of you, I think you'll be able to find these books, and recover them. I wish that I was able to come with you, but I can't leave the Archive.'

Will sighed noisily in the background. He had been making a great show of inspecting the various paintings, but the blank piece of wall he was now standing in front of made it obvious that all his attention was on the conversation.

Horatio, though, was looking at Tilly with much more interest than he'd shown before.

'You can remove items that you didn't take inside the books yourself?' he asked and Tilly nodded.

'That's a curious skill to have acquired, girl,' he said. 'Where might you have picked that up?'

'That's not relevant right now,' Artemis said, and Tilly was relieved she was keeping some of her secrets.

'I see,' Horatio said. 'And is it just books she can lift?'

'I don't *lift* anything,' Tilly said, offended. 'But no. I've . . . acquired other things too. Bits and pieces.'

'Could you remove people also, do you think?' Will piped up, dropping any pretence that he wasn't eavesdropping.

'I'm not sure,' Tilly said. 'I've never tried.'

'I see,' said Will thoughtfully, stroking his goatee.

'Well, we can work out what you can do and what you can't as we go,' Horatio said. 'If you can be trusted.'

'How dare you!' Tilly said. 'How do *we* know we can trust you?'

'I'm the most trustworthy sort of person to do business with,' Horatio replied, 'because I don't care about any of this. I work, and I get results, for those that pay me my fees, and Ms . . . Ms . . .'

'Artemis will do,' she said. 'Or you can call me the Bibliognost.'

'Well, yes,' Horatio stumbled on. 'Anyway, this lady here has agreed terms that ensure I'll be trustworthy. Can you say the same?'

'We're not being paid anything,' Oskar chimed in. 'We're doing this because it's the right thing to do.'

'But almost everyone thinks they're doing the right thing,' Horatio said smugly. 'Them's the most dangerous folks to work for in my experience. But for now I think we can probably agree to work amicably enough together?' He stuck a hand out.

There didn't seem to be any other option, not to mention any other way back home. Tilly shook it, and so did Oskar.

'That's settled then,' said Horatio.

'The question that forms,' Will said, coming closer to the group, 'is how *you* found your way here yourself, good sir?'

'The same way any of your other visitors do, or did,' Horatio said. 'I found a map. Or rather I was sold a map. I was curious as to where it might lead, and here I am. I know a business opportunity when I see one. And the best kind of deal is where everyone gets what they want, as seems to be the case here. Now, can we get on? I have things to do, places to see, books to find.'

'Do you mean to return to London?' Will asked Tilly and Oskar. 'Oft I have imagined what it would be to feel the breeze off the Thames on my face again.'

'Can we go via London?' Tilly asked hopefully. 'Maybe my family could help; they know a lot about bookwandering. Actually, my grandma might be particularly useful; she used to be the Cartographer at the . . .' She tailed off, remembering what Milo had said about Horatio's feelings about the Underlibraries.

'I know where you mean,' Horatio said. 'And we'll have to see about getting former Underlibrary employees involved, especially if they want to see the Quip.'

'You will have to trust Mr Bolt as to the best route and direction,' Artemis said to Tilly and Oskar. 'That's what his expertise in this mission is after all. But there's no harm in allowing these two a moment at home, or in garnering help from elsewhere if need be. And, if our theories are correct, a visit to the Underlibrary might become a necessity in finding these books – however you feel about it. And remember, I'll be keeping an eye as well, and Mr Bolt knows how to get in touch.'

'I do,' he assented. 'And remember, this time you two'll be paying the fee for travelling on my train.'

'We barely have any money,' Tilly said. 'My mum gave us some dollars – are they any good?'

'Oh, it's not your money I want,' Horatio said. 'It's your imagination.'

32

A FIRST-TIME CUSTOMER DEAL

They said a polite goodbye to Will, who watched them mournfully as they followed Artemis and Horatio through the gardens back towards the train station. For a second, he looked like he was going to shout after them, but seemed to change his mind at the last moment.

'Come on then,' Horatio said. 'No time to waste.' He didn't hold a hand out to help either of the children onboard, but let them clamber up themselves.

The carriage they climbed up into was very fine. It was a mixture of Victorian steampunk and old-fashioned elegance. There was a lot of dark wood and deep-pile carpet, but the room was also full of

elaborate clockwork devices. There was a complex system of cogs and pulleys that ran round the top of the carriage. Two chutes – one empty and

one full of what looked like wooden balls – started by a desk in a corner of the room, while the other end disappeared through a gap in the carriage wall towards the engine.

Horatio and Artemis climbed in behind them, and he went straight to the desk to open a large ledger, dipping a quill into the inkpot that rested next to it.

'Firstly, Ms Artemis,' he said smoothly, 'I am still owed your payment for the first journey these two made.' He wrote something down in the ledger as Artemis sat on a stool by the desk and picked up one of the wooden balls from the chute and held it tightly in both hands. She closed her eyes and nodded to Horatio, who turned over a large hourglass filled with black sand on the desk.

And then . . . nothing.

Artemis simply sat there, eyes closed, silent until the sand had drizzled through the hourglass and Horatio gave a cough to signify it was done. Artemis popped the ball into the empty chute by the desk and, without warning, it was sucked up and disappeared through the gap. She repeated the process again – to pay for both of them, Tilly realised.

After the two orbs had been sent through, Artemis brushed her hands together, then shook Horatio's.

'Happy?' she said.

'Of a sort,' he replied. 'As close to happy as I'm likely to get, so long as people are paying their dues. Quip can't run on promises and goodwill: she needs the ideas and the imagination to go.'

'So you've told me before,' Artemis said. 'Now, Tilly – are you happy to go next?'

'Yes,' she said, 'but I don't know what to do.'

'Oh, don't worry – it's really very simple. Just take a ball, hold it tightly and think.'

'Think what?'

'Anything,' said Artemis. 'You can daydream, or make a shopping list, or recite a poem in your head.'

'We prefer good ideas,' Horatio said. 'But as you're so young, and it's your first time riding our Quip, I won't be picky. See it as a first-time customer deal. And don't worry: I have no idea what you're thinking – the only person that gets to see

what's inside your head is Quip as she burns it up.'
He turned and scribbled in his ledger again before
picking up a great ink stamp next to the book and
thudding it down.

'What are you writing down?' Oskar asked,
peering at the page.

'Just your names,' Horatio said. 'And stop
spying, boy. Our passenger records are absolutely
confidential. Many of our clients value their privacy
very highly and don't want nosy little boys reading
their business. Now you, girl, what's your full
name?'

'Matilda Rose Pages,' Tilly said, sitting down on
the stool and taking an orb, which was smooth and
much colder than she was expecting. 'And I can just
think of anything at all?'

'Anything at all,' Artemis said.

'Does it hurt?' Tilly asked nervously.

'Not in the slightest,' Artemis reassured her. 'Are
you ready?'

Tilly nodded and Horatio turned the hourglass

over. Tilly's mind went absolutely blank and she looked at the hourglass to see that the grains of sand were barely falling as all that was in her head was worry about thinking good thoughts.

'Why don't you close your eyes?' Artemis said gently. 'And think about your favourite book perhaps?'

And so Tilly did. She tried to blank out the sounds and smells of the train and the nervousness in her stomach that she couldn't quench about working with Horatio, and that when it boiled down to it the Archivists hadn't really been that much help at all, and her worries about explaining to her family that it might all have been for nothing if they couldn't find these books. Instead, she thought about Anne Shirley and what she would have to say about all of this. Tilly remembered visiting Green Gables for the first time and walking through the idyllic woods with Anne and Oskar as they first learned about bookwandering. She thought about how Anne always saw the best in everyone and everything, about how she always tried to do the right thing, and . . .

'You're done,' Horatio said.

Tilly's eyes opened, and where she really was rushed back in. She looked at the ball in her hands and noticed that it was smoking slightly, with the same black, glittery dust that she'd seen billowing out of Quip's chimney.

'What *is* that?' she asked.

'It's magic,' Horatio said. 'Book magic.'

'It doesn't look much like book magic,' Oskar said. 'I thought it was all sticky and black.'

'That's what it looks like when it's extracted violently,' Horatio said. 'When it's taken unwillingly. It's how the Underlibraries get their book magic, but you don't have to do it that way. That there is what it's supposed to look like.'

Tilly remembered what Milo had said – that book magic wasn't a very good name for it, because it wasn't really to do with books at all, it was to do with stories.

'Were they lying when they said it didn't hurt?' Oskar said, nudging her and distracting her from her thoughts.

'No, it's fine,' Tilly said. 'Really, you can't feel anything at all. I just can't believe book magic is so easy to get.'

'Why don't the Underlibraries get it like this?' Oskar asked as he closed his hands round a new wooden ball.

'I wonder if it's ever even occurred to them,' Horatio said. 'Perhaps they always believed they could just take what they wanted. Now stay quiet while the boy pays, and we can be on our way.'

Once Oskar and Tilly had officially paid for their journey onboard the Sesquipedalian, Artemis stepped back down on to the platform, after kissing them both formally on the cheek.

'It has been a pleasure to meet you,' she said. 'I hope that you and Horatio are able to work together to help save the world of stories, and that you'll come and tell me what you've found? And I—'

But she was interrupted by an undignified yell that came from beyond the golden gates. A figure burst through them, before pausing to catch its breath, hands on knees, huffing and puffing.

'Wait!' the figure called, out of breath. 'I wish to come too!'

It was Will.

33

BOLDNESS SHALL BE
MY FRIEND

Everyone stopped and stared at Will as he dragged himself over the last few metres to the carriage, cheeks red and hair messy. Tilly couldn't help but notice that there was a smile on Artemis's face, as though a plan had come together nicely. Tilly wondered if Artemis was telling them everything she knew about the situation.

'Forsooth, I have not exerted myself so for many years,' Will puffed, before looking up at their shocked faces. 'Do not stare at me agog,' he said. 'Mistress Tilly, you can remove items from stories – correct?'

'Yes,' she said slowly.

'Like . . . me, mayhap?'

'What?' she said.

Will took her hand and kneeled in front of her. Tilly was sure she heard Oskar try to suppress a snort of laughter. 'I believe,' said Will, 'that you may possess such powers which may allow me – who had previously been trapped deep within Story, without any hope – to accompany you out of this foul place. By which I mean no offence, my lady Artemis,' he said, dipping a bow in her direction.

'None taken, Will,' Artemis replied. 'In fact, I took the liberty of collecting a few of your personal effects as you toured the Archive with Tilly and Oskar.'

She handed over a small satchel to Will, who looked at her, caught halfway between amazement and suspicion.

'I see you had prepared for this eventuality,' he said slowly. 'I might even be so bold as to say it was no accident that it was I you paired with these two adventurers in the first place.'

Artemis simply smiled.

'So, it will work?' Will asked her. 'If Tilly

accompanies me, I shall be free?'

'I don't know for sure,' Artemis admitted. 'There's a risk in leaving, of course, but I believe there is logic to support the idea that it will work as you hope. All characters are able to leave their books, of course, for varying amounts of time, and indeed I wonder, Tilly, if you might have more control over that process than others, if you were to practise.'

'But I am not a character,' Will said, bristling. 'I am a person.'

'Of course,' Artemis said. 'But you're still bound by Story, and Tilly has shown that she's able to manipulate the borders of this place more than others. And who knows? You may be able to repay the favour to Tilly and help her on her quest, as it's by her means you can hopefully leave, as you've wished for so long.'

'*Hopefully?*' Will repeated.

'As I have said, nothing about this is certain,' said Artemis. 'But I am sure that if you're brave enough there are many here who'll be curious to see how you fare.'

'Boldness shall be my friend,' Will said, steeling himself. 'There is no darkness but ignorance, and I find that I long to know what might lie outside these walls, if Tilly will consent to take me. And I swear I shall try to aid you as best I can – however little use it may be.'

Tilly turned and pulled Oskar to one side. 'What do you think?'

'I think he's actually quite annoying, but why wouldn't we give it a go?' Oskar said. 'I trust him more than Horatio, to be honest. Also, imagine everyone's faces at home when we rock up with actual Shakespeare! Honestly, Tilly, it'll be worth it just to see your grandad's face.'

And Tilly couldn't help but agree on both counts as they turned back to the waiting adults.

'As long as you promise not to die horribly if it doesn't work,' Tilly said, looking at Will. 'I *won't* be responsible for killing Shakespeare.'

'Hang on, hang on,' Horatio said. 'It's all well and good giving your permission, girl, but none of this lies with you two. It's me who decides who comes aboard this train. And what happens if her magic doesn't work properly? I won't be held responsible if this fool dies – again – when he tries to leave.'

'Will is an adult,' Artemis said. 'And the risk is his to take. Not yours, or Tilly's. No one will lay this at your feet if it goes awry. I promise.'

'And can he pay?' Horatio said.

'What is your fee?' Will asked. 'For I have no money, nor lands, nor anything of value.'

'Ah, lucky for you, that's not how we do things around these parts,' Horatio smiled. 'You pay in ideas, and I'll warrant yours are particularly fine. Quip'll run beautifully on what's inside your head, I reckon.'

'Oh! Such flattery,' Will said. 'I shall happily trade you an idea or two to ride aboard such an excellent craft. Would you like it in prose or poetry?'

'Neither,' Horatio said, taking a ball and throwing it to Will – who dropped it and had to scrabble around to pick it up again. 'Come and sit here, and I'll do all the work for you.'

Will shrugged and climbed on to the carriage, but, after Horatio had explained what to do and set the hourglass running, no sand at all trickled through.

'Unfortunately,' Artemis said, watching from the platform, 'I think you'll find that Will may be unable to pay in the manner you require. I don't think he's sufficiently, well, *real* in any human sense. He's essentially pure book magic, and so, short of tossing him in the furnace whole, I don't think you'll get much from him.'

Horatio looked appraisingly at Will.

'Good sir,' Will said, stepping backwards. 'Are you in jest?'

'Of course, you fool,' Horatio said. 'Times aren't yet so hard as to resort to burning writers.'

'Perhaps in payment I could sign something for you,' Will offered, 'if 'tis still worth anything. I assure you it was in my time.'

'I don't want your—' Horatio started, but then paused. 'Do you know, Master Shakespeare, I have some lovely original folios of yours that are absolutely crying out for a signature, or a note of any sort.'

'Hang on,' Tilly said, remembering what Orlando had told her. 'Original folios? Oh my goodness – *you* have the Source Editions of Shakespeare's plays, don't you? That's why we can still bookwander into them because they're here!'

'Not all of them,' Horatio said proudly. 'But most of them. And it sounds like any book is much safer on board the Quip than in the hands of your Underlibraries. And Mr Shakespeare,' he added, his manner increasing in politeness by the word, 'if you'll come with me, I'm sure we can make a deal that suits us both.'

34

ENDINGS AND BEGINNINGS

Horatio stuck his head out of the door of the payment carriage.

'Milo!' he yelled. 'Are you ready?'

'Yes!' a voice called from the engine room in front of them.

'Then fire her up!' Horatio said. 'You can go and watch if you want,' he said to Tilly and Oskar. 'Tell Milo to bring you to the dining car afterwards and we can see where we stand. Quick, up and over before we pick up speed.' He gestured at the door.

A ladder made of silver rungs was set into the side of the carriage and they climbed up it on to the top of the train. The Quip was barely moving yet, but it still felt incredibly precarious as they clambered up and then down into the next carriage, the engine cab. Unlike a regular steam train, which would have a huge coal-car for fuel, on the Quip there was simply a cage collecting the wooden balls charged with book magic that were sent through from the carriage they'd just left.

'I didn't think I'd see you two again,' Milo said, grinning widely at them, winding his yellow scarf round his neck an extra time to keep it safe from the pistons. Gusts of sparkling book-magic smoke were seeping out of the edges of the engine and the circular opening, which was obviously meant for the orbs to be dropped in.

'How long does one payment last?' Oskar asked as Milo grabbed one from the cage and popped it in, causing another billow of smoke.

'Depends who it's been paid by,' Milo said. 'But whoever's ideas they are, they take us pretty far. We usually only need one or two for a journey, which is why we can leave the engine untended sometimes once we get going. We're nearly full steam ahead.'

'Your uncle said that you should bring us to the dining car once you're ready, by the way,' Oskar said. 'And I am starving.'

'Nearly there,' Milo said, eyeing the level of glittering smoke in Quip's engine and checking a gauge on its side. 'And we're good.'

The three of them climbed back up out of the engine cab on to the roof of the train. Tilly braced herself for having to withstand the wind to stop from falling off, but, as they poked their heads above the canopy of the cab, there was no resistance at all, just a gentle breeze, as though they were on a leisurely countryside walk, not on top of a train going at full speed. And even stranger was that, as they travelled, the world around them started to melt away into blackness. The red brick of the Archive dissolved into what looked like the white stone of the labyrinth and then into inky emptiness. There was nothing to see apart from a smattering of faint light in every direction. It was like looking up into the Milky Way on a clear night.

'Are these the Endpapers?' Oskar asked in wonder. 'I thought you said you don't stop there very often.'

'These aren't technically the Endpapers,' Milo said. 'Although it's what the Endpapers are made of. This is pure Story. It's how we get around.'

'It's . . . beautiful,' Tilly said, standing on the top of the train and drinking it all in. 'Kind of terrifying, but beautiful. Like being in space.'

'It's quite something, isn't it?' Milo said. 'I never really get bored of seeing it. All the endings and beginnings and memories and half-thought-up ideas all waiting to be used and formed, and our little Quip pushing through it all, powered by imagination. It's at times like this that I'm glad I'm here; gives you a bit of perspective, doesn't it? Oh shoot – keep steady – we're about to go round a plot twist!'

The train swerved abruptly, and it took everything for Tilly and Oskar to stay on top of the train. Once they'd regained their footing, the three of them just sat there for a moment, racing through the expanse of glowing darkness. It was awe-inspiring and quite lovely, until Tilly felt a strange sensation in her fingertips. She glanced down and there were tendrils of smoky book magic sliding across her hands. She shook her hands vigorously, trying to get rid of them, just as Horatio stuck his head out of a window further down the train.

'Matilda!' he shouted. 'You need to come quickly – it's Will!'

Oh no. She'd forgotten all about Will. What happened if Artemis was wrong, and he couldn't leave the Archive, and it was her fault? What would even happen to him if they couldn't get him back in time? She could see from Milo's and Oskar's faces that the same thoughts were racing through their brains.

'We need to hurry,' she said as the three of them ran for the ladder.

35

AN EXTREMELY
ILL-MANNERED QUESTION

The three of them climbed back down as quickly
as they could and ran through several carriages,
the ones at the front of the train linked by covered
walkways, not the precarious chains and gaps they'd
had to jump over at the back. Milo led them through
a set of grand double doors that opened on to a long,
plush dining room with tables set with crystal glasses,
silverware and thick white napkins. But there was
barely time to take in any of the luxury of the dining
car as Will was lying on the floor between two tables,
seemingly unconscious.

Tilly and Oskar rushed over and dropped to their
knees by his side. Alarmingly, his edges seemed to

be blurred, as though he were dissolving from the outside in, like a sugar cube in coffee.

'Will?' Tilly said, gingerly touching his shoulder. The moment she made contact with him, Will took a deep, shaky breath.

'Tilly?' he said weakly. 'You have returned?'

'I'm here,' she said. 'Are you . . . are you okay?' But, as they watched, and as Tilly kept her hand on Will, his edges started to firm up, and within a few moments he was back to normal, although breathing heavily and very pale.

'I am . . . recovered, it would seem,' he said breathlessly.

'Thank goodness,' said Oskar. 'Imagine having to explain this to your grandad, Tilly.'

Tilly just glared at him. Did this mean that Will had to stay by her side from now on?

Will was sitting up, his colour returning to his cheeks, although he leaned dramatically against a table, seemingly enjoying the care and attention.

'Leaving the Archive seems to be all right,' said

Horatio grimly. 'But only when you're together. Looks like you might need to stay a bit closer in the future, Matilda, or he might not make it back to London.'

A few minutes later, the four of them were sitting at one of the dining-room tables, with Milo standing hopefully next to them and Will rubbing his hands together as though he were trying to get rid of pins and needles.

'Tilly, please assure me you will not stray so far from me again,' Will asked. ''Twas most alarming.'

'How long do you think we'll need to stay together?' Tilly said a little nervously, worrying that perhaps they hadn't thought this all the way through. 'When we get out of Story, it'll be more normal, right? I haven't been next to the key all the time and it's still here.'

'I do not know,' he said woefully. 'Let us proceed very carefully until we are sure and hope this will be resolved once we have escaped the clutches of Story.

I had the most unpleasant sensation deep within me, as though my very essence were being erased. And I still cannot shake the feeling in my bones.'

'That sounds awful, Mr Shakespeare,' Milo said, staring at Will like a fan who had unexpectedly bumped into their favourite actor.

'Go on with you,' Horatio said, flicking his wrist at Milo.

'Can't he stay and eat with us?' Tilly asked.

'Of course not,' Horatio said. 'He has chores to do. The dining car is for paying guests only.'

'I'd really like him to stay,' Tilly said, hoping she sounded braver than she felt. 'And, if you want us to help you, then we want Milo to help too.'

'I'm not sure you have anything to bargain with, girl,' Horatio said, looking irritated.

'You need me to get the missing books back,' Tilly said. 'You've got no other way to get them out.' She hesitated. 'So I think I do, actually.'

Horatio looked at her for a long time, then sighed. 'We'll come back to that once we've ordered,' he said.

'And fine, he can stay for now, but don't think this is how it's going to be.'

Milo's cheeks were pink with excitement as he slid into the booth next to Tilly and Oskar.

'So, can you even eat?' Oskar asked Will, trying to change the subject and take the attention off Milo.

'What an extremely ill-mannered question,' Will said. 'Do I have a mouth? And teeth? A stomach?'

'Okay, okay, you can stop there,' Oskar said. 'I get it! I was just asking! Artemis said you were made of book magic – who knows? I'm just trying to make conversation!'

'I grant that there is a difference between the wants and the needs of the body, however,' Will said. 'Take care to ask what you really want to understand, Oskar. I do not require nourishment, but I am able to eat, and take much gratification from it still. It is one pleasure we were able to take comfort in at the Archive – and I have become a baker of some skill. Scott was most envious of my delicate morsels, I assure you, although he did deign to share with me a recipe for something called a cinnamon roll, which I developed quite the taste for over the years.'

'So, where are you travelling to, Mr Shakespeare?' Milo said politely. 'If you don't mind me asking?'

'I suppose I shall go wherever Tilly desires for now,' he said. 'As it appears it is her presence that allows me to stray so far from the Archive. I do hope to see London once more.'

'But you can't just stay with me forever,' Tilly said, worried.

'Forever is such a dramatic word,' Will said. 'We shall proceed most carefully once we disembark and see how the situation stands outside this Story purgatory.'

'But you're going to help us as well, aren't you, Will?' Tilly said. 'With the missing books and the Underwoods and the Underlibrary?'

'I cannot see what help I should be,' Will said, leaning back and thinking. 'I suppose that I am skilled in discerning the wants and weaknesses of my fellow men, so I may be of some service in that regard.

Indeed, it may even be that the universe is presenting me with one last opportunity for greatness. I have long said to myself: Will, be not afraid of greatness when it presents itself, as though a cloak to be put on. For some are born great, some achieve greatness and some, well, some have greatness thrust upon them. And, as I am to be your constant companion, I shall embrace the path laid at my feet.'

'So . . . yes?' Oskar said.

'Ay,' Will said, glaring at Oskar. 'I will help.'

36

GREEN EGGS
AND HAM

Alongside all the fancy glassware and cutlery on the table was a pile of menus. Horatio gestured towards it.

'Come on,' he said. 'Get yourselves fed and fit. Starved children are of no use to me.'

Inside the powder-blue menus were lists and lists of every kind of food you could possibly imagine – and what book they were from. There was clam chowder from *Moby Dick*, or a picnic with all the trimmings from a Famous Five book. And you could follow it up with apple pie from *The Railway Children*, or some Turkish delight from *The Lion, the Witch and the Wardrobe*. There was a full afternoon-tea spread from *Alice's Adventures in Wonderland*, glasses of raspberry cordial from *Anne of Green Gables*, and you could even order a gin cocktail from *The Great Gatsby* if you were old enough. The menu also listed something described as pickled limes from *Little Women*, but Tilly didn't think they sounded very appetising.

'Who makes all of this stuff?' Oskar asked in wonder.

'Our chef, Madeleine,' said Horatio. 'Our customers expect a level of luxury onboard the Sesquipedalian that I am happy to provide, and a level of whimsy that . . . well, people are happy to pay for.'

'We borrowed her from a book,' Milo explained.

'So, she's . . .' Oskar started.

'A fictional character, yes,' Horatio said, glaring at Milo. 'Not that we usually advertise that fact. And here she comes now.'

A woman with red hair swept into a tight chignon swept over to take their orders.

'How ingenious,' Will said, seemingly unperturbed

by Horatio's illicit catering business. 'Now, I think some of the Queen of Hearts' jam tarts should suit me, and a cup of the Mad Hatter's tea.'

Tilly plumped for the apple pie that came from *The Railway Children*, together with a glass of Anne's favourite raspberry cordial. Oskar dithered, sorely tempted by a slice of the enormous chocolate cake from Roald Dahl's *Matilda*, but in the end going for some green eggs and ham from Dr Seuss. Milo started to order something, but Horatio glared at him. 'The boy will have plain porridge,' he said. 'From *Oliver Twist*.'

Madeleine nodded her head, and left. Milo just stared down at the table, and wouldn't make eye contact with either Tilly or Oskar.

'Won't someone notice she's missing from her

book?' Tilly said. 'She must be a Source character to have stayed out of her book for so long?'

'Not much gets past you, does it?' Horatio said, begrudgingly impressed. 'But no, no one will notice – she's from a book that basically no one has read. Madeleine was an ingenious find on my predecessor's part. I don't even have the Source Edition to send her back to if I wanted to – no doubt it's tucked into some dusty corner of an Underlibrary, or hidden somewhere clever.'

'Was your predecessor a book smuggler too?' Oskar asked, and Horatio shuddered.

'We don't use the s-word onboard this train,' he said. 'We run a respectable, if private, business. It is the rules of bookwandering that are out of sync with what readers want, not us. But yes, of course I had a predecessor – how old do you think I am? Although she wasn't quite in the same line of business as we are; the Quip has a good few years on me. The former conductor ran it as a novelty – a jaunt through Story, dinners from your favourite books, a chance to hobnob with your favourite characters, that sort of nonsense.'

'That's not allowed, surely?' Tilly asked.

'Well, of course not,' Horatio said. 'All highly illegal if you consider the Underlibrary laws as set in stone. But shinier and more glamorous than my work, and so it was inevitable it would attract the wrong sort of attention. And, when she was in a tight spot, I was happy to help her evade official eyes, and took Quip off her hands at the same time. And I imagine Quip was in business before she bought her anyway; this is a train that has mischief in her very soul.'

Within a surprisingly short amount of time, Madeleine returned, pushing a trolley containing everything they had asked for.

'Green eggs are better in theory than practice, aren't they?' Oskar said, looking at his plate – which contained a very large ham leg and a pile of bright green fried eggs – rather apprehensively. He took a forkful and closed his eyes as he ate. 'Oh, not bad at all!' he said. 'Tastes like pesto!'

A bowl of porridge was set down in front of Milo,

who said thank you politely, and started eating. Tilly moved it out of the way without saying anything.

'Here, let's share,' she said. 'I won't be able to eat this whole slice anyway.'

'Are you sure?' Milo asked, looking longingly at the apple pie.

'Of course,' she said. Oskar nodded too, his mouth full of green eggs, and pushed his huge plate into the middle of the table.

Horatio shook his head wearily as if he didn't understand them at all, silently sipping a cup of black coffee. Will nibbled his jam tarts and the three children shared an excellent if mismatched meal.

37

FAVOURS ARE GOOD TO HAVE IN STOCK

'Are you finished?' Horatio said, eyeing the empty plates strewn round the table. 'To business then.' He rang a bell to signify he wanted the table cleared. 'Artemis believes the clue to what is happening at your Underlibrary lies in what's happened to the books that are going missing. Or that they're linked, at least.'

'Yes, and—' Tilly started.

'It wasn't a question,' Horatio interrupted. 'And she has paid me to help you find them. The theory being that should they be hidden inside layers of stories, or other books, as Artemis believes, and should we be successful in tracking them down, you'll be able to bring them back out into this world because of your particular abilities?'

Neither of them said anything.

'That *was* a question,' he said.

'Yes,' said Tilly. 'Although I'm not sure I quite see the link with the Underwoods.'

'I imagine the theory is that, as someone or something is causing havoc by hiding books, and as the Underwoods are stirring up *other* sorts of trouble, it's not outside the realms of possibility that they're either involved in, or at least aware of what's going on with, these lost books. But what they get up to at the Underlibraries is the least of my concerns. Now where on earth is Madeleine to clear all this mess?'

He rang the bell again and glanced in frustration at the door through which the chef had left. But Madeleine didn't reappear.

'Milo, go and see where she's got to,' he said. 'Make yourself useful and take a pile of these plates while you're at it.'

Milo didn't protest, but quickly stacked up as many dirty plates as he could carry and went to track down the chef.

'So,' Horatio said after Milo had gone, 'I won't beat around the bush, Tilly. Your skillset is of great interest to me, if you can do what you say you can. Both in search of the books on Artemis's list, and in the future. I could pay you well to help me acquire items that were previously . . . inaccessible to me.'

'Are you offering me a job?' Tilly said in confusion.

'Of a sort, yes,' Horatio said. 'It would be more on a freelance basis.'

'But I'm twelve,' she said. 'And I don't want a job. I want to work out how to stop the Underwoods, and make sure everyone can bookwander again. I thought that's what we were doing. And then I want to just go back to normal and go to school and be at home and not go on any adventures for a bit or have to save anyone or anything.'

'Personally, I don't really want to go to school,' Oskar said. 'But I agree with the rest of it.'

'*You* were not being offered a job, boy,' Horatio said.

'We're kind of a package deal,' Oskar said.

'And we don't want a job!' repeated Tilly.

'Just bear it in mind,' Horatio said. 'And anyway I need to know you can do what you say you can – would you be happy to demonstrate for me?'

'I can demonstrate when we go and find the books Artemis has paid you to track down,' Tilly said firmly. She suddenly wanted very much to be back at Pages & Co. and to talk to her grandparents and her mum about what they should do next.

'Here's what I suggest,' she said, trying to sound businesslike. 'You take us back to London now. Tomorrow you can come to the bookshop to pick us up and we'll go and get the books – that way you have a chance to do some research into where they are, or however you usually find books.'

'An interesting suggestion,' Horatio said. 'And certainly one I'm open to. But, unfortunately for you, the price of a ticket to London has just gone up.'

'That's not fair,' Oskar said.

'I never promised fair,' Horatio said.

'What do you want?' said Tilly nervously. 'More imagination?'

'A favour,' Horatio said, with a smile like the Cheshire cat.

'What sort of favour?' Tilly asked.

'Well, favours are the sort of things that are good to have in stock,' Horatio said. 'If I knew what I needed now, I would have asked for it, but I'm always keen to collect favours from useful people.'

'And I'm a useful person?' Tilly said, not sure if that was the compliment that it sounded like at face value.

'Anyone who can do something no one else can is useful,' said Horatio. Again, Tilly felt as though something more sinister lay behind Horatio's smooth words.

'Will?' Tilly said, turning to him in frustration. 'Aren't you going to help?'

'What would you have me do, child?' Will said.

'The man has named his price, Tilly. I am sure you . . . we can think of something once we have arrived. What harm is a favour?'

'Don't you care about saving bookwandering?' Oskar said to Will.

'Oh, child, hark what I say to you. These are such slight moments of history. Everything will come good again, I am sure of it. I do not embroil myself in the politics of bookwanderers any more for my heart has been disappointed too many times.'

'But this isn't really about politics,' Tilly said, desperately disappointed. 'I mean, it is a bit, I suppose, but it's about reading, and freedom, and imagination.'

'Ah, child, I wish I were not the one to reveal the truth to you,' said Will. 'For you will not get to be too much older before you understand that is not what stories are for. Their nature will always be warped by those who seek to use them for power and control.'

'You're wrong,' Oskar said vehemently.

'Tilly, Oskar,' Will said more gently. 'I say these words not to be cruel, or to hurt you. I have seen the world as a man, as a writer, and I have seen it go on and on and on as an Archivist. I have seen the same problems again and again, and reading is nothing but a merry distraction from it. A way to escape problems and cares, ay, but not a way to solve them. I wish 'twere otherwise.'

'I don't agree with you,' Tilly insisted. 'And I'll prove it to you, one way or another.' She turned to Horatio, full of frustration and anger, feeling she couldn't place her trust in any of the adults around her. At least, if she owed Horatio a favour, he wouldn't be able to give them the slip and not help them find the books on Artemis's list. 'Fine – one favour,' she said. 'Now take us home.'

'Did you just agree to a favour?' Milo said as he re-entered the carriage, pale-faced with concern.

'It's none of your business,' Horatio said. 'Now, where has Madeleine got to?'

'She's gone,' Milo said.

'Gone? What do you mean, she's gone?'

'I mean she's not anywhere on the train – she's just vanished.'

'But . . . that's impossible,' said Horatio. He frowned. 'Well. One more thing to worry about. But, before I deal with that – you two, where in London do you want to be dropped off? Pages & Co.? Whatever's going on in Story is making it harder to park up Quip. We need to know where to make the gap a little further in advance. I have another stop to make before my next delivery – there's some last books I have to track down for that client, and then I need to find Madeleine, and only *then* can I start locating these lost books for you. So, if you want to find them, I suggest you let me know where you're going as quickly as you can. My patience is wearing thin.'

Tilly was about to ask him to take them as close to Pages & Co. as the train could get when she glanced across at Will, leaning his forehead against the train window, and she had a different idea. She stood up and gestured for Horatio to follow her a few steps away from the table and, checking that Will wasn't listening, leaned in and updated their destination.

'It makes no matter to me,' Horatio said when he heard where she wanted to go. 'But one more thing to remember,' he said, turning to speak to Tilly and Oskar. 'If I find out that you've spread the word about this train and our work beyond your immediate family, I will provide no further assistance in your quest – do you understand?'

Tilly and Oskar nodded as the train whistle started to blow.

38

MY SOUL IS IN
THE SKY

The train stopped at a very small platform under a bridge over the River Thames.

'Mind the gap,' Horatio said.

They hopped from the step of the Quip across a channel of sparkling magic and landed on the cobblestones. Tilly, Oskar and Will watched as the Sesquipedalian chugged away, its engine dissolving in a cloud of glittering book magic. The last thing they saw before it vanished into the evening air was Milo, sitting on the back of the train, where they had first spotted him, waving goodbye.

And with that they were resolutely back in the real world – with the addition of William Shakespeare.

The first thing that Tilly and Oskar did was to pull out their phones, and switch them on.

'How long have we been gone?' Oskar asked. 'We've been so deep in Story I feel like it could have been anything from an hour to a year. Hopefully, not the last one,' he said, feeling a bit nauseous at the thought.

Tilly checked her phone screen. 'We've not even been gone a day,' she said, pointing to the date. 'We left for America this morning.'

'I'm never going to get used to how time works when we bookwander,' Oskar said, rubbing his head. 'Well, at least my mum won't be worrying yet.'

Tilly knew the same couldn't be said of her grandparents. She texted them, and her mum, to let them know that they were safe and back in London and that she would call them soon. The moment the messages were sent, her phone screen lit up with her grandad trying to phone her, but, as guilty as Tilly felt, she cancelled the call and turned her phone off.

'Where are we?' asked Oskar, looking around.

'In London,' Tilly said. 'Southwark to be precise. We're here to remind Will of a few things.'

'I see the river still smells much the same,' Will said. 'If not worse. Is this where your family resides?'

'No,' said Tilly, getting her bearings to make sure she knew where she was going. 'You don't recognise where we are?'

'Of course not,' Will said. 'London hardly looks the same as the last time I walked these streets.'

'Some bits do,' Tilly said, taking Will's hand and leading him round the corner, where a round white building with wooden beams and a thatched roof stood next to the river.

'Oh,' breathed Will. 'It is still here? I had imagined it would be long lost to the river, or fire, like the first time. Or to neglect and irrelevance.' Tilly felt Will's grip tighten round hers as he looked up at the Globe theatre.

'It's not technically the same building,' Tilly admitted. 'But I think it's pretty much in the same place, and looks the same – is it how you remember it?'

'It is,' Will said, his other hand resting on his heart in wonder. 'I feel as though my soul is in the sky, observing this moment from above. May we enter?'

'We can try,' Tilly said. 'I'm not sure if there's anything on, or if they'll let us in without a ticket, but we can see.'

They crossed the street and walked up the steps, through the gate in the wall that surrounded the theatre. It was fairly quiet apart from a few tourists taking photos, and the doors to the Globe were shut fast.

'Ah, there is no one here,' Will said. ''Tis but a relic.'

'No, sir,' said an usher, eyeing Will's outfit. He was perched on a folding stool in the courtyard by one of the doors. 'There's a performance on, so the crowds are all inside.'

'Would you permit us to enter?' Will said quietly.

'I'm afraid I can't do that, sir,' said the man, who barely looked to be out of his teens. 'Once it's started, the doors stay shut.'

'I would so dearly love to see it,' Will said, and

Tilly could see the man decide that Will was probably one of Those Fans who took everything a few steps further than he was comfortable dealing with.

'It's really a very special occasion,' Tilly tried. 'Our friend is not in London for very long and this place means a great deal to him.'

'Well, it means a great deal to a lot of people,' the man said. He looked at Will and Tilly and Oskar and sighed. 'It's the interval soon,' he said. 'I can't let you in, but you'll be able to get a glimpse inside once the doors open. It'll be about five minutes now, I think, if they went up on time.'

'What play is it?' Tilly asked, fingers crossed it was actually a Shakespeare play.

'It's *A Midsummer Night's Dream*,' the usher said.

'Perfect,' Tilly grinned.

The three of them lingered by the doors, Will lost in his own thoughts, and Tilly and Oskar struggling to suppress yawns.

'Tilly, do you have any cash?' Oskar asked, eyeing the ice-cream stand that was setting up its wares in advance of the interval rush. Tilly took her purse out of her backpack; they still had all the dollars her mum had given her, but they'd spent most of their British money on the breakfast at the airport, which had only technically been that morning, but felt like weeks ago.

Oskar ambled over to the woman selling ice cream with the couple of pounds Tilly had shaken out of her purse, before returning empty-handed and affronted.

'Four pounds fifty!' he said. 'For one ice cream! And it's not even sunny!' But he was saved from further outrage by the wooden doors of the theatre swinging open and a torrent of people spilling out into the courtyard, making beelines for the toilets or the bar.

'Come on, Will,' Tilly said, pulling him forward excitedly. The three of them went to stand by the door and stare into the theatre, watched by the eagle-eyed usher.

A wooden stage stuck out into the pit where some of the audience were waiting, stretching their arms, and peering up into the exposed sky, hoping it wouldn't rain. The stage itself was dressed with vines, flowers and fairy lights wrapped round its columns and along the edge of the stage. Around the periphery of the theatre ran wooden seats and balconies of benches, everything in golden brown wood. Tilly had visited the Globe twice before – once on a school trip when they were given a tour of the building, and once with her grandparents and Mum to see a play about a woman called Emilia who was said to have inspired Shakespeare. Tilly reminded herself to ask Will about her later on and realised that there were probably quite a *lot* of questions people would like to ask Shakespeare, given the chance.

For the moment, though, Will was simply staring, transfixed by the sight in front of him.

''Tis as if I have been taken backwards through time,' he said. 'So much of this place is just how my memory keeps it. Oh! We spent good hours here.' He stood, facing the empty stage, and closed his eyes, summoning the ghosts and memories of past actors, filling the benches with the rich, the notable and the royal; and the pit with the poor and the rowdy.

Tilly closed her eyes too and she almost felt transported back to Elizabethan London herself. The noise and chatter of the audience would not have sounded so different, or the smell from the Thames, or the breeze from the open roof, and the chilly edge to the spring evening air.

They were jerked back to reality by a bell ringing to signal that the second half was about to begin. Will, who was standing closer to the stage than the others, was quickly swept up in the tide of people returning to their seats, or jostling to make sure they had a good view from the pit.

'Will!' Tilly shouted, realising they hadn't tested if he had to stay near her now they were out of Story. But, as he was pushed right to the very front, they could still seem him clearly standing there, entranced by the stage. Tilly and Oskar started to try and push their way through the people to get to him.

'Hey there!' the usher shouted, having lost sight of them in the crowds. 'Has anyone seen a dude dressed like Shakespeare and two kids?'

Tilly could hear him shouting, but no one paid any attention, everyone in the pit focused on getting the best view they could, so she grabbed Oskar and let them be carried by the crowds closer to Will. After a few moments, the audience settled and silenced and a tall man entered and started speaking.

'I wonder if Titania be awak'd;
Then, what it was that next came in her eye,
Which she must dote on, in extremity.'

Tilly saw that Will was speaking the lines along with the actor playing Oberon. As the play progressed, the audience laughed, and cried, and cheered as one, and Will stood in the middle of them all as if he were seeing his words performed for the very first time. For a brief moment, the clouds above their heads parted, and the spring moon shone down on Will and his audience, and Tilly saw him wipe a single tear from his eye.

They stayed for the whole second half of the play,

even though Tilly felt a little guilty about not buying tickets. But she did think that bringing Shakespeare to his own play perhaps excused them, especially in the cause of rescuing bookwandering – something she felt that the Globe would surely be onboard with, whether they knew it existed or not.

After the play finished, Will didn't move as the crowds started emptying out, but walked towards the stage and touched the boards of it gently with his fingertips.

'To think that this remains still,' he said quietly to himself. 'That these words are still spoken, and this stage still stands. That the audiences still come, and that my words still stir their hearts.'

He leaned forward and pressed his forehead to the wood, as though in prayer, before taking a deep breath and turning back to Tilly and Oskar.

'Is this play performed often?' he asked, looking nervous as to what they might tell him.

'Yes,' Tilly said. 'It's performed, and read, and studied all over the world, Will. Children read it in school and actors study it at university, and there are plays and films and books all inspired by your stories – not just this one, but all of them. I think there's even a show in New York where you can run around after the actors and be part of the story. Almost everyone in the world knows your words, and they mean so much to so many people. How can you say that none of this matters? It *must* matter, Will.'

'I see your purpose in bringing me here, child,' Will said, smiling at Tilly. 'I . . . I had not imagined that this could be possible. I thank you, truly. I know you did it because you seek my aid, but, whatever the route that has brought me here, I cannot be anything other than glad and grateful in my very soul. To know I hold a place in people's hearts so many years after I have gone . . . 'Tis a gift that you do not know the worth of. I am in your debt.'

'Great,' Oskar said, giving Tilly a thumbs up. 'Will's onboard. But what *with*? What do we do now?'

'Firstly, we need to go home,' Tilly said. 'To Pages & Co.'

39

SLIGHTLY LESS NORMAL THAN EVERYTHING ELSE

Tilly knew that if she called her grandparents they would immediately insist that they got a taxi home, but she was happy to have the journey on the Tube to get used to being back in London, and out of the layers of stories they had been in.

'Doesn't it feel like we were there for days, or weeks?' she said to Oskar as they sat on the familiar seats of the Northern line. They had seated Will in between them to ensure he stayed put.

'I can't believe it's the same day,' Oskar said. 'I'm glad my mum won't be worried, but no wonder I'm so exhausted.'

It wasn't long before they both fell asleep on the train, their heads resting on Will's shoulders.

Tilly woke up as they passed through Camden Town station and a big crowd of tourists piled on.

'Tilly, might you have a quill and some paper to hand?' Will whispered to her. 'For new inspirations strike me every moment I am here, observing life as as it is now.'

Tilly dug around in her backpack and produced a notebook and a pen, and enjoyed watching Will trying to negotiate a biro as he scribbled lines down – covering them with his hand so no one could read them. Despite Will's obvious resemblance to the world's most famous playwright, no one on the Tube batted an eyelid, used to seeing all sorts of people and outfits, and the journey up to north London went smoothly.

They got off the train and started to walk up the hill towards the high street and Pages & Co. Even though they'd only left that morning, it felt like a lifetime had passed. Tilly checked her phone again and saw that she had several text messages from her grandparents, but she didn't open any of them, wanting just a few more moments of respite before she had to deal with their questions and worry. She hoped that Bea had explained everything to them so they wouldn't be too angry with her and Oskar. She steeled herself to explain to them that, although she'd been right about the Archivists, they hadn't been as much help as she'd wanted, and all she and Oskar had were a few more clues, and a lot more problems that needed fixing.

But the normality of the high street was soothing to her as she walked past the places she knew and loved, all shut up tight for the night. The Italian deli where they were always secretly given any leftover Portuguese custard tarts, the café that advertised every kind of breakfast you could possibly imagine and, of course, Crumbs, the bakery that Mary ran. It was all so thirst-quenchingly, gloriously normal and Tilly felt it wash over her as they headed up towards the shop.

Will was there, of course, slightly less normal than everything else, asking Oskar question after question about how various objects worked, and why different things were as they were. He paused from his questions to scribble in Tilly's notebook, having mastered the pen.

'Here we are,' she said to Will, pointing proudly at the outside of Pages & Co. Its tall windows seemed like they were welcoming her home, and through them she could see the shop, dark and calm after-hours. Tilly felt an ache in her heart, one that used to be uncomplicatedly settled by being at home in Pages & Co., but that now had sharper edges and a more difficult shape to grapple with. She found her keys in her backpack and opened the door to the bookshop, hearing the bell jangle over their heads.

'Tilly!' a voice called almost immediately and the three of them looked up to see Grandma and Grandad running towards them. They gathered Tilly and Oskar up into a huge group hug before noticing Will.

Grandad cocked his head, clearly trying to work

out why he was so familiar. 'Have we met?' he asked.

'Grandad,' Tilly said, relishing the moment. 'This is William Shakespeare. He's one of the Archivists, and he's come to help.'

'Oh,' Grandad said. 'Right.'

'It's actual *Shakespeare*, Archie!' Oskar said gleefully. 'You don't seem very excited.'

'I . . . I am,' he said. 'It's just— Tilly, we need to tell you something. Your mum . . . the Underwoods have her.'

40

Hot Buttered Toast

Tilly went pale.

'What do you mean, they have her?'

'She went to the Underlibrary and gave herself up to them – to try and protect you,' Grandad said, looking as though telling her was causing him physical pain. 'She didn't warn us, or I promise we would have stopped her, Tilly. We didn't know she'd taken you or Oskar to the airport, or that she'd gone to the Underlibrary, until she called us from there – I don't think she came back here from Heathrow before she went to find the Underwoods.'

'But what use is she to them?' Tilly said. 'I don't understand why she'd do that.'

'We don't know what she's offered them,' Grandma said. 'She just called to say where she was, and where you were. She said you were safe and with friends . . . in America. How are you even here?' she asked. 'Did you go to Washington?'

'Yes,' Tilly said, feeling scared and exhausted and confused all at the same time. 'But we went to find the Archivists, and we went right inside Story, and you know what time is like when you bookwander. So here we are.' Tilly swayed a little on her feet as everything overtook her.

'Come on, sit down, both of you,' Grandma said, shepherding the three of them into the kitchen. 'You all need a cup of strong, sweet tea and to tell us what's happened.'

'No,' said Tilly, trying to keep a clear head. 'We need to go and get Mum. Now.'

'You're no use to her like this,' Grandma said sternly. 'You'll only put her in more danger if you go now. I promise you, we'll get her back, even tonight if we can. But the two of you need to eat and drink something, and shower, and well, we'll need to work out what to do with *you* as well,' she said, looking Will up and down.

'A pleasure to meet you,' he said, dipping into a low bow, and reaching out for Grandma's hand to kiss. 'These two children are a credit to your name and your establishment.'

'They most definitely are,' Grandad said proudly. 'By the way, Oskar, your mum thinks you're with us until tomorrow, if you're happy to stay?'

'As if you even need to ask,' Oskar said.

A few moments later, they were sitting at the familiar kitchen table, hands wrapped round mugs of tea, and a plate of hot buttered toast between them. Tilly and Oskar were trying to tell Grandma and Grandad everything that had happened to them and Tilly felt cold all over when she got to the bit in the Library of Congress.

'Oh no!' she said, remembering. 'Orlando and Jorge – they'll still be prisoners of the American Librarian.'

'The American Librarian?' Grandad repeated. 'You mean the librarian in charge of the Library of Congress?'

'No,' Oskar said. 'It's way worse than that. The Librarian at the American Underlibrary. Jacob Johnson is working with the Underwoods – he's in on it too. And he has Orlando and Jorge.'

'Okay, okay,' Grandad said, his head in his hands. 'Well, that's another thing we need to sort out. Elsie.' He looked at Grandma. 'Who do we know at the American Underlibrary who might be able to help? Does Amelia know anyone? Could you give her a call and see if she can find out where these two – Orlando and Jorge?' Tilly nodded her confirmation. 'See where they are and get them out if they're not safe?'

Grandma nodded, steely focus written across her face, and went to call Amelia.

Meanwhile, Tilly and Oskar finished telling Grandad about their journey to the Archivists, Artemis's theory about the hidden books and Horatio.

'I'm sorry the Archivists weren't much help,' Tilly said. 'After I made such a fuss about finding them.'

'But they were,' Grandad said. 'For one thing, to prove that they exist – that's quite an achievement, Tilly. I can only apologise for not believing you. I should have trusted you from the start. But, even if they didn't give us an easy way to fix it, this Artemis woman has helped. She's shown us the thing that holds it all together – that books are going missing. It's somewhere to start. If the Underwoods are involved, as it would be sensible to assume, and we can find out what they're trying to do with the books, then we'll really be getting somewhere.'

'But how long is that going to take?' said Tilly. 'Horatio won't be getting in contact until tomorrow. And when are we going to get Mum back?'

'We need to have some leverage to offer,' Grandad said. 'And we need to know what she's offered them. And we need to keep you safe, Tilly.'

'But I want to—'

'Your mum has decided to sacrifice her own

freedom for now in order to keep you safe and we must respect that, Tilly, however hard it is. We won't achieve anything by putting you both in danger, by just turning up there without any extra knowledge, or a plan. She said you would know what to do when you got back . . . And we do have more of a plan now – we suspect the Underwoods are involved in hiding books so they're breaking the chain of imagination. And, of course, we also need to decide what to do with Mr Shakespeare here,' he said, eyeing Will a little nervously. 'You said he might have to stay with you at all times?'

'Possibly,' Tilly said. 'We haven't really had time to test it properly outside Story.'

'We didn't really think it through,' Oskar admitted.

'I can only apologise for the inconvenience my presence causes,' Will said. 'I freely admit that my exit was motivated solely by my desire to find a way out of that godforsaken Archive, and I was focused only on my own escape. I was drunk on the idea of freedom and I now understand that I bring your family even more complications at a time of great strife. But I swear to you that I am for your cause. Tilly and Oskar have demonstrated to me the worth of your goals and I would be honoured to fight alongside you. Mayhap I shall be able to offer some wisdom once the situation has become clearer. I have spoken with many bookwanderers over the decades and I earnestly hope I may be of use.'

'Well, thanks, Mr Shakespeare,' Grandad said.

'Please, call me Will,' he said, and Grandad just nodded. Tilly realised he was more than a little bit starstruck.

'Have we got any way of contacting Mum?' asked Tilly. 'Has she got her phone with her?'

'If she does, she's not answering it,' Grandad said. 'And I don't want to risk sending any of our plans via text if she's with the Underwoods, especially as she believes you to be safe with her American friends. We cannot give the Underwoods the power of knowing you're back in London. I know it feels impossible, but you have to let your mum do what she's chosen to do for now.'

'I know,' said Tilly, trying to force herself to think as rationally as she could through her exhaustion and worry. 'So what do you think we should do?'

They talked through the options and, by the time the toast was finished, they had a plan. In the morning, they would split into two teams. Grandma would go with Tilly and Oskar to meet with Horatio and start tracking down the missing books. Grandad and Amelia would go and get Bea back. Tilly desperately wanted to help her mum, but she knew she needed to work with Horatio, and that, as former Librarians, Grandad and Amelia were best placed to find Bea and get her out safely. It wasn't a solution. But it was somewhere

to

start.

41

WHAT A THRILL TO BE BOOKWANDERING AGAIN

It felt as though she had only put her head on her pillow a few moments before, but when Tilly was shaken awake and glanced at her alarm clock it was the middle of the night.

'Not again,' Oskar said, stirring from the air bed on the floor. 'Didn't we already do this? Who is it this time?'

'I have dreamed up a plan,' Will said, sitting at the foot of Tilly's bed as though it were the most normal thing in the world to be woken up by Shakespeare.

'Can't it wait until morning?' Oskar yawned.

'Perhaps,' Will said. 'But I believe you will be keen to hear of it now. I have realised what the best course of action is to save your gentle mother.'

This woke Tilly up much more quickly. 'What is it?' she asked.

'I shall offer these people, these Underwoods, *myself* in exchange for her safety,' Will said proudly.

'Huh?' said Oskar.

'I was thinking on what you have shared with me thus far,' he explained. 'And please do enlighten me if I have misunderstood any of the pertinent facts. Whatever they are working towards, these Underwood siblings desire Tilly for her blood because 'tis partly of this world, and partly of the world of stories, correct?'

'Yes,' Tilly confirmed.

'So, if they seek to steal the immortality of stories, which they believe is running through your veins, then surely a being of pure story would better serve their goals? I am not a person as you are: I am made of story and memory and imagination now. And therefore I suppose that their purposes would be better met by what I am than what you are, Tilly.'

'But I don't want you to do that,' Tilly said quietly. 'I

don't want you *or* my mum to have to give yourself to them instead of me.'

'Child,' Will said gently. ''Tis true they seek *what* you are, but do not imagine they care *who* you are. If I can offer them what they desire, it will be of no difference to them. And know that I do not actually wish to give myself to them, only to parlay with them and retrieve your mother, and we can proceed from there.'

'But what happens if you get too far from me?' Tilly said. 'And you start . . . disappearing again.'

'I was able to stray a little further from you back in Southwark so perhaps the effect is lessening,' said Will. 'And, regardless, 'tis a risk I am willing to take. If I cannot leave you, Tilly, what would we do? Would I stay with you until you are old and grey? I have long yearned for purpose, and a noble path has been presented to me. I beseech you, let me walk it.'

'Grandma and Grandad won't let you,' Tilly said. 'They'll want to keep talking and planning and look for the missing books first. They're not going to let Shakespeare sacrifice himself.'

'Then let us not inform them of what we have planned,' Will said. 'Did you not tell me you were able to reach the Underlibrary by some secret means?'

'Tilly can get there through the Endpapers,' Oskar said. 'But we can't bookwander, remember?'

'But we can,' Tilly said, 'if we choose the right book. Because Shakespeare's Source Editions aren't in any of the Underlibraries – they're on the Quip. We just need to go to the very end of one of your plays, Will, and the Endpapers will take us straight to the Underlibrary.'

'Will the Underwoods be there at this time of night, though?' Oskar said.

'If they're keeping Mum there, then maybe,' said Tilly. 'Or they will be in a few hours. Let's go first thing in the morning, before Grandma and Grandad are up. Set an alarm for six a.m., Oskar.'

Oskar groaned, but acquiesced, put his pillow over his head and went back to sleep.

'Are you sure?' Tilly asked Will.

'It would be an honour,' he replied.

Their alarms went off while it was still dark outside, and Tilly and Oskar forced themselves out of their warm beds. Will was still sitting on the end of Tilly's.

'Have you been there all night?' she asked warily.

'Oh, I suppose so,' he said, giving himself a shake. 'I do not require sleep, but I am able to . . . let my mind rest. 'Tis the way I can best describe the sensation. I am not sleeping, but I am not awake.'

'Like a computer on standby,' Oskar suggested.

'I do not know what this standby of which you speak means,' Will said.

'Never mind,' said Oskar, stretching and heading to the bathroom.

'Could you give me a minute to get ready?' Tilly said awkwardly.

'I do apologise,' Will said, standing up and wandering over to the door. 'One forgets so quickly what it is to be human. I shall return anon, and we can begin our travels.'

A little while later, the three of them were assembled downstairs, the copy of *A Midsummer Night's Dream* that Orlando had given Tilly in front of them, open at the last page. Tilly had written Grandma and Grandad a note, left on her bed, saying they were going to get Bea back – and not much else. They crept through the door into the bookshop, where they could bookwander from.

'What happens when you bookwander, Will?' Oskar asked, taking him firmly by the arm.

'I do not know,' Will said cheerily. ''Tis not at all possible from the Archive. What a thrill to be finally wandering again. I had ne'er thought I would have the chance again.'

'Right then,' Tilly said, and read aloud the last speech in the play.

Pages & Co. was sucked down and under their feet and they found themselves back in the enchanted forest of *A Midsummer Night's Dream*. Thankfully, Titania and Oberon were nowhere to be seen. There was only Puck, standing in a clearing, although the sounds of music and laughter could be heard echoing through the trees from a party some way off.

'How is it that we access the Endpapers?' Will

whispered as Puck recited his final speech.

'We just wait,' Tilly hissed under her breath. 'Keep hold of us both and, when the play ends, you'll see.'

She and Oskar were steeling themselves for the very strange sensation they knew was coming.

As Puck finished speaking, the air suddenly shimmered and sparkled and then Puck was talking again, but backwards, before everything started rushing and blurring. The whole play was rewinding around them, and the three of them held on to each other tightly as the leaves danced in the air and they were surrounded by glimpses of light and movement until everything dropped into blackness.

There was a brief moment where Titania was in front of them, and Tilly could have sworn that she made eye contact – just for a fraction of a second. Then Tilly's head was spinning, and she felt gingerly with her fingertips to reassure herself they were standing on solid ground. She breathed a sigh of relief as she felt wooden floorboards and edged her way slowly over the floor until she found the wall, then a door, then the light switch.

They were in the same sad office that the Endpapers had spat them out into before, except this time it wasn't empty. Decima Underwood was sitting behind the desk.

'We wondered when we'd see you,' she said, with a cold smile. 'And you've brought a guest. How lovely!'

42

WE DO NOT HAPHAZARDLY GO INTO THE BREACH

Where's my mum?' Tilly said immediately, but Decima ignored her question.

'Follow me,' was all she said, standing up and leaving the office, not even checking to see if they were following her. They weren't sure what else they could do.

'Good lady,' Will started as they walked after her down the long, familiar corridors of the Underlibrary, 'would you be so kind as to introduce yourself?'

Decima ignored Will too and simply kept walking until she opened the door to a large room in which a fire was burning. The fireplace was somehow familiar to Tilly, but she couldn't quite place why. She gave an involuntary shudder when she saw it, but it could have been because of the person standing in front of it: Decima's twin brother, Melville.

Decima went to stand next to him.

The last time Tilly had seen the Underwood siblings, their skin had been covered in tattoos from where they'd tried to put book magic directly into their bodies, to steal its immortality. Some tattoos were still visible, poking out of Decima's sleeves, and one creeping over the top of Melville's shirt collar. Even more alarming was the fact that they seemed to have got even younger – they both looked disconcertingly youthful and healthy. Clearly, they'd made progress in their experiments with book magic.

'Matilda,' Melville said silkily. 'What a pleasure to see you again. As reckless as your mother, I see. And you too,' he said, glancing at Oskar. 'And . . .' He looked Will up and down, clearly unsettled by the obvious . . . Shakespeare-ness of him.

'William Shakespeare,' Will said. 'And I would say it was a pleasure, but I do not believe it will prove to be so.'

'I don't follow,' Melville said. 'You've brought some down-on-his-luck actor with you, pretending to be Shakespeare? I don't understand your strategy here.'

'Down-on-his-luck actor?' Will said, incensed. 'How dare you! I am William Shakespeare, formerly of Stratford-upon-Avon, currently journeying from the Archive to assist these young bookwanderers.'

'Surely not,' breathed Decima, coming and standing a little bit too close to Will as if she didn't believe he was real. 'It's impossible.'

'I assure you it is not,' Will said.

'You found the Archive?' Melville said to Tilly and Oskar. 'But you're children. How did you even . . .' His voice petered out, clearly unable to wrap his head round them having achieved something like that. 'Where is it?'

'I couldn't tell you,' Tilly said. 'You have to have a map.'

'Well, where is your map?' demanded Decima.

'We don't have it any more,' Tilly said.

'I understand why *you* are here, Matilda,' Melville said. 'We knew that once your mother turned up here, you wouldn't be far behind. And we assumed the other one would be with you too, as he always seems to be.'

'Rude,' Oskar said under his breath.

'But bringing an Archivist with you?' said Decima. 'Bringing an Archivist to *us*? I can't possibly imagine your logic! But I suppose this is why you and your family keep threatening to get in our way without ever succeeding. You'll see we're making great strides in our research! And to be presented with such a . . . resource.' She continued staring at Will as though he were a scientific specimen, not a person.

'A resource, madam?' Will said, indignantly.

'Why, yes,' said Decima. 'For you're clearly not made of the same stuff as us, are you? Why you died in . . . what was it – 1616, I believe?'

'Ay,' Will said. 'My former life was cut short in that year.'

'So, what sustains you now if not book magic?'

Decima said. 'The very thing we're so keen to learn more about.'

'Indeed,' Will said. 'We assumed your interest would be piqued thus. And you do not give us credit enough for reason behind our action; we do not haphazardly go unto the breach. I am willing to offer myself in exchange for these two leaving here unharmed – and with Tilly's mother.'

'A noble offer,' Melville said. 'But, when we have all of you here, why would we let *any* of you leave until

we have a greater grasp of what you can offer us?'

Tilly realised that, in her desire to rescue her mum, they had played into the Underwoods' hands. She looked nervously at Oskar and Will.

But Will was taking a step forward, his hands visibly sparking with book magic.

'Let me offer you further motivation,' he said, and reached out to touch Decima's hand with one finger.

The touch was gentle, but Decima froze, and there were sparks as their hands connected. She stared at hers in horror as it started to visibly age, the skin changing from smooth and flawless to wrinkled and age-spotted.

'What did you do?' she said, clutching her hand to her chest. '*What did you do?*'

43

A TWIST IN FORTUNES

'As you correctly divined, I am made of story,' Will said. 'And I am claiming some of it back from you who use it improperly. Do not think this is an unequal negotiation.'

'How dare you steal it from me?' Decima said, gazing at her hand in horror.

''Tis not yours,' Will said. 'The Archivists have not been asked to help protect bookwandering for many years, but now we have been pulled back into the fray. I come to protect stories, and you have been weighed and found wanting. Now, shall we try to come to an agreement?'

'Give it *back*,' said Decima, fury written across her face.

'I cannot,' said Will simply. 'Be grateful I did not take more. I could if I wanted to.'

'You can have Beatrice,' Melville said quickly, while taking a step further away from Will. 'We don't need her.'

'What did she offer you?' Tilly asked.

'She said that, as she'd been pregnant with you, she had some small fraction of book magic within her,' Decima said, holding her hand behind her back. 'And we were willing to see if that were the case while she was with us – we're not so proud as to ignore every avenue presented. But really we were keen to indulge her as we knew eventually you'd come to find her. I believe the threat of limiting bookwandering for all children – something we don't even yet know if we can achieve – would have worked eventually, but this certainly added more urgency. And look, you've behaved exactly as we expected. Well,' she said, looking uneasily at Will, 'not *quite* as expected, granted.'

'Ay,' Will said. 'It would serve you well to remember I am well versed in how to tell a good story. One must always reserve some knowledge until towards the end, and a twist in fortunes adds a certain excitement to proceedings. And, of course, you would be wise also to recall that the villains can never triumph. Now, shall we agree some terms?'

'You want Beatrice to be able to leave with these two,' Melville said. 'That's fine, we agree. We agree.'

'Nay,' Will said. ''Tis not so simple. I would not sacrifice myself to you in a way that also furthers your schemes. My second and final requirement is that we sit and discuss the future of the British Underlibrary, and your control over bookwandering.'

'And we get you in exchange for that?' Decima said. 'Just a conversation?'

'Ay,' Will said. 'Let us see what can first be achieved through words.'

'Why of course,' Melville said, exchanging a smirk with Decima. 'Let's see how far words get us.'

'Do not underestimate them,' Will said. ''Tis easy to promise words, but you must choose them carefully. Now, if you would be so kind as to bring Beatrice here, so we are assured of her safety, then we can proceed.'

They waited in slightly awkward silence as Melville spoke briefly into a phone. A few minutes later, the door burst open and Bea ran straight over to Tilly.

'You brave, wonderful girl,' she whispered. 'I knew you could find them. Are they here?'

'Sort of,' Tilly said, not wanting to explain in front of everyone that the Archivists had not provided as neat a solution as she had hoped. 'Um, Mum, meet Will Shakespeare.'

Will bowed to Bea, who did a small double take, but quickly took it in her stride.

'There,' Melville said. 'Now, shall we talk? Let's go somewhere more private, and more secure, until this conversation is finished.'

The group passed through the double doors that led to the main hall of the Underlibrary. It was usually a place that made Tilly feel full of wonder and excitement, but it was empty and dark now and their footsteps echoed eerily up to the high ceilings. There were only a couple of librarians on duty, and they avoided eye contact and stayed silent as the group walked by.

Instead of passing through the hall to the corridor on the far side where Tilly and Oskar had been before, they went to the circular desk in the middle of the floor. Decima lifted up a section of the desk that was hinged, and gestured for them to follow. The desk itself was a circle around a tall wooden card catalogue – a cabinet of tiny drawers on all sides that housed records of every book in the Underlibrary. Built into the cabinet was a door and Decima took a delicate golden key from a chain around her neck and slotted it into a matching keyhole. She pushed on the door – which had no handle – and Tilly saw a flight of stairs disappearing down into the dark.

'Why is everything so unnecessarily spooky?' Oskar asked, rolling his eyes.

In answer, Decima reached out and flicked on a light switch that illuminated the stone steps easily.

'Fine,' Oskar said. 'It must be you that makes it spooky.'

'Why are you here again, boy?' Melville asked.

'I am a key member of this team,' said Oskar.

'And if you haven't worked that out by now,' Bea said, 'then more fool you.'

44

THE SOURCE
LIBRARY

The stairs curved downwards, and Tilly, Oskar and Bea followed the Underwoods in a silent line. The steps ended in a small antechamber dominated by a large black door with several bolts and locks on it.

'Welcome to the Source Library,' Melville said. 'You should count yourselves fortunate that you're seeing this place. Few bookwanderers would ever be given the opportunity.'

So, this was where it was, Tilly thought. The place that housed the special Source Editions of almost every book first written in English. The books that were supposed to be kept protected so that no one could alter their stories forever, but were now bound by the Underwoods so they could further control bookwandering. The Source Library was shrouded in mystery and secrecy, and it was hard not to feel intimidated by the huge, locked black door.

Tilly expected Melville to produce some sort of ancient key, but in fact he went over to a small hatch on the side of the door and slid it open to reveal a

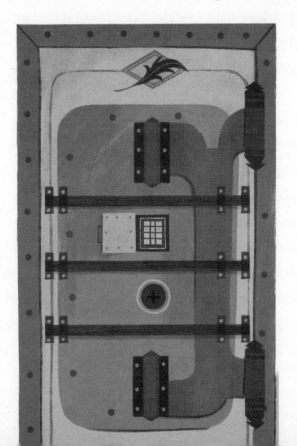

high-tech-looking number pad.

'A new addition,' he said smugly over his shoulder. He keyed in numbers that Tilly and Oskar couldn't see, and suddenly the locks all began sliding out of their bolts, springing apart in a chain reaction around the edge of the vast door. Once they were all open, Melville grasped the huge handle and heaved it open. The lack of light and the vastness of the metal door made Tilly feel as though they were deep underwater, entering a submarine.

She wasn't sure what to expect on walking through the door, but what she was met with were shelves and shelves and shelves spreading out into a hall that was as dark as the Archive had been bright. The shelves stretched away from them in both directions, and it was impossible to see how big the room truly was. It had an eerie, cold atmosphere, with its high ceilings and endless bookshelves, and it felt abandoned and unloved. Tilly wondered if it had always felt like this, or if it was because the books in here had all been bound and were being kept captive as part of the Underwoods' machinations. Row upon row of books usually gave Tilly the feeling of limitless possibility, each book a portal to another world, a new way of looking at things, a new character to meet – but these books seemed to absorb adventure and deaden its promise.

Decima switched on another set of lights, which only barely took the edge off the darkness that seemed to be seeping deep inside their bones the longer they were in the Source Library.

'Follow me,' she said, and led the group to the right, skirting the edge of the great room.

'I can't say this feels good,' Oskar whispered to Tilly. 'You realise this is the second time we've ended up in some sort of creepy basement with these two, and fool me once, et cetera . . .'

'At least Mum's here and safe. Safe-ish,' said Tilly.

'And Will,' Oskar added.

'Who'd have thought we'd ever be saying that?' Tilly managed a small smile.

'He kept it quiet that he could use book magic like

that, didn't he?' Oskar said quietly, and the two of them glanced back at Will, who looked deeply unsettled by all the dark shelves looming around them.

'I don't know if he realised he cared enough to use it until yesterday,' Tilly pointed out.

The Underwoods took them to the far edge of the huge hall where a nondescript door led them into an antechamber. A wooden printing press stood at one side, currently still, but with freshly inked plates visible from recent use.

There was also a far more advanced version of the laboratory that Decima had constructed in the book of fairy tales that Gretchen had led Tilly and Oskar into at Christmas. There was a great vat in one corner, bubbling with black, sticky liquid. It was book magic – but it was the tar-like goo that sucked light into it that Tilly and Oskar had seen when the fairy tales were ripped apart. It was the opposite of the beautiful sparkling substance they had witnessed onboard the Sesquipedalian. It was hard to believe they were both essentially the same thing. And even more ominous than the vat of book magic was the contraption that had been built above it, which looked like a smaller version of the machines that crushed up cars into tiny cubes of metal.

'You will remember, Matilda,' Decima said, 'that, when we last saw you, we had been exploring the possibilities of borrowing some of the natural properties of book magic.'

'You mean stealing,' Tilly said shortly.

'We are not stealing it; we are utilising it more effectively,' said Melville.

'Now,' Decima went on, ignoring both her brother and Tilly, 'you will also remember that we were having some teething problems. Our experiments only worked within stories, not out here, but you will have no doubt noticed we're currently very happily residing here in London, having escaped the unpleasant effects of ageing. Until you started interfering – again.' She frowned down at her hand. 'Even this is fixable, as you will see. We have made great progress – it's remarkable, don't you think?'

Decima waited, as if she were a proud science teacher waiting for her class to ask enthusiastic questions. 'Humour me,' she said, smiling without it reaching her eyes. 'Ask me how we did it.'

But still no one said anything until Melville chipped in.

'Do go on, Sister,' he said, glaring at the others.

'Now, if Matilda had been more willing to help,' Decima went on, 'I think her . . . let's say her substance would have had much the same effect. But you will see we have evolved beyond relying solely on one rebellious child. Because what we needed was simply a more potent form of book magic. Fairy tales were far too unpredictable, and their magic was the same, and the books we created solely for the purposes of our experiments on our printing press here did not have strong enough roots. They remained untethered from the wider power of stories because they weren't created to be read and shared, it would seem. Eventually, we realised where we were going wrong – and that the answer was right on our doorstep. Here in the Source Library.'

Decima picked up a book from a table by the side of the cruncher and placed it between its jaws. She pressed a button and the contraption jerked into life, its jaws slamming into the book from all sides, as black fluid dripped down into the vat.

'But those are Source Editions,' Tilly said, turning pale. 'If you destroy those, then every edition of the book across the whole world will blink out of existence. Oh . . .'

She exchanged a look with Oskar and Will, the horrible truth dawning on them all simultaneously.

'*That's* why the books are disappearing,' Oskar said. 'They're not being hidden; they're being destroyed. Permanently.'

45

THE CHAIN of
WRITERS AND READERS

'But . . . but this is monstrous!' said Bea.

'Oh, don't be so sanctimonious,' Decima said as the last remaining drops of book magic were squeezed from the book in the grip of the machine. 'We have thought this through, and we're starting with the books that have the least importance.'

'Because you think no one will notice,' Oskar said.

'But someone *will* notice,' Tilly said. 'All books have their readers. And, even if someone didn't notice one book vanishing, you're destroying the chain.'

'The chain?' Melville repeated dismissively.

'The chain of writers and readers,' Tilly said. 'You're taking imagination out of the world and that affects everyone, even if they've never heard of an individual book. And you have no idea what will happen if you destroy a book! You can't possibly know who's read it or what it means to them!'

'What happens if a book has helped heal a broken heart?' Bea asked, her voice full of quiet fury. 'What happens to that heart? What happens to the couple that fell in love because they both loved the same book, and you wipe that book from their memory?'

Tilly and Oskar exchanged a glance, remembering the couple at the airport, who had gone from loved-up honeymooners to leaving separately within minutes.

'You say you've thought it through, but you have no idea what you're doing!' Bea finished. 'And it's immoral! Who knows what damage you've already wreaked? You can't possibly understand or know the changes you've effected.'

'A drop of imagination and magic is removed from the world every time you destroy a book,' Will said. 'Imagine not knowing that.'

'What nonsense,' Melville said. 'There's no *chain*.

Not everything has to have some grand meaning. It's nowhere near as dramatic as you're all making out. And, if you're trying to elicit some sort of emotional response, I assure you it won't work. None of the books we're converting are well read – no one cares about them!'

'*Every* book written has been cared about by at least one person,' Bea said. 'Even if it's only the writer. You underestimate the power of stories – as you always have done. No one could ever trace the impact one book has had on the world.'

'And even if you don't care about all of that,' Oskar added, 'I would have thought it was pretty obvious that you need people to care about books and stories enough to have something to be in charge of. If no one cares about reading, there'll be no bookwanderers, and no Underlibrary.'

'There's no reason at all to think that what you've said is true,' Decima said, trying to disguise the slight wobble in her voice. 'Sapping imagination! Honestly, you're all delusional. You're so used to the nonsense peddled at your silly little shop about *connection* and *meaning*. I know what Archie Pages is like, all his mumbo jumbo about the importance of reading.'

Tilly took a deep breath.

'You're wrong,' she said calmly. 'It's like my mum said: there isn't a book out there that hasn't meant something to someone at some point. A story doesn't get told if it doesn't mean something. Wasn't there ever a book you loved so much that no one else had heard of?' Tilly said. 'Not even when you were children?'

'We don't go in for such sentimentality,' said Melville.

'But you must have loved stories once,' Tilly said. 'Otherwise you wouldn't be bookwanderers. Can't you remember what it felt like to love books, not just want to steal from them?'

'No,' Decima said shortly, although she still looked slightly uncomfortable. 'It's been a long time since I was so naive about stories. We've grown up, and so should you all. Now, pull yourself together, Brother.'

Decima walked over to the vat of book magic and raised the arm that Will had taken the magic out of and plunged it straight in. She held it there for a few seconds before pulling it out and looking at it in satisfaction.

'Good as new,' she said. 'I will need to add some more of the book magic for a longer-term effect, but this will do for now. I hope you'll see that all you have are party tricks and self-righteous rhetoric. And that is no match for science and determination, and, I assure you, we are very determined. It won't be long before you come to us, begging for a drop of what we have to offer, of that I have no doubt.'

'You'll see that ours is the way of enlightened thinking.' Melville smiled coldly. 'We're no longer stuck in past darkness, shunning progress.'

'There is no darkness but ignorance,' Will said. 'Let me make that *very* plain.'

'Even if you keep denying that what you've already done has caused horrible damage,' Bea said, 'what will you do when you've used up the books that you believe people won't notice? This can't last forever. You may have managed to convince enough librarians here – although I doubt anyone upstairs is aware of the extent of what you've hidden away down here – but, as soon as it becomes public knowledge to bookwanderers, you can't hope to get away with it.'

'Let me set you straight immediately on one thing,' said Melville. 'I think that you'd be surprised how many of the people upstairs do, in fact, know what we're doing and have, indeed, helped us with it. You should not assume that everyone here shares your beliefs; some of our esteemed colleagues upstairs are very much onboard with our plans to protect bookwandering, and take back control. And our friends extend beyond this Underlibrary, I assure you.'

'Oh, we know,' Oskar said. 'We've spoken to Jacob Johnson.'

'How very enterprising of you,' Decima said. 'But I assure you we know all about your little escapade in the Library of Congress.'

'Are you letting him use the book magic too?' Oskar asked. 'Did he have tattoos under his suit?'

'We're still testing the side effects,' Decima said smoothly.

'Oh, I get it,' said Tilly. 'You're not sharing.'

'We are making sure we're confident as to the process,' Decima said. 'I would not wish to burden any of our colleagues unduly. We're doing everyone a great service by testing the effects of book magic on ourselves – and future bookwanderers will be grateful for our work and our sacrifice.'

'The only sacrifice being made is of stories that belong to everyone,' Bea said.

'Oh, would you stop being such a self-righteous bother of a woman!' Melville said, losing his temper. 'I was elected as Librarian in order to shepherd in a new era for British bookwandering and that is what I intend to do.'

He pulled himself together, smoothing his hair down and taking a deep breath. 'I look to a future where our resources are harvested efficiently and where there can be a smooth, continuous and consistent message from the top. There's more to books than curling up in a corner with a cup of tea.'

'You're right that there's more to it than that,' Tilly said. 'But not the things that you think. And you still haven't said what you'll do when you run out of books.'

She saw Decima and Melville exchange glances at her question, in a way that made her feel distinctly uneasy.

'For one thing, I'm sure we will master our printing press in time,' Melville said. 'We will be churning out Sources that work properly before you know it. But, in the meantime, we have plenty of books that we believe will cause the smallest of ripples when utilised, if they do at all. Should a few hearts break here or there, that's something we're willing to let happen in pursuit of the cause. None of your imagination chain nonsense has any basis in science. Not to mention that we have all sorts of exciting . . . opportunities on the horizon, such as Mr Shakespeare's presence, for example.'

'Ay,' said Will, looking a little nervously at the cruncher, which was still dripping with the dregs of the Source Edition it had obliterated.

'You look as though we're about to put you between its jaws,' Decima laughed.

'You do not intend that?' Will said. 'I assure you, I would put up some fight – you have many years that I would happily reclaim from you.'

'We're not monsters,' Melville said, sounding almost frustrated that he had to keep defending himself.

'A most learned man once said,' Will offered, 'that the fool doth think he is wise, but the wise man knows himself to be a fool. I would think on those words.'

'I don't even know what you mean,' Melville said, waving Will's words away as if they were a bad smell. 'But come now, the death of an author is not what we're aiming for . . . Although I suspect you're not operating on the same scale of death and . . . *aliveness* that we are.'

'Of that you may be quite sure,' said Will.

'You on your high horse,' Decima said dismissively. 'How is our work any different from your situation? As far as the rest of the world knows, you died in 1616 and that was that. But in fact you chose to live forever – what gives you that right, but not us?'

'Firstly, I did not choose this story,' Will said. 'The Archive pulled me to it because of the worth of my words, one might even go as far as to say my legacy – something you clearly strive for and are falling far short of. I rather think the desire to live forever should preclude someone from doing so. Getting what you want is a dangerous thing—' But Will was interrupted by a knock at the door.

'Excellent,' Melville said. 'We can finally be done with all this fussing. We're talking round in circles and our guest is here: one who will also be able to provide the answer as to where we'll be getting more stock of lost and forgotten Source Editions. Enter!'

And the door opened to reveal Seb, accompanied by Horatio and Milo Bolt.

46

THE FOX AND
THE MOON

'What are *you* doing here?' Oskar said to Horatio. 'I thought you were on Artemis's side?'

'And I thought you two would have picked up by now that I'm not on anyone's side other than my own,' said Horatio. 'Don't take it personally; it's just business. There's no conflict in me helping you with what Artemis paid for and fulfilling this order as well.'

'You know this man?' Melville said.

'We've met,' Tilly said cagily, not wanting to give the Underwoods any extra information about the Archive.

'You two really do have a talent for sticking

your noses where they don't belong, don't you?' said Decima. 'I'd almost be impressed if it wasn't so damnably annoying.'

As she spoke, Seb had walked over to stand with Tilly, although he couldn't make eye contact and break his cover as a spy who was actually reporting back to Amelia and the Pages family about what went on at the Underlibrary. Seb hadn't seemed to react when he saw that they were all there, and so Tilly assumed that her grandparents had read the note she had left and asked him to track them down. Tilly was reassured that Grandma and Grandad knew where they were – and that Seb was with them.

Tilly turned to Horatio. 'What are you giving them?' she asked, looking suspiciously at the large cardboard box that Milo was carrying.

'Books, obviously,' Melville said. 'Mr Bolt here – who you seem to know somehow – is an expert at tracking them down, and we have hired him to find us Source Editions that are currently outside the jurisdiction of any of the Underlibraries.'

'How can you say there's no conflict?' Oskar said crossly to Horatio. 'You must have known all along what was happening to the missing books! You would have led us on a wild goose chase.'

'I would have done what I could to try and find *those* particular books,' Horatio said. 'It's just that some of them may have ended up being unable to be found – or indeed the trail may have led you here.'

Melville turned to Horatio.

'*How* do you know these people?' he asked. 'And who is Artemis?'

'That has nothing to do with what you've hired me for,' Horatio said. 'So I'll not be answering that. Your books are here; what any other clients have engaged me to do is between me and them.'

'I trust you have succeeded?' Melville said, still clearly unsettled that Horatio had met Tilly and Oskar before.

'I always do,' Horatio said. 'If the price is right. And so here you are. A selection of lost and forgotten Source Editions for you to do with as you like. I am uninterested in why you require them.'

'But I thought you said that it *was* in your interest to keep the balance of bookwandering steady?' Tilly said.

'It is also in my interest to keep my bank balance steady,' Horatio said. 'No one cares about these books, they do not upset the balance in terms of my business, my train or my clients, and therefore I am happy to provide the required service. I have been careful with what I've procured, I assure you.' He turned back to the Underwoods. 'We have one box here and one more just outside to be brought in once we've been paid appropriately.'

Horatio gestured to Milo, who put the large box at Melville's and Decima's feet before scurrying back behind Horatio. He was avoiding making eye contact with Tilly or Oskar. Melville bent down and neatly slit the box open with a penknife he produced from his pocket. He pulled out the top few books, but barely looked at their covers.

'They're definitely Sources?' he asked Horatio.

'Absolutely,' he confirmed.

'Where did you get them from?'

'That would be telling,' said Horatio. 'I'm afraid I cannot reveal my methods. Especially not to the Librarian of an Underlibrary. I'm sure you understand.'

'Hmph,' Melville snorted dismissively. 'I think it's time for you to go. But first I'll check the authenticity of your stock.' He took one of the books he was holding and, before anyone could stop him, he put it between the jaws of the crushing machine, and within moments another Source Edition had been turned into sticky black pulp.

'Oh!' Decima breathed as the book magic dripped down the claws of the machine, putting her hand to her chest. She staggered backwards slightly and felt for the wall behind her to steady herself. She looked to Melville for support, but he, too, was pale and wobbly.

'Did you feel that as well, Sister?' he said, his hand

on his heart. 'I feel . . . cold inside all of a sudden. And such pain. *Such* pain.'

'I feel as though I've just learned a horribly sad piece of news,' Decima said, trying to pull herself together.

And then, to everyone's amazement, Melville started to cry. Clearly mortified about showing weakness in front of the others, he scrubbed at his cheeks with his shirtsleeve.

'I'm just very tired,' he said. 'Running the Underlibrary is a huge task, and no one understands. I just feel suddenly . . . empty.'

'It's that man,' Decima said, pointing at Will. 'You've done something to us.'

'I did not lay a hand on you, madam,' Will said. 'Not this time.'

'Well, whatever it is, it can be easily fixed with another dose of book magic,' Decima said, grabbing another book at random from the box that Horatio had brought and hitting the buttons to control the machine.

But, once another book had been destroyed, the

effect was even worse, and this time Decima burst into tears.

'You've brought us defective books!' she shouted at Horatio. 'What are these things? Are they even Source Editions?' She pulled another book out of the box and looked at it.

'Oh . . .' She stopped, tears still running down her cheeks. 'It's . . . it's *The Fox and the Moon.*'

'Why . . . why do I know that title?' Melville said, tears still escaping. 'Have we bookwandered there?'

'We used to read it together when we were children,' Decima said. 'But Mother threw it away when she said that we'd got too old for stories. I'd forgotten all about it. We used to act it out, do you remember? I'd make you be the moon so I could be the fox.'

'What was the other book?' Melville said slowly. 'The one we just pulped?'

'There's no way of knowing,' Decima said, her voice growing icy as she stood up straight again. 'And it doesn't matter. I see what you're doing.' She turned and glared at Tilly. 'I don't know how you've done this, but it won't work.'

'How I've done what?' Tilly said, as confused as the Underwoods were.

'You've weaselled your way into some record, and found the books we read as children, and you're going to trick us into destroying them to prove some stupid point,' she said.

'I have no idea how I would even know what books you'd read as kids!' Tilly said. 'It's just a coincidence! But now you can see how awful what you're doing is!'

'I don't believe you, child,' said Melville. 'Three books that had that impact on us – you must have been behind it.'

'I swear I wasn't!' Tilly said. 'I would never destroy two Source Editions just to make a point! Who would do something like that! Oh . . .' She stopped and turned to look at Horatio. Tilly thought for a second that he'd winked at her, but it was impossible to tell in the gloom. Melville and Decima followed her glance, but by that point Horatio was studiously focused on his notebook.

'Did I miss something?' he said, looking up innocently at them all staring at him. Melville and Decima were becoming more and more unsettled by the second.

'Regardless of how this has happened,' Bea said, 'Melville, Decima, surely you can now see why we care so much about convincing you to change your plan? Every time you destroy a Source, there's someone, somewhere who will feel what you've just felt. Is it worth it?'

'For the greater good, yes,' Decima said, but she sounded unsure.

'We'll get over it,' Melville said. 'And so can everyone else. Our cause is more important than a brief moment of heartache.'

'It's not a *cause*!' Tilly said, losing patience. 'You just want power! Can you just stop being so selfish for one moment!'

'That's enough,' Decima said. 'You've distracted us

with your schemes for long enough. Seb, take them upstairs and escort all of our guests to somewhere secure – yes, including Mr Bolt and the other boy. After we've inspected their delivery further, I think we need to sit down and have a chat. Make sure they are in *separate* rooms as well. We'll have some guards sent down to meet you at the door back up to the main atrium. Got it?'

Seb nodded, unable to do anything else without blowing his cover.

'Good,' said Melville. 'It's time you all understood who's in charge.'

47

EACH BOOK IS ITS OWN MASTER

Tilly let herself be swept along by Seb's guiding arm as he ushered them back into the main hall, taking care to shut the door behind him. They retraced their steps along the edge of the room, Tilly's mind busy with worries about getting too far from Will, and leaving him in the hands of the Underwoods, even if it had been his idea to take that risk.

'Did you know?' she said quietly to Horatio as they walked past rows and rows of shadowy bookshelves.

'Know what?' he said.

'That those books meant something to the Underwoods?'

'How could I possibly have known that?' he said, looking straight ahead. 'It would take someone of unusual skill to have learned such things, wouldn't it? Or access to a very particular archive of information.'

'But you didn't even know about the Underwoods until . . . Oh.' Tilly paused, realising he hadn't been telling them even half of what he knew. 'I suppose you must have.'

'A word of wisdom,' Horatio said. 'Never underestimate what I know. Or who I know. My business runs as much on information as it does on imagination.'

'But you were helping the Underwoods by bringing them books,' Tilly said, confused.

'If you're looking for a hero, I suggest you keep looking,' Horatio said. 'I was doing a job I'd been hired to do. Generally, I'm inclined to let people get on with whatever they want to do, but when people start meddling with my business, and members of my staff go missing, well then, I can't quite turn a blind eye.'

'Your staff?' asked Tilly.

'Madeleine,' Milo supplied. 'Our chef. You know

how she vanished? Well, we never found her and so my unc— And so Horatio thinks her Source has been destroyed.'

'So she's just . . . gone? Forever?'

'Yes,' Horatio said shortly, and Tilly couldn't tell if he was angry, or upset, or both.

'I'm sorry,' she said.

'Honestly, I think Source Editions cause more problems than they're worth, if destroying them makes such trouble,' Oskar said. 'Whose idea even were they – in the first place?'

'I'm not sure,' Seb said. 'It's a very old practice.'

'And they're there to protect stories,' Bea said automatically.

'But they're not doing a very good job!' Oskar retorted. 'Stories are being destroyed forever and the Underwoods are using the power of the Sources for their own devices! The exact opposite of what's supposed to happen! They're stealing all the book magic!'

'True story magic, and imagination, will last longer

than the Sources those two have access to,' Horatio said. 'But you're right that they are using a concerning amount, considering the impact it's having.'

'But, Milo, I thought you said story magic could never run out,' Tilly said.

'I think I said that there's enough to go around if it's shared fairly,' Milo said. 'That's not the same thing.'

'If it's shared fairly . . .' Tilly repeated, her steps slowing to a halt as she thought. They were nearly back at the door, and she needed time to think through an idea that was tickling at the edge of her thoughts. 'I wonder if . . . You can't make a *new* Source Edition – that's right, isn't it, Mum?'

'As far as I know,' Bea agreed.

'That's correct,' Horatio said. 'If one is lost and still in existence, then it's impossible and, of course, if it's destroyed, all traces of the story will disappear so there's nothing to make into a new one.'

'And if they're lost and unbound like the Shakespeare Sources you have –' Tilly paused to raise an eyebrow at Horatio – 'then everyone can still bookwander in them?'

'Sure,' Oskar said, trying to follow her logic. 'But we can't just lose all the Source Editions – where would we put them?! There's thousands of them in here.'

'So, what if there were no Source Editions in the first place?' Tilly said quietly.

'You can't just unmake a Source Edition,' Bea pointed out.

'Why not?' Tilly said. 'How are they made in the first place?'

'They just start out as regular books,' Seb said. 'But they're stamped with book magic and become part of the Source Library. But you won't get the librarians to agree to stop that process.'

'They're too fond of being in charge,' Horatio chimed in, earning a glare from Seb.

'But that's the regular book magic, right?' Tilly said. 'The black stuff that comes when stories are broken or hurt – what we've always been told is the only way to get book magic. But what about what you use, Horatio?'

She turned to Bea. 'Mum, when we were travelling through the layers of Story, and when we were on Horatio's train, the Quip – book magic isn't supposed to be like this! That black sticky stuff is what you get when it's stolen – the real book magic is so beautiful. It's glittering and airy and free.'

'It's like levelled-up book magic,' Oskar said. 'It's made of imagination and ideas – it's not to do with the paper and ink and stuff – that's what *books* are made of, not what stories are made of.'

'Do the Underwoods know about this?' Bea asked Seb and Horatio.

'I don't think so,' said Seb. 'You heard them – they couldn't get their printing press to make books that had much magic in them at all.'

'For all of their grandstanding, they don't truly understand what makes stories work,' Horatio said.

'And surely they'd be using it already if they did,' Seb pointed out. 'They wouldn't have to destroy

Sources to get it, which comes with risks they wouldn't take if they didn't have to.'

'So what do we do?' Oskar said, eyes alight with the prospect of A Plan.

'Okay, so if it's the stolen book magic that's taken from broken stories that makes Source Editions,' Tilly said slowly, 'is there perhaps a reason to hope that pure story magic might change them back again? I mean, turn them back into normal books and stop them being Source Editions? If the Underwoods can't access the magic that they're getting from the Sources, then they're stuck, right? The other Underlibraries won't let them just waltz in and destroy their Sources. Even someone like Jacob Johnson wouldn't give them free rein when he understood what was happening, surely?'

Horatio looked begrudgingly impressed.

'I've . . . I've never thought of that,' he admitted. 'But the logic is there up to a point, although it's untested as far as I know.'

'But is it safe?' Bea asked. 'Can we be sure it would

work? Might it not have the same effect? What would happen if all the copies of all the stories disappeared?'

'But we're not removing the book magic,' Tilly said. 'We're removing the stamps and the limits. All books have real book magic in them already – we couldn't get rid of that if we tried, unless we completely destroyed them like the Underwoods are doing.'

'But how?' Oskar asked. 'How could we possibly get hold of enough book magic to do that? You've seen how many Source Editions there are downstairs. There's no way to spread it through all the books quickly enough.'

'We need more magic, you're right,' Tilly said, trying to get her brain to speed up. 'Horatio, how would we do that? How do those wooden ball things work?'

'Wood soaks up imagination particularly well,' Horatio said as if everyone should know that. 'It's why we make books out of paper.'

'You two travelled through the paper forest, didn't you?' Milo said. 'That place is made from your own imagination.'

'I'm not quite sure I'm following your logic, Tilly,' Seb said nervously. 'You think that if you put in this pure story magic – that you say is different from the book magic we usually use – a book will cease to be a Source Edition?'

'I don't know if it'll work,' Tilly said. 'But yep, that's kind of what I was thinking. It's like the reverse of how you make a Source, right?'

'Well, I think it's worth a go,' Oskar said. 'If the Underwoods don't have any Sources, they don't have any fuel. Not to mention that no one's actually managed to explain to me why we need Sources particularly convincingly.'

'They protect a book's very existence,' Seb said. 'They keep the original edition safe from people bookwandering in and altering details – it's why they're kept down here.'

'But that doesn't actually answer the question, does it?' Bea pointed out. 'Now that I think about it. Because, if there are no Sources, then there's no way to change the books – each book would be its own master.'

'But . . . but . . .' Seb stuttered, clearly flummoxed at the principle that his whole job was built on being yanked out from under him. 'But there must be a reason for them. They can't just be . . . *unnecessary*.'

'You've always got to think about who is making the rules,' Horatio said. 'And who for. People with power often want to control things, but that doesn't mean it's the best way to do something. In fact, that's rarely the best way to do it.'

The six of them stared at each other, each taking in what they'd realised with varying levels of enthusiasm.

'Well, let's test it then!' Tilly said, fizzing with adrenalin. 'We're surrounded by Source Editions to try it out on in here! We can go and change something *tiny* and see if it stays when we leave the book.'

'That way we'll know if it's safe to do that to the other books,' Bea nodded.

'One small problem,' Seb pointed out. 'We're surrounded by *bound* Source Editions.'

'Don't you know how to unbind them?' Oskar

asked. 'You're a librarian after all.'

'Well, yes, in theory, I suppose,' Seb said nervously. 'Pass me one over. I have a bad feeling about this, I must say.'

Tilly grabbed a book from a nearby shelf. 'Here we go. We can test it on . . . Oh, okay. Well, this is a Sherlock Holmes book.'

There was a pause. Then Seb held out his hand to take the book.

'Very well,' he said. 'What's the worst that could happen?'

'Well, it's a classic,' said Oskar. 'So we could ruin something that generations of people have loved.'

'That was a rhetorical question,' said Seb, with a glare at Oskar. 'But nevertheless here we go.'

48

DO NOT WANDER

Seb opened up the Sherlock Holmes novel. On the title page there was a stamp in black that showed the British Underlibrary logo. It was an open book, like at the American Underlibrary, but with a key at its centre. Text underneath the logo read **'Designated Source Edition. Do Not Wander'**. Seb turned the page to where the story started, and across the first word there was a smear of black book magic.

Seb tutted. 'Whoever did this did it with very little care,' he said. 'The Underwoods have had their underlings down here doing their dirty work and clearly not much attention has been paid. They've made a right pig's ear of it. Goodness knows who's slipping in and out of these books – there's enough gaps left. But hopefully that makes it easier to unbind.'

'How do you do it?' Oskar asked, fascinated.

'You let the story know that you want to read it,' said Seb.

'Sorry, what?' Horatio said.

'It's really not a complicated process, sir,' Seb said. 'The main barrier to unbinding these books is that they're being protected by lock and key – and fear. Books *always* want to be read.'

He laid a gentle hand on the cover of the book, closed his eyes and breathed in deeply. Taking his hand away, for a fraction of a second there was the outline of his handprint in shining gold, which faded away immediately.

'It's story magic,' Tilly said. 'You've had it all along.'

'All readers do,' Milo said. 'You just have to know how to use it.'

Seb opened the book again and, as they watched, the crude, sticky magic faded away and, even though there was no breeze deep underground, a ripple flickered through the pages, almost as if the book itself was breathing a sigh of relief.

'Just . . . a few thousand more to go . . .' Oskar said, looking around.

'First, we need to test whether this works,' Tilly said. 'Now the book is unbound, we need to see if we can make it truly free – and all the copies of it, wherever they are in the world. Are you ready?'

The others nodded and Tilly, feeling slightly self-conscious, held the book tightly between her hands. 'Do I just . . .?' She was about to ask how she should do it, but of course it was her plan, and no one had the answer. So she closed her eyes and thought of Pages & Co., and Anne, and Alice, and Oskar, and her family, and everything she had seen and learned since she first discovered she was a bookwanderer. She felt her fingers start to spark with glittering book magic, but it quickly fizzled out like a damp sparkler.

'I don't think that was enough,' she said, disappointed. 'It is a Source Edition, I suppose – it probably needs more welly. Maybe we should all do it at the same time?'

So all six of them took hold of the narrow book. Tilly couldn't know what each of them was thinking about, what stories meant to them, but within seconds the air around the book was sparkling with magic and the book was glowing as they channelled pure imagination into the Source Edition.

'How do we know it's worked?' Milo said.

Seb opened the book and let out a low whistle. He held it out so everyone could see, and before their eyes the **'DO NOT WANDER'** stamp faded into the paper and disappeared.

'But how can we tell if the story is still protected?' Oskar said. 'That we haven't broken . . . well, everything?'

'I suppose we go and look,' Tilly said, turning to Horatio, who nodded briefly.

'Yes, you just need to get inside the book and change something and see if it sticks,' Horatio said. 'Just the smallest, smallest thing, in case it hasn't worked, and you change something forever.'

'Are we all going?' Milo asked eagerly.

'No,' Seb said firmly, one eye fixed anxiously on the door that led back up to the Underlibrary. 'If it hasn't worked, then we can't risk causing more damage to the Source. I really shouldn't be letting you do this at all.' He looked distinctly nauseous and was fussing with his bow tie.

'I'll go,' Tilly said. 'It's my plan.'

'Which means I'm obviously going too,' Oskar said.

'Two is more than enough,' Seb said, before Horatio could volunteer to go too – he clearly wanted to see for himself if the book magic had made any difference. 'We'll stay here and keep watch – you should only be gone for a few seconds in our time. In and out, remember – and only change the tiniest detail.'

Tilly nodded and opened the book at random, linked arms with Oskar and read them to 221B Baker Street.

49

'PLAYS THE VIOLIN WELL'

'I enumerated in my own mind all the various points upon which he had shown me that he was exceptionally well-informed. I even took a pencil and jotted them down. I could not help smiling at the document when I had competed it.'

The room that appeared around them was a pleasant, airy sitting room with comfortable-looking furniture and wide windows. For the famous abode of an infamous detective, it was actually rather generic; there were books and papers on tables, and a pipe on the mantelpiece, but it was disappointingly unmysterious. The sound of talking came from somewhere nearby, and Tilly knew that this wasn't the time to explore – they certainly didn't have time to try to explain to Sherlock Holmes why they were in his apartments. If any fictional character could deduce what was going on, it was him.

Tilly and Oskar started to look around for something they could change, comparing the details in the room to what was written down – it had to be something in the text for the experiment to work. And it had to be small in case it *didn't* work.

'Look, here!' Oskar called, pointing at a journal lying open on a desk. In it was a list of observations that John Watson had made about Sherlock Holmes that was mirrored in the Source Edition they were holding. It read:

SHERLOCK HOLMES – his limits

1. Knowledge of literature – nil.
2. Philosophy – nil.
3. Astronomy – nil.
4. Politics – feeble.
5. Botany – variable. Well up on belladonna,

opium and poisons generally. Knows nothing
of practical gardening.

6. Geology – practical but limited. Tells at a
   glance different soils from each other. After
   walks, has shown me splashes upon his
   trousers and told me, by their colour and
   consistency, in what part of London he had
   received them.

7. Chemistry – profound.

8. Anatomy – accurate, but unsystematic.

9. Sensational literature – immense. He appears
   to know every detail of every horror
   perpetrated in this century.

10. Plays the violin well.

11. Is an expert singlestick player, boxer and
    swordsman.

12. Has a good practical knowledge of British
    law.

'We'll just change something on here!' Oskar said.
'This doesn't seem super important, right? I've not
read the books, have you?'

'No,' Tilly admitted. 'And, in hindsight, maybe we should have experimented with something we knew better. And that was less beloved.'

The noise of people talking started to get distinctly louder. 'This'll have to do,' she said, and grabbed a fountain pen lying on top of the journal. She scanned down the list, looking for the thing that seemed like it would have the least impact on the story.

'This!' she said, crossing out violin and writing piano in scratchy writing above it. 'How much difference could that make?' she said.

'Let's get out of here,' Oskar said, opening the Source Edition up to the last page to read themselves back to the Underlibrary. But, just at that moment, the door to the room opened and two men walked in.

'Hey there, what are you doing in here!' the shorter man said. 'This is private property! Sherlock, shall I ring for Scotland Yard?'

But the taller man with the piercing eyes was looking them up and down.

'Girl of about ten,' he said to himself. 'Ink on fingers

– not familiar with a nib pen, necklace with a bee on it – likely of sentimental value, potentially belonging to her mother or grandmother. Boy of similar age, acts like a brother to the girl, and holding a book with . . . my name on it. Peculiar . . . Both look distinctly like they are doing something wrong.'

'I'll say, Sherlock,' the other man said. 'They've broken in!'

But Sherlock simply cocked his head as if he couldn't quite work them out. He took a step towards them.

'Time to go, Tilly!' Oskar said urgently.

'It's like in Latin or something,' she said, panicking as she looked at the last line of the book.

'Just sound it out!' Oskar shouted. 'Quickly!'

'*Populus me sib . . . sibilat, at mihi plaudo, ipso, no ipse, domi simul ac nummos contemplor in . . . arca,*' Tilly said, almost in a shout, and, to their relief, before Sherlock could take the book from Tilly's hands or John Watson could summon Scotland Yard, 221B Baker Street melted around them and they were back in the Source Library.

Bea, Horatio, Seb and Milo were there, waiting.

'You were barely gone a second,' Bea said, relieved. 'How did it go?'

'Let's find out,' Tilly said, flicking back towards the beginning of the book to find the page with the list on it. She ran a finger down and stopped. 'There, look,' she said triumphantly. 'It hasn't changed!'

'Oh, thank goodness,' Seb said, letting out the breath he'd been holding.

'*Number ten – plays the violin well,*' Oskar read triumphantly. 'It's still exactly the same. We haven't ruined Sherlock Holmes! And, more importantly, this isn't a Source Edition any more . . .'

But, before they could decide what to do next, there was a clang that echoed round the hall.

'It's the guards,' Seb said, looking pale. 'We've kept them waiting too long.'

'Okay, listen to me,' Horatio said, quickly taking

charge. 'Milo and I will go with Seb. Hopefully, the guards have not been told how many to expect, and well, I'm sure I can provide some sort of distraction if need be. I think Matilda might need a few more moments in here.'

'To save Will?' she said.

'Well, there's no harm in trying,' he said. 'But I meant to carry out your plan to free the Sources.'

'Oh yes, right,' she said. 'Of course.'

'We need to go,' Seb said, hurrying Horatio and Milo along.

'Hey, Milo!' Oskar said just as they turned their backs. 'Is there any way we can contact you? Do you have a phone . . . or a computer we could email you on?'

Horatio rolled his eyes, but Milo's face lit up.

'There's no computer or mobile phones on the Quip,' he said. 'They don't work in Story. But you can write to me.'

'But where do we send it?' Oskar asked.

'If you address it to Milo Bolt, the Sesquipedalian,

and put it in between the back cover and the last page of a book – next to the Endpapers – it'll get to me.'

'It just magicks its way there?' Oskar said sceptically.

'Is that just one step too far with the whole magic thing?' Milo laughed.

'Fair enough,' said Oskar.

'But I wouldn't worry too much about keeping in contact,' Horatio said, with a sly smile. 'Remember, Matilda, you still owe me a favour. I'll be in touch.'

50

CHOSEN ONES

Bea, Oskar and Tilly stood in the chilly hall of the Source Library, hiding among the shelves, listening to the great door clang open and shut as Milo and Horatio left with Seb. Tilly felt very far from the other end of the hall where the Underwoods still had Will; she hoped that he was able to stay this far away from her safely now they weren't travelling through Story.

'There's *a lot* we need to catch up on once we've dealt with this,' Bea said. Tilly nodded, hoping there was a point in the not-too-distant future where they'd all be able to sit down with a hot chocolate and compare stories about magical trains and mysterious Archives – and whatever was about to happen here.

'Well, at least we've got one question ticked off the

never-ending list,' Oskar said cheerfully. 'Why the paper forest had all that stuff in it from places we'd bookwandered.'

'At this point in time, that's what you're thinking about?' Tilly said, incredulous.

'Yes!' Oskar said. 'It was never explained! I hate it when stuff like that is left hanging! It's why the pirate ship from *Treasure Island* was there, and the lamppost from Narnia – it all came from our imagination. And that's why we thought we might be back in *A Midsummer Night's Dream*, because we'd just bookwandered there!'

'*A Midsummer Night's Dream*,' Tilly repeated. 'That's it!'

'That's what?' Oskar said confused.

'The last piece of the puzzle!' said Tilly. She checked the shelves to try to get her bearings before leading them back into the depths of the Source Library. 'I have an idea to help us free the Source Editions – but we can't do it by ourselves. Horatio's not the only one owed a favour. It's time for me to call in one of my own. Just trust me, okay? Even when you see who I mean.'

'So cryptic.' Oskar grinned. 'You know it used to be me convincing you to do things like this. But I think the time has come to make peace with the fact that the majority of our madcap plans are now definitely your idea.'

'Does that make you the sensible one then?' Tilly said.

'No way!' said Oskar.

'Someone has to be the sensible one,' Tilly said.

'I am more than happy to take that label,' Bea said.

'You took two children to the airport in the middle of the night and sent them to America, Bea,' Oskar pointed out. 'So you do not get to be the sensible one.'

'Right,' Bea said. 'Fair enough.'

'Honestly, I think the time for being sensible passed a really long time ago,' Tilly said. 'Maybe no one has to be the sensible one.'

'It's clear who the chosen one is, though, eh, Tilly?' said Oskar, good-naturedly poking her in the back.

'Well, I hereby designate us all chosen ones,' Tilly said.

'So we're all special?' Oskar asked.

'Or we're all normal,' Tilly said.

'I think they might be one and the same when it comes down to it,' said Bea.

'Where are we going, Tilly?' Oskar hissed as he and Bea followed her between the shelves, watching her check the spines of the books they were passing.

'We need a bit of backup,' Tilly said, stopping and pulling a book down. 'And, now we know how to unbind the books, we can ask some friends.'

Tilly showed Bea and Oskar the cover of the book she had found.

'*Anne of Green Gables*,' Oskar read. 'Of course.'

'You want to pull Anne out of the book?' Bea said. 'But that's not how it works.'

'Mum, I don't have time to explain properly,' Tilly said. 'But you remember what Horatio was saying about who makes up the rules? Well, there are some other bookwandering rules I think it's time to break.

It's like Milo said – we've all got book magic in us if we know what to do with it.'

Tilly copied what Seb had done with Sherlock Holmes and laid a hand on the cover. She felt a little bit silly, but she thought intently about how much she wanted to read it, and asked the book to let her in, and immediately the black mark over the first word faded.

She quickly turned to a page near the beginning that described Anne, and whispered the passage as quietly as she could, but nothing happened.

'Don't be dispirited, sweetheart,' Bea said. 'It was a lovely idea, but I don't think even you can completely break the rules of bookwandering. Now, what had you—' But she was cut off.

'What a strange, unpleasant feeling this place has,' a high Canadian voice said behind them. The three of them whirled round to see Anne Shirley standing there, shivering slightly.

'Tilly!' she said happily. She bobbed a curtsy to Bea. 'And lovely to meet you,' she said. 'My name is Anne. Spelled with an "e".' Tilly reminded herself how lucky she was that characters could remember her even after she'd left their books, something she was hoping would come in useful again very shortly. 'Now, why on earth are you here and . . .'

Tilly shushed her quickly with a finger to her lips. 'We have some more people to find, and then I'll explain everything,' she said.

They made their way from the Ms for Montgomery to the Cs for Carroll, which took them much closer to the room the Underwoods were in with Will. Tilly pulled down the Source Edition of *Alice's Adventures in Wonderland* and before long Alice had emerged, alongside the Mad Hatter and the White Rabbit.

Oskar eyed Anne and Alice, who were looking at each other warily.

'How exactly are they going to help?' he asked.

'Because they're still Source characters for the time being,' Bea said, realising what Tilly was planning, 'they're the most powerful versions of these characters you can get.'

'And they're going to be on *our* side, obviously,' added Tilly. 'They're made of pure imagination – if anyone can help us to unlock the Source Editions, it's them.'

'Unlock the what?' Alice said.

'Okay, gather round,' said Tilly. Anne, Alice and the other Wonderlanders huddled round her, and she explained where they were and what was happening.

'And so we need your help,' she finished. 'We need your magic – we need to set all your books free so you aren't trapped down here any more. We need as much imagination as possible.'

'But what do we do?' Alice asked. 'This is a very curious plan, Matilda, and it sounds like ever such a lot of effort.'

'I'll tell you once we've got more people,' Tilly said. 'And I think I need to ask one person in particular. Now, get as many characters out of their books as possible, but quietly, please!'

Alice and Anne hared off, their feet silent on the stone floor, and started pulling down book after book, passing the message on to those who were newly arrived.

Before long, the spaces between the shelves of the Source Library were full; there were princesses and pirates, wizards and talking animals, and everything in between. Tilly could see some of her favourite characters talking to each other, and many, many more than she didn't recognise.

But the noise was getting impossible to ignore. Tilly gestured to Anne and Alice who, with Bea, spread the word through the bustle of fictional characters. There was an unmistakable glitter and sparkle to the air lighting up even the darkest corners of the Source Library. Tilly and Oskar led the way back through the shelves towards the room where the Underwoods and their awful machine were, and where they hoped Will still was.

Then the door suddenly swung open, and Melville strode out, looking cross.

'I thought I told you to . . .' He stopped as he saw what was in front of him, and his knees buckled underneath him. 'Who . . . What . . .' He stumbled backwards towards his sister.

'I'm afraid that we have some unfinished business here,' Tilly said, hands on her hips. 'And I've brought some friends to help.'

Tilly gestured for the characters to stay where they were, and walked towards Melville and Decima – who thankfully still had Will with them.

Melville tried to disguise the fear on his face as he shoved Will forward to stand in front of them. Will's hands were smeared with a black, sticky liquid that was keeping them bound together.

'No more of your tricks!' Melville cried. 'You'll see Mr Shakespeare is unable to try anything like he attempted upstairs. He's bound, like these books are. I don't know how you have amassed so many people or who exactly they are,' he said, a little shakily. 'But be assured we still have the upper hand here, Matilda, unless you wish to physically overthrow us – and, even then, I promise you we have more than one way to evade you here. Who is that rabble anyway? Are they armed?'

'You don't know?' Oskar said gleefully, realising Melville hadn't worked it out yet.

'What do you mean, boy?' Decima said.

'Go and take a closer look,' Bea suggested, a small smile on her face.

Decima shoved Melville aside and her face fell as she recognised enough characters to know what Tilly had done.

'But it's impossible,' she said. 'These books are bound. There's no way to do this so quickly.'

'I think you'll find there is *always* a way,' Tilly said. 'Especially when it comes to stories. A friend once told me I should try and make a little room for the impossible to happen.'

'Oh, that is excellent!' Will said. 'May I borrow it for what I've been working on?'

'Shut up,' Melville hissed. He turned back to Tilly. 'So what? It's all well and good showing off that you can bend the rules – but we already knew that. You're going to make fictional characters fight us? When we have the power to destroy their stories once and for all at our fingertips? You've not thought this through.'

'I promise you I have,' Tilly said, and she pulled out the copy of *A Midsummer Night's Dream* that Orlando had given her, crossing all her fingers that this last gamble would pay off.

'*Ill met by moonlight, proud Titania!*' she shouted and suddenly the Queen of the Faeries **shimmered** into being before them, looking even more magnificent and more terrifying in the real world than she did in the forest.

51

WHAT A WASTE OF IMMORTALITY

Titania was taller than all of them and she seemed to be lit from within. Her hair floated around her, and so did her blue-and-gold dress, neither paying attention to the laws of gravity. She was like a cloud of magic, the air sparking and sparkling about her.

'How . . . how are you doing that?' Decima said, staring in terror at Titania. 'You can't . . . It shouldn't . . . That's not how it works!'

'My lady,' Tilly said, attempting a curtsy. 'You promised me a favour and I need your help now. These people are trying to destroy Story and use its magic to gain power. I ask you now to help me free all the stories here.'

'*What would you have me do, child?*' Titania said.

Tilly bobbed up on to her tiptoes and whispered something into her ear.

Titania smiled, nodded and held out her hand. Tilly felt a jolt run through her fingers as they touched, but she kept a tight hold and concentrated on the play she was holding. As Tilly and the Queen of the Faeries joined hands, and joined magic, the air filled with the scent of caramelising sugar with a coppery burning smell and something else that was altogether impossible to describe.

Magic, Tilly supposed.

'How does she even know who you are?' Decima said, horrified. 'She shouldn't know who you are – what witchcraft are you using?'

But Tilly did not break her concentration to explain to Decima how her half-fictional nature worked.

'Stop it *right now*!' Melville said, panicking. 'Sister, what are they doing?'

But all Decima could do was stare helplessly at Tilly and Titania as pure story magic sparked around them. Tilly heard a gasp from her mother and a low,

'*Wowww,*' from Oskar and she knew it was working.

'*Concentrate, Matilda,*' Titania said to her.

'*It is just beginning to grow.*'

For, around them, a forest was sprouting from the pages of the play. Between them, Tilly and Titania were pulling Shakespeare's enchanted wood from *A Midsummer Night's Dream* into the Source Library, and its vines and trees and leaves were spreading throughout the whole place. Flowers sprouted at the base of the shelves and wound their way up, right to the ceiling. And it just kept growing, until it had taken over the Source Library completely.

Soft grass grew under their feet and vines crept over their heads so you could barely see the concrete ceiling above them. The air felt lighter and brighter, although the smell of fire and sugar and magic was still present, combined with the lush, fresh scent of growing things.

Melville and Decima looked very small amid the beauty of the forest, hemmed in by an army of fictional characters.

Titania released Tilly's hand and looked about her in satisfaction.

'Consider now your debt be paid?' she asked Tilly.

'I do,' Tilly said. 'Thank you.'

Titania gave Melville and Decima a supercilious stare before melting away into nothingness, leaving her forest behind her. There wasn't one corner of the Source Library that wasn't touched by it.

'What are you doing, Matilda?' Decima said, regaining her composure. 'This may look impressive, but you realise your mistake? You have brought to our door more resources than we could possibly ever use.' She laughed coldly. 'This forest can be cut down and pulped for book magic. And these characters too. Some will have to be returned to their Sources, of course, otherwise people will notice their absence, but you have hand-delivered to us a wealth of book magic.'

'You're missing one crucial thing,' Tilly said. 'The same thing you've always missed. You don't understand book magic at all. It isn't that black stuff you steal and rip out of books – that's only a faint reflection of what book magic is. True magic – the magic of stories and imagination – is what brought all these characters here, and it's what's brought the forest to you. And it's what's going to stop you.'

Tilly signalled to the assembled book characters, who turned and pressed their hands to the nearest branch or vine, the wood conducting their magic straight into the books.

Inspired by the fire that had spread from scroll to scroll in the Library of Alexandria and how quickly it had burned, Tilly had asked each character to donate a small portion of their book magic. It started to flow directly from them, conducted by the forest itself, so that the books on the shelves began to light up and glow as the book magic spread through their pages.

'What are you doing?' Decima said.

'I'm setting the Sources free!' Tilly said. '*We're* setting them free. In a few moments, none of these books will be Source Editions any more. They'll just be normal stories, magical in the way *all* stories are.'

'How dare you?' Decima said. 'You stupid little girl. You have no idea what you're doing. Do you think your fellow bookwanderers will be happy to hear of the damage you've caused? Do you think the Underlibrary will look kindly on this, regardless of who your grandfather is? How you've fallen from your high horse, chastising us for utilising Sources when you are trying to destroy them all in one fell swoop!'

'But you want to destroy stories, not Sources,' Tilly said. 'And it's the *stories* that are important. I think that maybe the Underlibraries have had too much control for too long. Maybe bookwandering needs a fresh start, a chance for stories to exist free of the Sources.'

'The Sources *protect* them, you foolish child,' Melville said.

'Not very well, if they can be stolen and destroyed by people like you,' Tilly said. 'Now they can be looked after by readers, as they should be.'

'And you think this is going to stop us?' Decima said, tearing her eyes away from the magic burning steadily through the whole Source Library.

'Well, yes, actually,' Oskar said, his hands on his hips. 'You have no Source Editions, so you have no power.'

'You forget what you have shown us,' Decima said, getting more and more manic with each word, her hair coming loose from its tight ponytail, her lipstick smudged. 'That we can use fictional characters themselves as a power source! And we still have Shakespeare here, and the rest of the Archivists can be found as well. This is just . . . a minor setback. A pause! We have the loyalty of the librarians. We have, we have—'

'You think they will side with two children who have just destroyed the entire British Source Library?' Melville sneered. 'You will never stop us; we have come too far and achieved too much for you to halt the tide of our progress.'

Tilly started to feel desperate. She had been sure that they would concede defeat as they saw their power source depleted, and the whole of the Source

Library freed from their control, but it only seemed to spur them onwards.

The Underwood siblings didn't even care what she was doing any more, but had turned their attention to the host of fictional character channelling their magic into the forest, a greedy look in their eyes.

Then Tilly heard a small cough and looked up to see Will trying to get her attention. She touched Oskar's arm so he was looking too.

'Sometimes,' Will said very quietly, 'to do a great right, you need to do a little wrong.' He gestured with his head to the copy of *A Midsummer Night's Dream* that Tilly was still holding.

Tilly looked at him, confused, until she realised what he was suggesting.

'But . . . it will ruin it.'

'It is only one copy,' Will said. 'And it is my creation; I give you permission. I brought Titania and Oberon into being, and I believe they are more than capable of dealing with such a challenge.'

'Stop whispering,' Melville said, taking notice of

their hushed conversation. 'Just stay still until this mischief you've wrought is done, and then we'll decide what to do with all of you.' He sighed as he watched the Source Editions become normal books, each one lighting up and sparkling as it was filled with pure book magic and freed. 'What a waste of immortality.'

'Actually, I think it's time for *us* to decide what to do with *you*,' Oskar said.

'What?' laughed Decima.

'Now,' Tilly hissed to Oskar. They darted forward, hands clasped tightly, and grabbed an Underwood each, and Tilly read aloud, again, the line to take them into *A Midsummer Night's Dream*.

'Titania,' Tilly said, nodding her head respectfully as the Underwoods lay sprawled on the grass, winded and gasping for breath from their unexpected bookwander. 'I'm sorry to trespass on your hospitality again, but we were hoping you might be able to take care of these two for a while. I promise this is the last thing I'll ask you.'

'*More humans?*' Titania sniffed.

'Yes,' Tilly said. 'And yours to do with as you like. Maybe torment these two with your tricks, rather than each other? Just be careful that they don't break anything.'

The Underwoods started to scramble back across the grass as the faeries approached.

'You can't just get rid of us so quickly!' Decima yelled, twigs stuck in her hair, and her dress ripped. 'We've found a way back to the Underlibrary once before! Is this your worst? IS THIS IT?'

'You're making the same mistake you've always made!' Tilly shouted back as Oskar flicked to the back page of the play.

'This story was never about you.'

52

PURE STORY

They landed back in the Underlibrary, to be met by Bea's and Will's shocked faces.

'Is that it?' Oskar said, scarcely able to believe they'd rid themselves of the Underwoods just like that. 'We just leave them there? We should've shoved them into a book somewhere ages ago!'

'I meant what I said in there,' Tilly said. 'Although I only worked it out just now. We've been so focused on them, but I think our story was always supposed to be about *this*: freeing stories, and understanding what book magic really is.'

Oskar held up a hand to give Tilly a high-five, but they paused midway when they saw the panicked look on Bea's face.

'It's all going wrong,' she said. 'The forest –

it's stopped working!'

Tilly and Oskar looked around them to see that, although the channels of book magic were still flowing through the trees, the Source characters themselves were starting to flicker and then disappear.

They ran over to where Anne was still sending book magic into the trunk of a great oak tree.

'Is it done?' she said faintly, and Tilly and Oskar looked on in horror as the edges of her started to dissolve away into pure book magic around them.

'Stop, stop, Anne!' Tilly said, terrified.

Anne pulled her hands away from the branch, but as soon as she did the magic started retracting towards her.

'Mum, what's happening?' said Tilly.

'It's too much,' Bea said. 'It's using up the book magic too quickly – the characters are fading away.'

'But they'll be fine, right?' Oskar said. 'They're still in their books.'

'Not while they're still Source characters,' Bea said, holding out the copy of *Anne of Green Gables*, which was now mainly empty pages, without any trace of Anne in it, as she flickered and sparkled in front of them. 'It's a catch-22,' Bea said. 'You need the *power* of the Source characters to stop the books being Source Editions. But, if these characters lose too much magic and fade away *before* they've changed all the Sources here into regular books, well, I think some of their stories will cease to exist.'

'But what do we do?' Tilly said, trying the stop the panic that was bubbling up inside her. 'I can't be responsible for removing these books from the world, from every reader! Anne, you need to stop – *please*.'

'I have to help you, Tilly,' Anne shrugged weakly. 'You're my reader.'

'It's not worth it,' Tilly said desperately. 'You mean too much to too many people. I'm not your only reader! We'll find another way. Maybe if I help? I'm half Story after all – and apparently it wants me back.'

She pressed her hands against a tree, but a gentle hand stopped her.

'I have a suggestion,' Will said, rubbing his wrists

where the book magic bond had been removed. He kneeled down in front of Tilly.

'Matilda, my dear one,' he said gently, his voice full of affection. 'So little but so fierce. You have given me the greatest gift a writer could ever wish to have – to know that my words have found a home in the hearts and minds of readers long after I am gone. Why should I linger when my words have found an eternal home? After all, we are such stuff as dreams are made of and our little lives are rounded with a sleep. It is time for me to sleep, and to dream. Let me give you a gift equal to that which you gave me. Send these characters back whence they came, protect them.'

And, with that, he stood up and walked towards the shelves, as the characters started to melt away back to their books. Bea checked *Anne of Green Gables*, and Anne was present and vivid on every page where she belonged.

She nodded to Will, who dipped into one last deep bow and pressed his hands to the great oak tree Anne had just left.

'Seek happy nights to happy days,' he said. 'And good ends to good books.'

And, with that, he closed his eyes and channels of pure book magic started streaming from his hands into the tree. Within seconds, it was coming from every part of him, imagination pouring directly from him into the books, helping free every single book there.

They could see it spreading throughout the whole forest, the whole library, flowing through it like electricity. And, as the light spread to every last book, Will started to fray and he himself finally turned into pure story, a constellation of shimmering, beautiful imagination that surged through the entire Source Library, filling the air with eddies and swirls of glittering magic, and the unmistakable smell of toasted marshmallows.

EPILOGUE
ONE WEEK LATER

Grandma, Grandad, Bea, Tilly and Oskar were sitting round the kitchen table in Pages & Co., eating home-made pizzas.

The copy of *A Midsummer Night's Dream* with the Underwoods trapped inside it had been bound with a neat cross of golden story magic over its first word. It was then entrusted to Amelia Whisper, who had been reinstated as Librarian of the British Underlibrary. What role the Underlibrary was set to play had not yet been decided.

'So what happens now?' Tilly said, before taking a mouthful of pizza.

'Who knows?' Grandma said. 'Everything is different and there are lots of decisions to be made. There are a lot of things to clear up and people to check in on.'

'Orlando and Jorge are safe, aren't they?' Tilly asked.

'Very much so,' Bea reassured her. 'Amelia called in some favours at the American Underlibrary and they're safe and well at home. One day we'll take a proper trip to America together and they can tell us all about it.'

'We did the right thing, didn't we?' Tilly asked. 'Freeing the Source Editions?'

'Tilly, you and Oskar did what you thought was right,' Grandad said. 'And that is all we will ever ask you to do. I find that I'm almost embarrassed, having been a Librarian for twenty years of my career, and a bookwanderer since I was twelve, that I never asked the questions you did about what book magic really means. We've only ever wanted for you to be brave, and curious, and kind – like your mum – and you two have demonstrated over and over again that is what you are.'

'So everyone can just bookwander where they like, right?' Oskar said.

'Yes,' Grandad said. 'People are truly free to chart their own course.'

'To seek their own adventures,' said Grandma.

'To find their own path,' Bea added.

'To be the heroes of their own story,' Tilly said.

'I'll drink to that,' Oskar said, and the five of them raised their glasses of raspberry cordial and clinked them together.

Later that night, Tilly sat in her favourite armchair on the first floor of Pages & Co.

The moonlight was shining through the windows and illuminating all the books, each one its own adventure, its own story that would meet each reader and welcome them in a way that was particular to them.

She curled her feet under her and looked at the notebook lying in her lap. It was the one she'd been given in Paris for Christmas by Oskar's grandmother.

She opened it to the first page, picked up the fountain pen she'd accidentally brought out of 221B Baker Street and took a deep breath.

Tilly and the Bookwanderers

she wrote on the first page.

By Matilda Pages.

She took a sip of hot chocolate, read it back, smiled and kept writing.

THE END

From the Record of Matilda Pages

· · · Matilda Pages remains in the non-Story world despite initial attempts to retrieve her. Monitoring will continue, and future plans will be put in place to ensure her return at the soonest possible convenience.

ACKNOWLEDGEMENTS

Thank you to my family, extended family, and friends for your love and support. Especially to my mum and dad and my sister Hester. Thank you always to Adam Collier.

Thank you to Paola Escobar for her beautiful illustrations.

Thank you to my agent, Claire Wilson, and everyone at RCW. Thank you to the wonderful team at HarperCollins Children's, especially Nick Lake and Louisa Sheridan. Thank you always to Lizzie Clifford, Sarah Hughes and Rachel Denwood. Thank you to all my foreign publishers, in particular to Cheryl Eissing, Lindsay T. Boggs and Tessa Meischeid at Philomel.

Thank you so much to all the booksellers, librarians and bloggers who have supported the books so far. A particular thank-you to all the booksellers and schools who welcomed me so warmly when I was on tour in the US last autumn. Thank you in particular to Tattered Cover in Denver, whose theatre-home I have borrowed for Shakespeare's Sisters, and to McIntyre's Books in North Carolina, whose wrapping room I have borrowed.

Thank you to Laura Gottesman at the Library of Congress for answering my queries about where classmarks would be shelved in the Library – and apologies for having to tweak it so that the Main Reading Room could be used as the setting.

Thank you most of all to every reader who has found and connected with Tilly's story.